THE SQUAD

PERFECT COVER

JEN

D1043520

Published by Laurel-Leaf
an imprint of Random House Children's Books
a division of Random House, Inc.
New York

This is a work of fiction. Names, characters, places, and incidents either are the product of the author's imagination or are used fictitiously. Any resemblance to actual persons, living or dead, events, or locales is entirely coincidental.

www.randomhouse.com/teens

Educators and librarians, for a variety of teaching tools, visit us at
www.randomhouse.com/teachers

Library of Congress Cataloging-in-Publication Data
Barnes, Jennifer (Jennifer Lynn).
The squad / Jennifer Lynn Barnes.
p. cm.
Summary: High school sophomore Toby Klein enjoys computer hacking and wearing combat boots, so she thinks it is a joke when she is invited to join the cheerleading squad but soon learns cheering is just a cover for an elite group of government operatives known as the squad.
ISBN 978-0-385-73454-7
[1. Spies—Fiction. 2. Cheerleading—Fiction. 3. High schools—Fiction. 4. Schools—Fiction. 5. Computer hackers—Fiction. 6. Humorous stories.]
I. Title.
PZ7.B26225Sqa 2008
[Fic]—dc22
2007009352

Printed in the United States of America
February 2008
10 9 8 7 6 5 4 3 2 1
First Edition

For Michelle, coach, friend, and honorary big sis, who really did tell me, "If you don't feel stupid, you're not doing it right."

CHAPTER 1
Code Word: Pom-pom

If you'd told me at the beginning of sophomore year that I was going to end up a government operative, I would have thought you were crazy, but if you'd told me I was destined to become a cheerleader, I would have had you committed, no questions asked. At that point in time, there were three things in life that I knew for certain: (1) I was a girl who'd never met a site she couldn't hack or a code she couldn't break, (2) I had a roundhouse that could put a grown man in the hospital, and (3) I would without question chop off my own hands before I'd come within five feet of a pom-pom.

I liked to fly below the radar. I was the girl slouched in the back of your geometry class, not the one shaking my booty on the field. In fact, in the year and a half since we'd moved to Bayport, I'd spent more time in detention than at pep rallies and considered myself lucky; unless *school spirit* referred to a school-board-sanctioned wine, I had no intention of buying.

And then, one day out of the blue, the note appeared in my locker.

Toby Klein—
You are cordially invited to an
information session on the Bayport High
Varsity Spirit Squad today at four in room
117. Go Lions (and Lionesses)!

The year before, a bunch of angry feminist mothers had sued the district for having a male mascot, so now we were officially the Bayport Lion(esse)s. I kid you not. That's just one of the many reasons I couldn't fathom the idea of actually supporting the school in any way, shape, or form. That and the fact that I'd had to forcibly remove a football player's hand from my brother's arm three times in the last month. Emphasis on the word *forcibly*. If they touched Noah again, someone was going to lose an arm. Go Lions!

I turned the note over in my hand. Wow, I thought, the God Squad must really be scratching bottom if they're recruiting *me*. Maybe they just couldn't stand it that there were actually a few sophomore and junior girls who weren't willing to sell their souls for cheerleading immortality. There was a reason the varsity cheerleaders were collectively referred to as the God Squad, and it wasn't because they were religious; it was because at Bayport High, they were gods: the ultimate social power. Most people did everything short of bowing down to worship them on a regular basis.

I was not most people.

Slamming my locker shut, I moved to throw the note away, but decided to save it for ammunition in case anyone in my carpool got too rowdy. As I moved to jam the invite into my pocket, light caught the letters, and for just a second, a few of them jumped out at me.

"Stupid glitter pens," I muttered, but automatically, my

mind began cataloging the letters I'd noticed. I stuffed the note into my jeans, took four steps down the hallway, and then stopped. My brain does tricky things with letters and numbers: scrambles them and unscrambles them, analyzes their combinations, looks for patterns. When I was little, I loved palindromes and anagrams and any secret language more complicated than Pig Latin. Standing there in the hallway, my letter-savvy mind did its thing, and I pulled the invitation back out of my pocket.

After a quick glance around the hall to make sure no one was watching, I held the small white card in the light again and, one by one, picked out the letters that appeared slightly more sparkly than their counterparts.

> Toby Klein—
>   You are **c**ordially invited **to** an
> infor**m**ation s**e**ssion on the Bayport High
> V**a**rsity Spirit Squad today at four in room
> 117. Go **L**i**o**ns (and Li**one**sses)!

There it was in black and white, or, more specifically, in hot pink glitter pen. COME ALONE.

After that, I really did throw the note away, because there was no way it had been written by an actual cheerleader. Most of them probably couldn't even spell *cordially*, let alone embed secret instructions in an invite to one of their oh-so-special meetings. Someone was definitely playing a trick on me, and I had a pretty good idea who that someone was. I also had a pretty good idea what I was going to do about it.

Proximity—namely the fact that my brother's locker was only three down from mine—was on my side.

"Very funny, Einstein." Since I'd trashed the message and therefore had nothing to throw at him, I settled for flicking my brother on the back of one of his ears.

"Hey!" Noah tried not to lose what little cool he had, but failed miserably. After glaring at me for a second (like that did any good), he changed tactics. "Toby," he said in a low whisper, "I'm working my magic here."

And that was why Noah kept getting attacked by football players with no necks and something to prove. No matter how many times I assured him that hot senior girls weren't under any circumstances interested in scrawny freshman goofballs, he still couldn't help trying out his "charms" on the older women.

It was a miracle he wasn't dead, and given the current circumstances, there was a decent chance that I was going to kill him myself.

"Work's over," I said. I didn't even spare a glance at the current object of his affection before literally dragging him to the side of the hall. "You got anything you want to tell me?" I asked. For a girl my size (five three), I can sound pretty mean when I want to.

"Ummm . . . not that I can think of," Noah said, giving me one of his most "charming" grins.

"Try harder."

"Well . . . I . . . uhhh . . . did tell Chuck that you'd take him home after school."

"Try again," I said darkly. That wasn't what I was shooting for. Still, I had to wonder if Noah had been planning on giving me any forewarning at all that Chuck I'm-in-Love-with-Noah's-Older-Sister Percy was hitching a ride home. That kid made Noah look like Prince Charming.

"I went through your lingerie drawer looking for gift ideas?" Noah tried again.

"You what?" I didn't know what was worse: the fact that my brother had seen my underwear, or the fact that he was probably on the verge of *buying* underwear for a senior girl whose boyfriend I'd inevitably be forced to physically restrain.

"Don't worry," Noah said quickly. "Your stuff didn't give me any ideas."

And now he was insulting my intimates. It was a miracle I'd let him live past childhood.

Noah wrinkled his forehead, completely unaware that I was plotting his death. "What *are* you talking about?"

"The note." I decided then and there that I didn't want to learn any more of the many reasons that I should have been interrogating him. "The card in my locker."

Noah continued with his blank look.

"The invitation from the Bod Squad," I said, using the term he and his friends had adopted for the God Squad.

At the phrase *Bod Squad*, Noah's eyes lit up. Before he could get any unsavory ideas, I plowed on. "You know, the whole 'come to our secret lair in room 117' thing."

Noah opened his mouth and then closed it again. "You're joking about the secret lair thing, right?" he asked a few seconds later. "Because if they did have a secret lair, that would be really hot."

"You didn't send it?" I asked. Noah was many things, but he wasn't a liar, or at least he wasn't a good one.

"Pretend to be a bunch of cheerleaders?" Noah asked.

Why did I feel like I was giving him ideas? I looked down at my watch. "Go to class," I said finally, not wanting him to be late for fifth period. "And stay away from my underwear."

A second later, Noah was jackrabbiting toward his next class and I was walking slowly in the general direction of my own. Personally, I wasn't in any hurry. It had gotten to the point where Mr. Corkin and I had an understanding: I hated his class, and he hated me. It was a give-and-take relationship, and because of that, I took my time walking down the hallway and stopped at my locker again, just for the heck of it. Who cared if it had been less than a minute since I'd visited my locker last? Who cared if the bell had just rung? Delaying the inevitable was an art, and I was an artist.

31-27-15.

My combination was an anagram of a six-digit prime number. The fact that I knew that should tell you a little bit about me.

I opened the locker, briefly wondered if there were any orange Tic-Tacs left inside, and then immediately stopped thinking about freshening my breath. There, on top of a history book I hadn't bothered to read, was another note.

> Toby Klein—
> You have been selected to attend a preliminary meeting with the Bayport High Cheerleading Squad! Congratulations. How does it feel?
> Go Big Gold!

How in the world had they gotten another note into my locker so quickly *and* without my noticing? Talk about strange.

This time, the invitation was written in purple gel pen, but when I held it up to the light, some letters were a shade darker than the others, like the note's author had traced them over twice. I quickly scanned the letters, but this time, they didn't spell anything.

"Miss Klein? Need I even ask if you have a hall pass?"

Our vice-principal didn't hate me nearly as much as he probably should have given my complete and utter lack of school spirit and my slight tendency toward jock-directed violence, but he was still the vice-principal.

" 'Fraid not," I said, holding up my hall-passless hands to illustrate.

"What's this?" Mr. Jacobson's eyes widened at the sight of the little white notecard. "You got an invitation to the Spirit Squad's information meeting?" he asked. "That's quite an honor."

And you wonder why I think this school's messed up.

"Yeah." I took in Mr. J's encouraging smile. "Whatever."

"Toby," Mr. J said, and I could feel a lecture coming on. "It's an honor to be selected. You should go."

I hated to break it to him, but there was no way in Hades.

"Can't," I said, trying to soften the blow. "I'm late for Corkin's class, and that means detention. Darn."

While Mr. J launched into a lecture on personal responsibility and trying to make things work, I played around with the letters in my head. YOERICUTUS?

YO RICE UTUS?

Nope.

STORY ICE UU?

Damn *Us.*

"Toby, are you listening to me?"

"Sort of."

Mr. J smiled despite himself. "I think it would be good for you to get involved with some extracurriculars," he said

7

finally. "You should go to that meeting this afternoon. Mr. Corkin can spare you for one afternoon detention."

Wait a second, I thought, had I just been given detention immunity? Maybe I would go to this "meeting" after all. If it meant being able to thwart Corkin's diabolical plan of sticking me with yet another afternoon of torturous doldrums, it was totally worth it.

"Toby, go to class." Mr. J's words interrupted my train of thought. Obediently, I turned in the direction of the history room, and suddenly, the correct anagram of the scrambled letters fell into place.

CURIOUS YET?

I hated to admit it, but by the time I broke the news of my vice-principalian pardon to my faculty nemesis, I definitely was.

Since when did cheerleaders write in code?

CHAPTER 2
Code Word: Boobalicious

They were the most popular, had the perkiest smiles, and wore the shortest skirts. They were the best, the brightest (yeah, right), and the most boobalicious. They threw the most exclusive parties, hooked up with A-plus-list jocks, and ate lesser females for lunch. They were the varsity cheerleaders, and I was at one of their meetings.

It was official: I'd sold my soul to get out of detention.

"As you know, very few sophomores make the varsity squad." Brooke Camden, squad captain (or, as I liked to think of her, head bitch), raked her eyes over the occupants of room 117. The other varsity cheerleaders smiled sick little grins, and Brooke continued. "Most of you tried out for the JV squad. Some of you made it, some of you didn't, but making JV is no guarantee. We only take the best. The rest of you will be cheering for freshmen until you graduate."

Ho-hum.

"We don't have tryouts, we don't care if your mom was a cheerleader at *her* high school, and we don't explain our decisions."

All hail Brooke, Queen of Cheerleaders!

I glanced around at the varsity hopefuls in the room. Half of them were on the verge of tears, one of them looked a single haughty smile away from a nervous breakdown, and a few of them, already JV cheerleaders themselves, seemed to be putting every ounce of energy they had into appearing popular, perky, and worthy of pom-poms.

Gag me. Was this really better than detention? I was starting to have my doubts.

As Brooke lectured on about the massive responsibility of representing all that was good and beautiful at Bayport High, I turned my attention to the other God Squad members in the room. As impossible as it seemed, I had to admit that, given the fact that the invitation had proved to be legit, there was at least a decent chance that one of them had encoded the secret messages into my notes.

I glanced at each of them and ran through their names in my head. Brooke, Tara, Tiffany, Brittany, Lucy, Bubbles, Chloe, and Zee. Brittany and Tiffany were twins, and Lucy might as well have been their triplet. They were blond, bubbly, and gorgeous, and had a combined IQ of 37. I immediately scratched them off my list of suspects. Chloe Larson, Brooke's second-in-command, was smarter than she let on, but also wouldn't have touched my locker with an eighty-foot pole. That left Tara, Bubbles, and Zee.

I couldn't bring myself to believe that a person named Bubbles could have encoded anything.

"Any questions?" Brooke asked, leaning back against the blackboard.

"I have a question." Hayley Hoffman raised one manicured hand into the air. She was exactly the kind of girl the God Squad was looking for: JV cheerleader two years running, blond hair that she bleached blonder, and social claws that consistently demolished anyone and everyone who stood in her way and half of the people who didn't. When Brooke inclined her head toward Hayley's raised hand, Hayley stared directly at me. "Was this meeting by invite only?" she asked. "Or could just anyone come?"

I didn't know whether to be angry that she was implying I wasn't good enough to attend the meeting, or deeply offended that she thought I wanted to be there in the first place.

"This meeting," Brooke said, her voice every bit as bright and deadly as Hayley's, "was your first audition." Her eyes flitted to the rest of us, making it perfectly clear that this message wasn't just for Hayley. "You came, we watched." She smiled, no teeth. "We weren't impressed. Any other questions?"

This time, there were no takers.

"In that case," Brooke said, "we'll be in touch."

And just like that, the meeting was over.

That's it? I thought. This was what I was supposed to be "curious" about? Forget curious. I was completely baffled.

The only thing I knew for sure was that Hayley was right—I didn't belong here. Of all the girls who'd received a summons to this invite-only meeting, I was the one who even a dumb four-year-old would have circled in one of those "which one does not belong?" tests. Besides Hayley, there were a slew of other JV cheerleaders, some of them sophomores and some of them juniors who hadn't been chosen for the God Squad the year before. Then there were the noncheerleading populars: the too-cute editor of the yearbook, the part-time model, and the girl whose hot older brother was newly single. Given the fact that Bayport was one of the richest school districts in the country, everyone in this room could just as easily have been auditioning for a television show called *Lifestyles of the Rich and Bitchy.*

Everyone except me.

Chloe Larson rammed her body into my chair and then proceeded to give me the evil eye. "Watch where you're going."

It was all I could do to keep myself from rolling my eyes. I was sitting down, and she had run into me. Cheerleaders: they thought they owned the air the student body breathed.

"I guess some people are just perpetually in the way, you know?" Hayley's words broke into my thoughts. I debated giving her a reason to get another nose job, but decided against it. I was a third-degree black belt; she was a junior-varsity cheerleader. Where was the fun in that?

Instead, I stood up, ready to go back to my normal life of beating up football players and hacking into the school's database to change my grades and Mr. Corkin's middle name. And that's when I saw another note. It must have been in my lap, because it fell to the ground when I stood. Hayley's eyes lit up, and she dove for it, but another manicured hand beat her there.

"I believe this is yours." Tara Leery was a British exchange student and, as far as I'd been able to tell, the cheer-leader most likely to have a functional cerebrum.

Tara handed the note to me, brushing her fingertips against the back of mine. She held my hand for a moment and then turned, and without another word, she followed Chloe "Out-of-My-Way" Larson out of the room.

I watched them leave and then looked back down at the note.

"Maybe someone's finally sending you the memo on

combat boots," Hayley said, and then, in a confidential whisper, she added, "For the record: so over."

"Oh," I said thoughtfully. "I got that memo. I filed it away with your boyfriend's petition for a brain and the lost-and-found ad for your virginity."

I admit it. I'm not the nicest person. I have been known, on occasion, to use my sharp wit and clever puns for evil, rather than good. I don't smile at people just because they smiled at me first, and if I have something to say to someone, I say it to their face. I am, in other words, the anti-cheerleader.

Hayley recovered from my below-the-belt comment about her none-too-secret loss of virginity to a delusional football player who had also slept with her best friend and somehow thought that neither girl would figure it out. Hayley made her best attempt at glaring me into oblivion, flipped her hair over her shoulder, and flounced off, four JV cheerleaders following in her wake.

"Was it something I said?"

As soon as she was out of sight, I decided to make one last concession to my curiosity, after which I would never even think the word *cheerleader* again.

I opened the note in my hand, half expecting another encoded message. No such luck. The paper was blank.

CHAPTER 3
Code Word: Perky

"What was it like? What were they wearing? Did they happen to mention—"

"How a dweeby little freshman could win their undying affection?" I finished Noah's sentence for him. "No."

My brother wasn't the least bit deterred. "Did you talk to Brooke at all?"

I groaned inwardly. He had to have a thing for Brooke Camden. Why couldn't he crush on someone his own age? Or better yet, someone from his home world, Planet Goofball.

"Well?" Noah prompted.

I scratched the back of my hand absentmindedly. "I went," I told him. "I watched. I wasn't impressed."

Noah wouldn't let the issue go. "Did you at least get a couple of phone numbers?"

"Noah, for the last time, if you're not careful, you're going to get yourself killed, and one of these days, I'm not going to be there to save you."

Most younger brothers would have been offended at the very thought of being "saved" by their five-foot-three-inch sister. Noah was not most brothers.

"Where else are you gonna be?" he asked. "Cheerleading practice?"

"In your dreams, Noah." I scratched the back of my hand a little harder and wondered if I was having an allergic reaction to something (probably Hayley Hoffman).

"You do realize that it looks like you have some kind of bizarre scratching tic, right?"

I ignored Noah's comment and turned my attention to my hand. What in the world was wrong with it?

"Maybe it's a psychosomatic response to your guilt for not getting me phone numbers."

I gave Noah a look and then used the aforementioned itchy hand to thwap him under the chin.

"Oh, come on, Toby. You know you love me." Noah grinned, and even though I didn't find him the least bit charming, I smiled back before flicking him again and heading for the sink. I stuck my hand under the faucet and turned the water on, and the instant the water touched my skin, my entire hand changed color.

"Teal?" Noah, who'd followed me into the kitchen, asked. "Doesn't really seem like your style, Tobe."

"Noah," I said calmly.

"Yeah?"

"Run."

He was smart enough to vacate the kitchen, leaving me staring at my own bright blue hand. I soaped up and scrubbed it, but the color stayed. Ready to seriously pummel something, I grabbed a handful of paper towels and tried to rub off the color. Nothing came off on the towels, but when I looked back at my hand, the color was gone.

"Wha . . . ?"

After a half second of deliberation, I turned the faucet back on and let a few droplets of water drip onto my knuckles, and as they wet the skin, the color reappeared. Carefully, I continued letting water drizzle onto my hand until the vast majority of it was again a bright, perky teal.

Wait a second, I thought. Perky . . .

I shook my head to clear it of ridiculous thoughts. The cheerleaders had *not* dyed my hand teal.

Or had they?

I ran the day's events over in my mind until I came to the part where Tara handed me the note, her fingers gripping mine for the smallest fraction of a second.

"I suppose she could have done this," I said under my breath, "but why?"

Of all of the God Squad, Tara seemed the least likely to torture an antiestablishment social reject such as myself. Then again, maybe I just had to accept the fact that this whole day had been one giant plot to get me to that meeting, dye my hand teal, and . . .

And what? Why go to all the trouble? We were talking about the prettiest, most popular, ditziest girls in school. I wasn't even sure they were capable of encoding notes, let alone using invisible dye to . . .

Notes.

The realization hit me, and slowly, I reached into my pocket and pulled out the blank sheet of paper from before. Someone had folded it like a note and somehow gotten it into my lap. When I'd dropped it, Tara had given it back to me before Hayley could open it. Tara, who had also possibly turned my hand an invisible teal.

I unfolded the paper and spread it out on the counter. It

was still blank, but looking at my hand, I had to wonder. Was it really blank?

I folded a paper towel in half and wet a corner. Feeling a little bit ridiculous, I gingerly rubbed the cloth over the note, leaving a dampened streak in its wake. The moment water touched the paper, bright teal letters leapt to life. Again and again, I wet the paper towel and dragged it gently across the note, until the entire message was revealed in ink the color of my wet hand.

> *Practice gym, 5:30, tomorrow morning. Be there.*

What, no "Go Lions!" or sis-boom-bah crap? Apparently, cheery cheerleader-speak was only for visible ink. Seriously, though, what was up with the cheerleading squad writing me coded notes and dyeing my hands with invisible ink? Was it the whole squad? I had always thought of them as being one massively popular person split into many bouncy parts, but Tara was the only one who'd actually been involved in this whole debacle, so . . .

Something else occurred to me then, and I backtracked. Tara had picked the note up and handed it to me, had coated my hands with whatever it was they were using for ink, but she hadn't handed me the note. She'd been on the other side of the room when it had appeared out of nowhere. The only one near me was Chloe. Chloe, who had crashed into my chair instead of giving it a berth the size of Montana, a more typical course of action.

"This is ridiculous." I tried to snap myself out of it, but couldn't deny the teal hand or the invisible message or the encoded notes in my locker. Something strange was going on here, and all evidence suggested that it had something to do with the cheerleaders.

I could only think of one surefire way to find out what was going on: be at the practice gym at five-thirty the next morning. Sure, it was obscenely early, but really, what was the worst that could happen?

CHAPTER 4
Code Word: Tumbling

"Cheerleading practice? You guys woke me up at this ungodly hour for cheerleading practice?"

I am not a morning person, especially when I'm expecting a revelation of some kind and instead get eight cheerleaders telling me to stretch out so we can tumble.

What the hell *was* tumbling anyway?

"We always practice before school," Bubbles said solemnly.

Why was I even talking to a person named Bubbles? Why? From the moment I'd gotten here, they'd all acted like my presence was nothing out of the norm. No one had said a word about why I was there. They'd just told me to stretch and gone back to stretching themselves, like I was supposed to read their warped little ponytailed minds.

"Can anyone here explain to me why I'm at cheerleading practice right now?" I asked, my voice dangerously pleasant. All seven of the other cheerleaders turned to their captain, and I awaited with bated breath the wisdom she was sure to impart.

"If you can't cut the hours," Brooke said, "don't join the squad."

"I'm *not* joining the squad," I said. "Why would I join the squad? I don't even like . . ."

I searched for something to go in the blank. People? This school? Any of you? More like (d) all of the above.

"I don't like . . . cheers," I finished, trying to be diplomatic. After all, they outnumbered me eight to one.

"Oh, really?" Brittany-or-Tiffany (it was impossible to tell the twins apart) asked, like I was trying to put one over on them. "If you don't like cheers, then why are you here?"

Because you told me to be here, I said silently, but I wouldn't admit that out loud. They'd ordered me here, and I'd dragged myself out of bed to come, under the delusion that I might actually figure out why they were messing with me in the first place.

"Don't be such a grumpy bear, grumpy bear," Lucy said in a voice so bright that the sound of it made my teeth ache. "It's not that early, girly!"

My left eye twitched at the rhyme, and when she flashed me a big, toothy smile, I lost it.

"No," I told her in a firm tone I usually reserved for household pets that were chewing on my boots. "I don't do perky before nine."

The entire squad frowned at me in one synchronized motion.

"So are you in or aren't you?" Chloe's tone was more command than question.

In for what?

"I'll teach you to do a herkie!" Lucy, completely unaffected by my "no" voice, bounced into the air and did some kind of funky cheerleading jump. "Now you try."

"In for what?" I asked Chloe, ignoring Lucy and trying to strike the memory of this moment from my mind forever. "In for what?"

I was getting really sick of asking.

Bubbles was the one who answered, her voice a reverent whisper. "The Squad."

This was just too much. Don't ask me what I'd expected, but it wasn't this. Invisible ink, encoded messages, and the night before, I could have sworn I'd seen someone in a cheerleading skirt standing on my front lawn, surveying the house, and now . . .

"You want me to be a cheerleader?"

"Give the girl a cookie," Brooke drawled. "She finally figured it out."

I opened my mouth to speak, but Brooke cut me off. "Most sophomores would die for this chance," she said. "Are you in or are you out?"

"Out." This had to be some kind of sick prank. Me on the God Squad? No way. This was just part of a time-honored tradition of high school cruelties: confuse the asocial bottom-dweller, convince her she's on the squad, and then dump her. Only this time, they'd picked the wrong bottom-dweller. I wasn't jumping for joy at their invitation; I was dangerously close to losing my infamous temper.

"Stop sending me letters," I said in a low voice. "Stop messing with my hands, and stop coming by my house late at night."

Eight pairs of eyes stared back at me, duly shocked.

"Toby," Brittany-or-Tiffany (the other one this time) said. "Why would we do a thing like that?"

I looked at each of them in turn, one suntanned teen queen after another. The twins appeared identically bewildered at

21

the very suggestion of harassment. Bubbles's bottom lip was sticking out in an exaggerated pout (who does that?), and bouncy Lucy was still very conscientiously instructing me on the finer points of the herkie. Brooke, every inch the head cheerleader, and Chloe, every inch her clone, stared me down. Meanwhile, Zee, who I knew only as the school's resident Asian party girl, inspected her nails, and quiet Tara offered me a weak half smile.

There wasn't enough brainpower in this room to dye Easter eggs, let alone my hand.

"You're right," I said, hands in my pockets. "You're cheerleaders, and I'm nuts."

Brooke nodded. "That's right," she said proudly. "We date football players and cheer for games and win all the spots on the homecoming court. We are the pride of the Lions. . . ."

"Lionesses," someone else murmured.

"The pride of the Lions/Lionesses," Brooke said. "We *couldn't* do the kinds of things you're talking about." As she spoke, the others circled around me in a way that was decidedly creepy, until all nine of us were standing at the very center of the gym, directly over the Bayport emblem on the floor. "After all, we're just cheerleaders."

With those seemingly innocuous words and a flick of her wrist, Brooke produced a cell phone and proceeded to dial a seven-digit number. I had just enough time to think one sarcastic thought (Who's she calling, the Spirit Police?) before the code she'd entered somehow triggered the emblem beneath us to fall from underneath our feet, a trapdoor of spirit built into the floor for reasons I couldn't begin to comprehend.

As I fell and the gym floor righted itself above my head,

Brooke's words repeated themselves over and over again in my mind.

We couldn't do the kinds of things you're talking about. After all, we're just cheerleaders.

Yeah freaking right.

CHAPTER 5
Code Word: Herkie

I won't repeat the words I screamed as I fell, but suffice to say, they weren't "Go Big Gold." I kept cursing when I hit the ground, but shut up the second I started bouncing.

"A trampoline?" I stared up at the ceiling and, for lack of a better audience, addressed God. "Why are you doing this to me?"

All around me, cheerleaders landed on their feet on the trampoline and bounced off to solid ground. Lucy herkied her way down, and the twins executed synchronized front flips.

"Why?"

"Why not?" This was Brooke, who, as far as I could tell, believed that she single-handedly put the *god* in God Squad. The cheerleading captain flipped to stand next to me, and I scrambled to my feet. Unlike the cheerleaders, I hadn't been expecting to fall, and I hadn't prepared a choreographed dismount. Instead, I'd more or less belly flopped, which, by the way, was totally going to leave a mark.

As I got my footing, Brooke appraised my movement. "You're fast."

"And you're crazy," I said. "What is this? I tell you I don't want to be on your stupid little squad and you literally knock me off my feet and drop me onto a giant trampoline? What is wrong with you people?"

Brooke lashed out with her right leg, and only a life's worth of training had me moving quickly enough to dodge the kick. I ducked, and her foot whizzed by my head.

"Like I said . . ." Brooke smiled again, that same toothless smile, as she threw a hard punch at my left side. ". . . fast."

I moved quickly, and her hand caught air. "Like *I* said . . ." I countered with my own punch. "Crazy."

My hand connected with her stomach, but she absorbed the hit, grabbed my hand, and sent me flying. I flipped, landed on my feet, and let my instincts take over. Kick after kick, punch after punch, we sparred. I was faster and stronger, but I also wasn't used to fighting on a trampoline. She was.

She leapt at me, her leg extended, and it caught me on the shoulder. I rolled backward, pushing off the tramp and back onto my feet just as she came again, her foot whipping into a high-velocity roundhouse.

All I could think in the fraction of a second I had to move was that she didn't know who she was messing with. That was *my* move.

I rolled to the side, and her roundhouse missed me. Before she landed, my foot snaked out and kicked her legs out from underneath her. She turned 360 degrees sideways in the air, tucked herself into a ball, and somehow managed to land on her feet. That gave me just enough time to survey my surroundings and begin forcing her toward the edge of the massive trampoline.

Left, right, left . . . I threw punch after punch at her, and Brooke dodged, her glossy ponytail flying back and forth with the movement. I advanced and she backed up until she was a single step away from firm ground.

Taking advantage of the trampoline under my feet, I bounced once, twice, three times, and sailed over her, landing in ready stance between two of the others, who didn't seem the least bit interested in the fact that their fearless leader and I were engaged in some hard-core hand-to-hand.

I crooked my finger at Brooke. "Enough with the trampoline," I said. "Let's play my way."

Brooke effortlessly flipped off the trampoline and looked down at her nails. "Nah," she said. "I'm tired of playing." She turned to the others. "You guys see what you needed to see?"

"Yeah."

"Yup."

"I'm good."

"Works for me."

"Welcome to the squad, Toby!" Lucy, who I could only infer seriously needed to switch to decaf, squealed at high volume. She threw her arms around me. "We're going to have so much fun!"

This was not happening.

I extracted myself from Lucy's grasp. For the first time, I really looked at the room around me, and the venomous response on the tip of my tongue faded into what in all honesty I would describe as incoherent mumbling.

"Wha . . . huh . . . whaaa?"

While the drop to the trampoline hadn't been more than eight or ten feet, I was now standing at the top of a spiral staircase. The others pushed and prodded me down it, and when I reached the bottom, all I could do was continue with my incoherent mumbling. The room was easily three stories tall, with thick white Plexiglas walls that looked like something out of *The Matrix*. I counted four doors, two staircases, and what can only be described as the world's biggest flat-screen television.

I couldn't help thinking of my flippant words to Noah the day before. Unbeknownst to me, the cheerleaders really did have a secret lair.

"Impressive, isn't it?" Tara took a step forward to stand beside me. Her low voice echoed in the massive space. "I'm sure you must be overwhelmed. We all were, at first."

"Maybe *you* were"—Chloe delivered the words with a patented Chloe Larson eye roll—"but I'm never whelmed."

"All right." Tara rolled with the punches. "We were all overwhelmed at first, except for Chloe, who is un-whelmable." Her low, even tone never changed, but the look in her eyes at the "unwhelmable" comment made me smile for the first time since I'd been told to stretch that morning.

"What exactly is this place?" I addressed the question to Tara, who seemed (teal hand incident aside) the least likely to force me to commit cheerocide.

"This," Tara said simply, "is the Quad."

"The Quad," I repeated.

The other girls nodded.

"The Squad Quad," Brooke said, and as she stepped forward, the other girls, even Tara, edged back. "An underground, state-of-the-art, soundproof, bulletproof, boyproof, waterproof, digitalized, motorized, tantalizingly secure fourteen-thousand-square-foot enclosure equipped with everything from radar to TiVo."

"TiVo," I repeated.

"Let me break it down for you, To-bee." Brooke broke my

name into two distinct syllables. "You're standing in the middle of one of the government's most elite operative agencies."

"Operatives." I couldn't seem to stop repeating everything she said.

"Operatives. Secret agents. Spies. *Charlie's Angels* meets James Bond meets *Bring It On*."

"Bring what on?"

Brooke gave me a look. "We're the best of the best. We're pretty, we're smart . . ." She arched an eyebrow at me, and I remembered the way she'd thrown me across the room. "We're in perfect physical condition, and best of all, we never get caught." She shot me a toothy grin. "After all, who's going to suspect the cheerleaders?"

Not me, that was for damn sure.

"You're telling me that Bayport High's varsity cheerleading squad is a cover for a group of government superspies?" She had to realize how ridiculous that sounded.

"You know, Toby, maybe you're not as slow as we thought."

I didn't have time to respond to that particular insult before Brooke lifted her hands and clapped eight times, a rhythm I vaguely remembered trying to scour out of my brain after the one mandatory pep rally I hadn't managed to skip the year before. As soon as Brooke finished clapping, the others repeated her motions, and the lights dimmed.

"Screen on." Brooke didn't sound like a cheerleader. I didn't have time to decide what she did sound like before the plasma screen in front of us turned on and an image appeared.

"Is that my yearbook picture?" I almost didn't recognize

myself. They'd blown the picture up to larger-than-life-size, and you could totally see up my nose.

"Wow. Talk about unfortunate photos." One of the cheerleaders let out a low whistle at the picture, but Brooke glared whoever it was back into silence.

"Toby Guinevere Klein. Born August nineteenth. Brown hair, brown eyes, medium skin tone. Five feet, three inches, a hundred and three pounds as of last Wednesday."

First the picture, now my weight and my hideous middle name. I couldn't wait to see what they pulled out next.

"Your father's a physicist. Your mother's a karate instructor. Your little brother, Noah—"

"Leave Noah out of this."

Brooke inclined her head slightly. "Fine. We'll get back to you."

That definitely sounded like a threat.

"Third-degree black belt, two suspensions so far this school year, a total of fourteen at your last seven schools, dating back to the third grade, when you belted a sixth grader in the groin for throwing gravel at your classmates."

I smiled. I'd almost forgotten about that.

"You're a novice computer hacker."

I narrowed my eyes. Who was she calling novice?

"Next." At her one-word command, the image on the screen changed (thank God), and I found myself looking at an extensive list of company names and dates.

"Look familiar?"

I skimmed the list: Freemont Electronics, Conley Anti-Virus, Semi-National Bank and Trust, the Girl Scouts of America . . .

"Vaguely familiar," I replied before she could continue.

"It's a list of every secure system you've breached in the last twenty-six months," Brooke said, and for the first time, I caught something that might have sounded like respect in her pretty-girl voice.

"Impressed?" I asked.

Chloe scoffed on Brooke's behalf. "Get over yourself, hacker spaz."

Apparently, a simple "computer geek" was too passé.

"Impressed?" Brooke repeated. "Puh-lease. This is kiddie play."

Hey! I was deeply insulted. That bank and trust one hadn't exactly been a piece of cake.

"What *is* impressive," Brooke continued, "is what you did twenty-six months ago." She turned her attention back to the screen. "Next."

I recognized the code the moment I saw it. "Oh," I said. "That."

"Yes. That."

Before I explain what "that" was, I'd like to take this opportunity to say that when I'd weaseled my way past the firewalls and hijacked one of the user IDs, I thought the site was fake, one of those things that a hacker will put up on the Net just to see if there's anyone better out there. I figured that if it was legit, I wouldn't break through, as simple as that—only not, because it was legit and I did break through. My bad.

"The Pentagon," Brooke said. "Not bad for a thirteen-year-old girl."

"I was almost fourteen." I glanced away.

"Four months later, your dad was transferred here," Brooke said. "And you've been lying low ever since."

There wasn't really anything to say to that. I had been lying kind of low. I mean, the Girl Scouts? Not exactly my best showing.

"Well, you're in luck, Toby." The no-teeth smile was back. "It's football season, the Squad needs ten members, and our hacker graduated last year."

"And if I say no?"

Brooke showed her teeth. "You won't." She walked over to a nearby conference table, and one by one, the other eight cheerleaders took their places, filling all but two of the seats. Brooke leaned back and hit some buttons on her chair's arm. The image on the screen changed again.

"Tara Leery," Brooke said. "Nice picture, by the way, Tare."

Tara mouthed a silent "Thanks," and Brooke looked back at the screen.

"British exchange student and linguistic specialist. Fluent in nine languages, functional in twelve others, Tara has a perfect ear for accents. If we come across it, she can learn to speak it."

Brooke tapped a button with her French-manicured nail, and the picture on the plasma screen changed. "Bubbles Lane, contortionist."

Brooke didn't elaborate, but Bubbles did. "I can put my feet behind my head."

I racked my mind for the proper response to her proud declaration, but the best I could do was a rather unenthusiastic "That's nice."

"It's even nicer when you need someone to fit in a duffel bag," Chloe said sharply. "Or when the bomb you need to deactivate is hidden in the back of an air duct with laser sensor triggers no normal person could avoid."

31

A bomb? Personally, I wasn't really sure Bubbles could deactivate a washing machine.

"And speaking of bombs . . ." Brooke paused as the screen changed again. "Lucy Wheeler, explosives and weaponry."

I thought of Lucy jumping around doing herkies like a four-year-old on reverse Ritalin.

"Explosives?" I swallowed hard. "Weaponry?"

Lucy beamed at me. "I *love* Tasers."

I took about five seconds to desperately hope they were joking.

"And right now, I'm working on the coolest bulletproof push-up bra." Lucy's smile grew, if possible, even brighter. "It's to die for."

Tasers and bulletproof push-up bras. In practically the same sentence. So wrong. So, so wrong.

As I digested the wrongness of it all, Brooke ran through the rest of the squad. Apparently party girl Zee was a professional profiler, the twins generally came in handy because there were two of them (I *still* maintained they had a combined IQ lower than that of the average penguin), Chloe was their resident "gadget girl in Gucci," and Brooke, as far as I could tell, was exactly what she had always appeared to be: a gorgeous, terrifying, manipulative bitch who could lie, cheat, and steal with the best of them.

"The entire squad is, of course, trained in hand-to-hand combat."

I thought about how close Brooke's roundhouse had come to taking me down. Could they all fight like that?

"You're serious about this." I don't know why I said it. I mean, the giant plasma screen with the access code for the Pentagon should have been a big clue, but somehow, I couldn't help asking.

Brooke looked straight through me. "We save lives, Toby. That's how serious we are."

I said nothing.

"We also cheer at games," she continued. "We chant and we yell and we do backflips for the football team so that no one ever suspects we're up to anything else."

"And herkies," Lucy added.

"And we do herkies," Brooke amended. "Think you can handle it?" She leaned back in her chair, and she must have hit the button again, because all of a sudden, the list of companies I'd hacked into reappeared on the screen.

"Are you trying to blackmail me?" I kept my voice even.

Brooke shrugged. "Is it working?"

I closed my eyes for a long moment and then opened them again. "Maybe."

Tasting victory, Brooke leaned forward. "You're either with us or you're against us," she said. Like that was original. "If you're with us, you'll learn how to break into any building, how to lie your way into or out of any situation, how to look like one person one minute and another the next. You'll go undercover, you'll have limitless access to highly classified technology, and if you make it through your first two years, by your eighteenth birthday, you'll be a fully authorized CIA operative. Sooner or later, you'll probably save the world." She paused. "Plus you're like totally guaranteed to be on homecoming court."

Yippee, I thought, glancing back up at the screen. Brooke hadn't mentioned what would happen if I was against them, but I could guess. Hacking wasn't exactly a legal hobby, especially when the Pentagon was involved.

"I'm sure you'll even come up against codes you can't crack," Brooke added offhandedly.

And that's when I knew I was going to say yes. After all, I was the girl who'd never met a code she couldn't crack, and I wasn't about to let some cheerleader tell me otherwise.

"I'm in," I said, "but I am *not* wearing one of those stupid skirts."

CHAPTER 6
Code Word: Bitquo

"You'll need to get outfitted," Brooke told me. "And not just for the uniform."

Apparently, my skirt stipulation had fallen on completely deaf ears.

"Chloe, you'll set her up with the basics?" Brooke asked.

Chloe nodded. "Earpiece, communicator, digi-disk, truth serum . . ."

"And for the love of all things good and popular, get her some accessories." Brooke spared me another glance. "Those boots are going to have to go." I opened my mouth, but she continued spitting out orders like I didn't even exist. "Tiff, you and Britt are on makeover detail. Lucy, minor explosives only, please, and Tara?"

"Yes?"

"You'll be her partner."

That was the best news I'd heard all day. It was almost enough to make me forget that the phrase *makeover detail* had ever exited Brooke's mouth.

"Tara will give you the 411," the totalitarian captain told me, "but first, we have a few Squad matters to discuss."

Brooke glanced from me to one of the empty chairs at the table and back again. I gritted my teeth, but took a seat. I waited for Brooke to begin another long soliloquy on the cheerleading spy business, but instead, she turned to Zee, who nodded.

"I added the most recent body language indices to our files," Zee said, "and ran another set of statistical analyses on the remaining candidates. Hate to break it to you guys, but Stephanie Stanton is out. She's too jittery, too nervous, and in combination with what we already know about her susceptibility to subliminal suggestion, she's too big of a liability."

Stephanie Stanton. Why did that name sound familiar?

"But . . . but . . ." One of the twins tried to object.

"I know, I know," Zee said. "Her brother is hot, but she'd totally crack under the pressure. She's a double blinker, and they can't keep secrets worth a damn."

"A double blinker?" I asked.

Unlike Chloe, Zee answered my question in a perfectly reasonable tone of voice. "She blinks twice as often when you look directly at her."

Okay, I thought, trying to keep up. Double blinkers = bad secret keepers. And this from one of the single biggest gossip-mongers at my high school.

"And the subliminal suggestion part?" I asked.

"Messages on the bathroom stalls," Brooke replied. "The Big Guys Upstairs engineer them, and we implant them as part of our screening process."

It was then that everything they were saying clicked into place, and I remembered who Stephanie Stanton was. She wasn't some enemy agent with a thick foreign accent.

She was the pretty sophomore who'd sat next to me at the meeting—the one with the newly single, hot older brother.

Brooke had said that the squad needed ten members. Counting me, we currently numbered nine.

"So who's still in?" Brooke asked.

Zee looked through her notes.

"Hayley Hoffman, April Manning, Kiki McCall . . ."

JV cheerleaders: my very favorite people.

". . . Courtney Apex, and Sarasota Bane."

The last two were names that, being the social butterfly I was, I didn't quite recognize, but when their pictures flashed across the screen, I vaguely recalled having seen them at the meeting.

"Ix-nay on the ane-Bay," twin-on-the-left said. I got the feeling that this was as close to speaking in code as she could come. "Split ends much?"

"Tiffany," Brooke said, her voice surprisingly patient, "we can't rule out a candidate because of split ends."

Immediately, twin-on-the-right (who my advanced powers of deduction told me was Brittany) jumped to her sister's defense. "We already have to deal with her." Brittany jerked her head toward me. "If we take another neg-soc on, people are going to start getting suspicious."

"Neg-soc?"

Zee had the decency to look slightly embarrassed. "Despite your special skills," she said delicately, "you have what we refer to as a . . . uhhh . . . a negative social index."

All things considered, that was probably putting it mildly.

"Okay," Brooke said. "Bane is out."

If Brooke's "we save lives" spiel was to be taken seriously, we were deciding in whose hands we should place the fate of the free world, and a candidate had just been eliminated because of split ends.

"I think we should kick out Hayley Hoffman," I said, taking a stand. The others looked at me, and I improvised. "Her bitquo is too high, and we're already at capacity."

"Bitquo?" Tara might have been fighting back a smile as she spoke. It was hard to tell.

I looked at Brittany (also known as Miss We-Already-Have-to-Deal-with-Toby-the-Social-Reject) as I answered. "Bitch quotient."

Needless to say, that comment did not go over terribly well.

"Hayley's a strong applicant," Chloe informed me tersely. "Her social index is in our ideal range, she's a solid athlete, a leader, and she lies outstandingly well."

"So Hoffman stays on the list," Brooke said, not even giving me time to come up with another clever retort. "What about Courtney Apex?"

She zoomed in on Courtney's picture, and I recognized her as Bayport High's own pseudoprominent cosmetics model.

"She's afraid of fire," Lucy said, wrinkling her nose. Apparently, to the too-cheerful (no pun intended) explosives expert, that was a cardinal sin.

"And she may be somewhat recognizable from that toothpaste ad," Tara added.

"I like her," Brittany said firmly. "Good bone structure."

Bubbles shook her head. "Too tall," she said. "I mean, can you imagine having to toss her over a security wall?"

"Apex is out." Brooke made the decision, and no one questioned it. "What about Kiki McCall and April Manning?"

For the first time in my life, I found myself cheering for April Manning, Hayley's second-in-command. Anyone (or, for that matter, anything) was better than Hayley Hoffman.

"April is solid," Zee said, slipping back into profiler mode. "She's not as aggressive as Hayley and often lets her take the reins, but doesn't show any signs of allowing herself to be manipulated. As far as I can tell, she doesn't have any kind of inferiority complex. . . ."

Like that was a problem among the pretty and popular.

"Her body language is very controlled, and most of her actions seem highly strategic. She's ambitious, but doesn't have anything to prove." Zee grinned. "Plus her dad's totally loaded, even by Bayport standards, and she throws killer parties."

"And Kiki?" Chloe asked.

"Obedient," Zee replied immediately. "She's the only child of an overinvolved mother and a somewhat distant father, leaving her desperate to please on both accounts. We may be able to use the obedience to our advantage if we can coerce her into aligning her loyalties with us, but I can't guarantee it."

Brooke frowned. "She *is* a legacy."

Legacy? Did that mean what I thought it meant?

The others were silent for a long stretch of time, and then Chloe spoke. "Kiki's out," she said. "She's got to be. Are we really willing to risk a people pleaser just because her mom was on a Squad back in the day?" Chloe's voice hardened. "She's only passably coordinated, she's had private lessons out the wazoo and she still can't tumble, and, correct me if I'm wrong, despite the fact that she was practically raised for it, she has no special skills whatsoever."

Brooke held Chloe's gaze for an uncomfortably long time. I might not have been the profiler here, but I was sensing some tension between the captain and Number Two.

Chloe looked away first, and then and only then did Brooke continue. "Zee?"

"I'd say out, Brooke," Zee said, almost apologetically.

"Out," Tara echoed.

"Out," Brittany and Tiffany said in one voice.

Bubbles and Lucy shrugged.

"Out," Brooke said finally. "So we're down to April or Hayley."

I was about to raise my bitquo argument again when Tara spoke. "Special skills?"

Brooke tapped the arm of her chair, and the girls' files appeared on the screen behind her. "Both have been in the program since the sixth grade," she said. "Both are exceptional cheerleaders. Our screenings suggest that Hayley has some aptitude for mountaineering . . ."

Hayley Hoffman? Mountaineering? Where did they get this stuff?

". . . and April is surprisingly good at picking locks."

"Lock picking," I said loudly. "Well, that settles it. April's our girl."

Anyone but Hayley.

"We haven't had a climber in a while," Chloe said slowly.

Climber. Mountains. Hayley.

"This may have escaped your notice," I said in the calmest voice I could muster, "but Hayley is evil." The others stared at me. "I know, I know—evil and cheerleading kind of go hand in hand. . . ."

I was getting off track here, and I wasn't winning any friends.

"But we're talking about saving the world here, and a person like Hayley? All she cares about is saving herself." I paused. "Plus she hates me, and as much as that doesn't hurt my feelings . . ." I scoffed at the very idea! ". . . it just wouldn't be good for Squad morale."

Silence.

"Uhhh . . . go team?"

Brooke rolled her eyes, but then she shrugged. "April?" she asked the others.

One by one, they agreed, except for Chloe, who probably wanted to pad the Squad with a few more people who shared her thirst for my blood.

"April's in," Brooke said, not sparing Chloe a second glance. "I'll pass our official recommendation on to my superior, and with any luck, we'll be cleared to extend April an invitation to join the Squad this afternoon."

Upon hearing this, I was both surprised and incredibly relieved. The surprise came because I never thought I'd live to see the day when Queen Brooke referred to anyone as her superior. And the relief? That came because if Brooke had superiors who had to approve her recommendations for Squad acceptance, that meant that the fate of the free world wasn't *entirely* in the hands of my high school's varsity cheerleaders.

Brooke cleared her throat and tossed her ponytail over her other shoulder. "Next order of business," she said. "The president called. There's been another leak."

CHAPTER 7
Code Word: Thong

"Three minutes until our holos expire. That means T-minus eighteen until showtime, people."

I stared at Brooke. It was funny—she said these things like I was supposed to have some earthly idea what she was talking about, which I most definitely did not. Between the whole "holo" thing and the half hour I'd just spent listening to a rundown on what appeared to be an information leak from the Pentagon/CIA (not me, I swear), I was more clueless than Alicia Silverstone in the title role.

"Can you do *anything* with her in eighteen minutes?" Brooke's question was directed at the twins, and it was all too clear to me that I was the "her" in question.

Please God, I thought, let the answer to that question be no.

"The hair's going to take at least an hour," Brittany (I think) sniffed. "And that's if we speed up the dye process with Chloe's little rearrangey thingy."

"Electron wave accelerator."

I took in Chloe's correction. I wasn't sure what was more

disturbing—the fact that the twins were discussing dyeing my hair, or the fact that they were planning on using an electron wave accelerator to do it.

"We could give her a wig," Tiffany (?) suggested. "And change the clothes."

"I like my clothes."

"Whatever." Brooke waved that comment aside with a flick of her hand. "Why don't you guys just work on clothes for now," she told the twins. "We've got to be back in the locker room in sixteen minutes, and Toby still hasn't seen the rest of the Quad. Tara, finish her preliminary debriefing and take her by weaponry and aesthetics."

Finally, Brooke turned to address a comment (or, as I could already wager was more likely, an order) to me. "Come back to the gym after sixth period. Starting today, you'll be excused from seventh for practice."

No more gym class with a neofascist softball coach yelling in my face? I could learn to live with that.

"Britt, Tiff, you guys can Stage Five her while the rest of us debrief April this afternoon."

"Stage Five?" This time, I couldn't keep the question in. If anyone was going to Stage Five me, someone sure as hell was going to tell me what a Stage Five was first.

"A Stage Five makeover," Brittany said, tossing her too shiny, too long, too gorgeous blond hair over her shoulder.

Tiffany leaned forward to examine my eyebrows. "Better make that a Stage Six."

Tara reached out and lightly touched my shoulder just in time to keep me from leaping at Tiff. I'd had just about enough of the criticism twins. "Fourteen minutes," Tara said. "We'd better get going." With the ease of a skilled

43

diplomat, she steered me away from the table, the twins, and Brooke's mouth, which was already issuing new orders at top speed and high volume.

"You'll get used to it," Tara promised.

"The twins or *Mein Kampf* Barbie?" I nodded toward Brooke.

"Both."

I followed her lead and we approached one of the far walls.

Tara gestured to a small, squarish panel. "This is a touch pad," she said. "You place your hand on it, like this." She pressed her palm firmly against the square. A small flash of light rose from the bottom of the panel to the top, like a wave of concentrated laser beams.

"Let me guess," I said. "It scans your fingerprints?"

Tara nodded. "Among other things."

"What other things?"

The door slid itself open, and Tara stepped through it. "You'll see," she told me. Tentatively, I followed her through to another large room, trying to prepare myself for everything from nuclear warheads to spirit sticks.

Instead, all I saw was another large, mostly bare white room.

"This is the guidepost," Tara said, walking to stand in the center of the room. "From here, you can go any direction. The girls' locker room is directly above us. Cars and bikes are downstairs. Tunnel on the left leads to the helipad. Tunnel on the right will take you out to the woods."

"Bayport High has a helipad?"

Tara smiled a real smile for the first time since I'd met her. "There isn't much that Bayport High doesn't have," she said. "Most people think we have ridiculously wonderful facilities because we're such a wealthy school district, but really, you'd be surprised what having a secret government project housed beneath your school does for funding."

"And no one thinks it's strange that we have a helipad?" I asked.

Tara answered my question with a question. "Does anyone think it's strange that we have four gyms, an Olympic-sized training pool, a near-gourmet cafeteria, the biggest theater in a hundred-mile radius, and one of the most comprehensive library collections in the state?"

"Point taken." Because now that she mentioned it, Bayport's facilities were pretty extreme, even for a school district as wealthy as this one. If I hadn't ever questioned that, there was a decent chance that no one did.

"The guidepost also serves as a loading center," Tara said, smoothly moving on.

I looked around and didn't see anything to load. Nothing could have prepared me for what happened next.

"WEAPONS, OKAY!" Tara switched into cheerleader drive so fast I almost choked on my own spit. Her yell was loud and singsongy, and there was no mistaking the cheesy grin plastered to her face: she was one "Go Lions" away from a halftime show.

"*What* was that?" I asked, but the sound of my words was completely drowned out by the whirring of the shifting walls. Panels flipped, walls moved, and an instant after Tara had spoken (or rather, cheered), the entire left side of the room was filled with rows and rows of guns, knives, and . . .

"Bobby socks?"

"We rarely carry traditional weapons," Tara said. "You'd be surprised how many ways you can incapacitate a grown man using a pair of bobby socks."

"Uh-huh."

"Bobby sock grenades, bobby sock handcuffs, chloroform bobby socks . . ."

"You know that you people are seriously sick, right?"

Tara shrugged. "You know that you're one of us now, right?" she countered.

"Is this it?" I asked, scanning the weapons on the wall and avoiding her question. "Guns, knives, bobby socks, ribbons, lip gloss . . . I don't even want to know what that thong is for."

"Don't worry," Tara retorted lightly. "That information is classified."

The sad thing was, I couldn't tell whether she was joking or not.

"As for the other part of your question," she continued, "we have entire storerooms and laboratories dedicated to equipment and weaponry, but if you need it for a mission, you'll find it here before you leave." She paused, and her eyes held mine. "Lucy and Chloe are better at their jobs than you probably think."

"It wouldn't be hard." The words left my mouth, and though she didn't glare at my cheerleader-directed animosity the way any of the others would have, I was briefly overcome by the realization that she probably knew eighteen ways to kill a person involving a bright orange thong. Showing more discretion than usual, I changed the subject. "How'd you get the weapons to appear?"

"Simple," Tara answered evenly, and then without warning, she let out another cheer-yell. "WEAPONS, LAST TIME!"

More whirring, and the panels rotated and moved until the room settled back into its normal configuration.

"So 'weapons, okay' brings them out, and 'weapons, last time' puts them away?" It was meant as a rhetorical question, but Tara answered it anyway.

"No," she said patiently. " 'WEAPONS, OKAY!' takes them out." Sure enough, at her call, the whirring began again. " 'Weapons, okay' won't do anything."

"You have to yell it?" I asked.

Tara shook her head. "You have to *cheer* it. The voice recognition software is programmed to read both your voice identification and a combination of your tone, volume, and cadence. It's an added security measure. It's hard to cheer under duress. This way, if someone's trying to force you to reveal our weapons supply, you probably couldn't do it even if you tried." She tucked a strand of stray hair behind her ear. "Your turn. And remember, don't just say the words. Cheer them."

"You're telling me that this room knows whether I'm cheering or not?"

Tara said nothing. A few seconds of silence later, she looked at her watch.

I got the point. "Weapons, last time." I did my best to sound less angry than usual. Nothing happened. Tara kept staring, so I tried again. "WEAPONS, LAST TIME." I settled for loud instead of peppy, and still, nothing happened.

"WEAPONS, LAST TIME." I put a little lilt in my voice, but the panels remained completely immobile.

"Smile," Tara advised.

I glared at her.

"The holos have been gone for twelve minutes," she said. "T-minus three minutes left."

"Holos?"

"Holograms. If anyone had happened to look in the door to the practice gym in the past hour and a half, they would have seen a very good facsimile of the cheerleading team practicing a pyramid. The technology is light-years ahead of anything currently on the market, but basically, imagine going to see a 3-D movie, minus the glasses, plus an absurd number of projection points too small for the eye to see, and you've got completely realistic-looking holograms. We keep the doors locked during practices, so no one has a chance to interact with them, and they're configured with each of the possible outside vantage points—the windows on the doors and the ones on the north and south ends of the gym—in mind."

My mind ran through the angles from which a viewer could potentially view the holograms, calculated the density of light needed, and went into overload when I started thinking of rendering real-time motion with that kind of quality. So this was where those hefty taxes my parents paid went to. Secret high-tech cheerleading holograms. Of course.

Tara, sensing my wonderment, patted me on the shoulder, but then continued talking in a tone so no-nonsense that I couldn't have disbelieved her if I'd tried. "A little over twelve minutes ago, the holos went into the locker room. The showers are on timers. We have to be back before they turn off." She glanced down at her watch.

"T-minus two minutes?" It was half guess, half sarcasm on my part. "And you want me to cheer."

"Smile," she told me, and I tried miserably to heed the advice. "You have to yell and bob your head a little and smile, and you have to mean it."

I sighed, but considering the fact that if I didn't smile and mean it, the Pentagon was probably going to swoop down and arrest me any second now, I had no choice but to give it a shot. "I feel so stupid."

Tara patted my shoulder. "Don't worry," she said, her lips pulling up on the ends. "If you don't feel stupid, you're not doing it right."

"WEAPONS, LAST TIME!"

As the weapons disappeared, I couldn't help but think that my life had now officially hit an all-time low.

We walked back to the center of the room, and Tara handed me a towel.

"What's this for?" I asked suspiciously. With my luck, it was probably one of Lucy's explosives.

Tara opened her mouth to answer, but was cut off when the ground beneath us began to move. I looked down and realized that we were standing on another emblem—this one containing a shield embossed with a sixteen-point compass star and an eagle—and that this circular emblem, five feet wide to the other's twelve, was rising slowly off the ground.

"Squad version of an elevator?" I guessed.

The ceiling's panels spread apart, allowing our Squad-evator to deposit us in one of the locker-room showers. A shower which happened to be turned on, full blast. Tara jumped quickly out of the way, but I got the "refreshing" benefits of the spray, straight in the face. Within seconds, the shower turned off, and I stood there, fully clothed and sopping wet.

"Tara?" I said calmly.

"Yes?" She bit back a smile, which I met with a glare.

"I think I know what the towel is for."

CHAPTER 8
Code Word: Boo

Trapdoors. Underground lairs, high-tech headquarters, and references to "the Big Guys Upstairs." Bobby sock handcuffs and lethal orange thongs.

I tried to take it all in stride. Really I did. I pride myself on being the type of person who doesn't get caught off guard, but the thing was, I'd been so soaking wet that the twins had somehow coaxed me into pulling the shower curtain closed, stripping, and giving them my clothes. I figured that the Squad had to have some kind of intense drying technology, but I'd been standing in the shower in nothing but my underwear and my combat boots for ten minutes, and Brittany and Tiffany still hadn't returned so much as a single additional article of clothing. First period was about to start, and, quite frankly, even a bulletproof push-up bra was starting to sound good.

"Here." A manicured hand thrust something over the top of the shower stall. It was pink and sparkly. Like I would be caught dead in pink.

"What's this?"

"Your shirt."

"No." I dragged the word out, trying to be patient. "My shirt is much bigger. And black."

"I suppose that's one word for it."

"Brittany!" I spat out one of the twins' names, figuring I had a fifty-fifty chance.

"Tiffany," the twin in question corrected.

"Tiffany," I said, my voice dangerously pleasant, "I want my clothes back, and I want them back now."

There was a long silence.

"Tiffany!"

Then finally, she began speaking again. "You know how sometimes in spy movies, they'll send someone a note and it will be all 'this message will self-destruct in ten seconds'? Well, your shirt . . ."

"Self-destructed?" I asked through clenched teeth.

"It was more like assisted suicide."

I wrapped the towel tighter around my body, threw the curtain back, and leapt at Tiffany.

She held her hands out in front of her body. "Stage Six!" she shrieked. "We've been authorized for a Stage Six makeover!"

I was about to show her six stages of pain, but when Brittany came sauntering over with something that looked suspiciously like lingerie and a teeny-tiny jean skirt, I realized I had bigger problems than pink sparkles.

"I don't do skirts."

Brittany was less than intimidated at the threat of impending violence in my voice. "You're the hacker. We do fashion." She held up the jean skirt. "Today, the entire school finds out you made the squad, and unless you want to blow your cover the first day on the job, you have got to get a sense of style." She leaned forward. "Stat."

I'm not proud to admit this, but five minutes later, I was sitting in first period wearing a pink sparkly shirt, a skirt so mini it might not have qualified as such, and my combat boots, which I'd managed to get back from the twins before they had them incinerated. I had come to the conclusion that Brittany needed to die. The verdict was still out on Tiffany.

"That's her?"

I heard the whispered question, but didn't tune in. Instead, I adjusted my highly uncomfortable strapless bra and played around with the idea of stuffing one of those "special" socks into Britt's over-glossed mouth.

"That's her. I heard she transferred here from Europe."

"Well, I heard that her dad is like this way-famous movie star, and she came here and changed her name because she's totally not talking to him right now."

They were speaking loudly enough that it was hard not to listen to them, but the teacher was busy reading some romance novel and didn't notice that the vast majority of the class wasn't exactly working out geometric proofs in our spare time.

"What's her name, anyway?"

"Toby Klein."

And that's when I realized they were talking about me. Silence fell over the classroom, and in one coordinated motion, everyone and their dog leaned toward me, Toby Klein, newly appointed member of the God Squad. They awaited my words with bated breath.

I narrowed my eyes at the whole lot of them, but they just stared curiously back at me. "Boo," I said, trying to dispel their interest.

One of the girls tossed her hair over her shoulder. "That's European for hot," she said loudly, and the entire class looked at me with newfound respect. For the first time in my life, I found myself wishing that a teacher would regain control of her class, but everyone was just way too far gone.

"Toby, you look like totally boo today."

Mortified, I glanced back down at my pink sparkly shirt and renewed my vow to terminate the twin fashionazis.

"Talk about boo, where did you get those shoes?"

And now my oversized, clunky, unfashionable boots, the one article of clothing that I'd managed to retain, were being called boo. It was beyond all tolerance.

"I am in hell."

The girl who'd asked me about my boots tilted her head to the side. "Is that in the mall?"

By lunchtime, I'd given up on the idea of homicide. I'd moved on to genocide. I would personally rid the school— nay, the world—of cheerleaders.

"Toby, sit with us."

"Look, there she is!"

"Her? They picked her?"

"Toby Klein? Who's Toby Klein?"

"I hear she's related to Calvin."

"Well, I heard that at her last school, she was like megapopular, but then her boyfriend died, and she swore off popularity forever, but the God Squad, they know these things, and . . ."

It was almost more than I could take. How anyone could think I was related to Calvin Klein was completely beyond me.

"I have died and gone to heaven."

This voice I recognized, and I turned my mutinous glare on Noah. "Don't start," I said, turning to face him and inadvertently giving him a good look at my oh-so-prissy ensemble.

Noah's mouth dropped open. "My sister's a girl," he whispered with faux shock.

"Noah . . ."

He recovered quickly. "And not only a girl, but a popular girl." The smile was back with a vengeance.

"I swear, Noah, one more word, and I'll . . ."

I cut off my threat when I overheard someone else I'd never met inviting me to sit at their lunch table.

A loopy expression spread across Noah's face. "All hail Toby, queen of the cafeteria!"

I grabbed his arm and twisted it behind his back.

"You do not want to mess with me right now," I said in a low voice.

"Point taken," he replied with a grimace, and then, despite the hold I had him in, he grinned again. "You're a cheerleader," he said, deliriously happy. "You can have cheerleader slumber parties. You guys can have naked pillow fights in our living room, and . . ."

The rest of the school might have done an instant one-eighty in their opinions of me, but Noah never changed. I didn't know whether to be comforted or pissed. I let go of his arm. "Get lost," I told him, pushing down the urge to ruffle his hair. Once an older sister, always an older sister.

"She told me to get lost," Noah said, letting his eyes get big. "Toby Klein told me to get lost! She spoke to me! She . . ."

I rolled my eyes and shoved him away. Once a little

54

brother, always a little brother. He ambled over to his own table, a god among hopeless freshman boys. I watched him, and when Hayley Hoffman sauntered up to me, I devoutly wished I could change places with Noah. Goofy freshman boys versus evil junior-varsity cheerleaders? I'd take the boys any day.

"You may have everyone else fooled with your little act, but you can't fool me," Hayley hissed, dispelling any fear I might have had that she, like everyone else, would be wowed by my newly awesome status. "You aren't from Europe!"

I rolled my eyes so far back in my head that I could practically see my own brain cells and didn't bother to answer Hayley, whose you-are-beneath-me tone hadn't undergone any alterations in the past twenty-four hours.

"In fact," she continued, "you haven't changed at all. Different clothes, same skanky little reject who likes to pretend she's better than the rest of us."

I forced myself to unroll my eyes and look back at Hayley. "But I *am* better than you," I said evenly. "Or didn't you get that memo?"

She tossed her hair over her shoulder, and I elaborated in terms she would understand. "Me God Squad, you lame."

I'm ashamed to admit it, but I enjoyed flinging it in her face. It was almost even worth admitting the fact that I was (technically) a cheerleader.

"I don't know what's going on with the varsity squad," Hayley said, "but believe me when I say I'm going to find out, and when I do, everyone will realize that you're still exactly what you've always been: nothing."

"Toby!" Lucy appeared out of nowhere and bounded over to where I stood. "We've been looking all over for you.

Our table's over there. I just know you'll love it." She flung an arm around my shoulder. "Don't you just adore Toby?" she asked my evil companion.

Hayley forced a smile onto her face. "Who doesn't?" she said. I for one knew the answer to that question. In fact, it was probably a pretty long list, but Hayley, Mr. Corkin, and a linebacker I'd kicked in the crotch last semester were probably all up there at the top.

"Come on, Toby," Lucy said again. "This is going to be so much fun!" And then she shrieked, high-pitched, girly shrieking that made me want to gore out my eardrums with a dull cafeteria knife.

"Bye, Hallie," Lucy called over her shoulder as she dragged me off. Hayley stared after us, smoke coming out of her ears and a giant sign saying *dismissed* flashing above her head.

I bit back a grin. "Her name's Hayley," I told Lucy under my breath.

The perky weapons guru nodded. "I know," she said, her voice never losing its cheerfulness.

She'd called Hayley the wrong name on purpose, just to get under her skin. Was it wrong that I found that kind of mind game suddenly endearing?

"Situation averted?" Brooke arched a single eyebrow at me with the question.

Lucy nodded. "Totally."

Brooke looked at me and then looked at an empty seat at their table. I could almost imagine the chair the way it would have appeared in a Hollywood movie: shining and bursting with light, the equivalent of a social throne. In the movie, there'd probably be some sort of majestic music playing in the background.

The thought of it all made me sick. I refused to be that

girl. You know the one—the dorky girl with glasses who's secretly beautiful and gets adopted by the popular people and turned into a shiny, sparkly person just like they are. Excuse me while I hurl.

So when I reluctantly took my seat, I stared at my shoes, reminding myself that this was who I was. I wasn't glittery tube tops. I was Salvation Army combat boots, and I liked it that way.

"Chip, this is Toby. Toby, this is Chip."

I didn't even look up to see who had made the introduction. I knew who Chip was. He was a rich-boy football player who was also our student body president (to Lucy's vice president, if that tells you anything). He was the guy in the movie who would fall for the newly It-ed It Girl.

"Heya, Chip," I said, slouching down in my chair.

Brooke kicked my shin hard under the table.

Do you want to ruin everything? her voice asked in my ear.

I noticed immediately that her lips hadn't visibly moved and that no one else had heard her.

"Earpiece." Her in-my-ears voice answered the unasked question. *"It's in your hair ribbon. I have the microphone in my tongue ring."*

The fact that she had a tongue ring took me by surprise. She struck me as more of the belly-button type.

"Look, I'm turning this thing off so I can eat, but for the love of Gucci, flirt with Chip. You have to be above suspicion, and that means you have to be just like the rest of us. Or do you want to blow our whole operation and compromise the safety of the free world?"

That seemed a little melodramatic to me, but all things said and done, I was still dealing with cheerleaders here, so I figured I'd probably need to get used to the drama.

"Toby totally has a thing for jocks." Chloe, shooting me the evil eye, flirted with Chip on my behalf.

Yeah, I thought. I have a thing for kicking them where it hurts.

"Does she now?" Another male slid into the seat next to me. I didn't recognize his voice, but something about his presence felt familiar.

"Oh, you know me," I said, prompted by another under-the-table shin kick.

"No," the boy said blandly. "I don't. Should I?"

He was exactly the kind of arrogant, pompous, gorgeous ass I normally tried to avoid. Heavy on the gorgeous.

"Everyone knows Toby," Zee said, tossing her shiny black hair over her shoulder. Watching the hair toss, it was hard to believe that the psychological profiler and the school's numero uno "exotic hottie" were one and the same person.

Then again, it was hard to believe that I was one "Go Lions" away from being the school's most boo combat-boot-wearing, European, Hollywood offspring of Calvin Klein. I rolled with the punches.

"Everyone knows me." I repeated Zee's words, and then couldn't resist pulling Mr. Gorgeous's chain. "Who the hell are you?"

This time, I dodged the shin kick with a microsecond to spare.

"Well, Everyone-Knows-Toby," the boy said, addressing me. "I guess you'll just have to find out."

Inwardly, I smiled a wicked little grin. I would find out who he was, and with the help of the state-of-the-art Quad facilities, with any luck, I'd also find some grade-A black-mail material to wipe that self-important smirk off his perfectly crafted face. All I had to do was make it to seventh period first.

"Well, I heard that she totally dated a prince."

"No!"

"Yes!"

"No!"

"That is so boo!"

Unless I found a way to tune out the rumors flying at warp speed through the halls, getting to seventh was going to be harder than I had anticipated.

CHAPTER 9

Code Word: Like, You Know?

By seventh period, I was exhausted. Actively hating your newfound popularity with a fiery passion can really take a lot out of you. And seriously, I was beginning to think that *everything* sucks more if you're wearing a miniskirt. As I opened the door to the practice gym, all I wanted to do was escape. And lose the miniskirt. And forget about the fact that Brooke had assigned the twins to Project Give-Toby-a-Makeover. Talk about mission impossible.

I'd like to say that I walked into the gym with my head held high, completely devoid of any fear. But a day of being "completely boo" had taken its toll on my morale, and truthfully, I would like to believe that the phrase *Stage Six makeover* could put fear into the heart of even the most stalwart social misfit.

"Toby! Hi!"

I didn't know whether to be glad that Brittany and Tiffany weren't waiting for me, or to groan at the fact that Lucy was. Don't get me wrong. I didn't completely despise Lucy for being the perky, happy soul that she was. I'm not entirely heartless, and especially after the way she'd put Hayley in her place at lunch, I even had what might vaguely pass as a fondness for the bouncy little weapons expert. It was just a very particular kind of fondness—the kind where I didn't want to spend any more time in her presence than was absolutely necessary.

"Toby! Hi!" Lucy tried again. I had a sinking suspicion that ignoring her wouldn't make her any less friendly, and I wasn't sure I could take "Toby! Hi!" on repeat indefinitely.

"Hey, Lucy."

"So how was your day? Probably pretty long, I guess. But good? It was good, wasn't it?"

I could only conclude that the speed with which Lucy was speaking was the result of some kind of highly classified government enhancement of her tongue muscles, because otherwise, it shouldn't have been possible.

When I didn't respond to her question, Lucy frowned. "So your day wasn't good?" Her voice fell, and I felt a little bit like I'd just slain the Easter bunny in front of a Sunday school class full of orphaned children. I tried to decide whether the fact that she'd wanted me to have a good day that badly was strangely endearing or exponentially creepy. In either case, it felt somehow wrong to sit there, letting the Happiest Girl in the World frown.

"My day wasn't that bad," I told her.

It was, you know, only horrendous.

Lucy gave me a tentative half smile. "It will get better," she promised me. "Things will settle down. Like with all the rumors and stuff? It won't last forever, and you'll get used to it, and hey, it could be worse, right?"

I didn't have the heart to tell her that in the mind of

Toby Klein, things couldn't get much worse than standing in the cheerleaders' practice gym, waiting like an inmate on death row for the makeover that was headed my way.

"Anyway," Lucy said. "The twins are prepping the salon, and the others are getting ready to debrief April, but Tara and Brooke thought you might still be a little confused about the way things work and stuff?"

I could tell from the tone of her voice that the words that had just tumbled out of her mouth were supposed to be a question, but they sure sounded like a run-on sentence to me.

"So I thought I'd show you my lab, and give you a rundown on Squad history and stuff."

Her lab? As in the lab where the girl who added *and stuff* or *you know* onto the end of every sentence fooled around with explosives and weaponry? Still, it beat the hell out of getting a makeover.

Lucy was oddly quiet as she took me down to her lab (no trampoline this time—apparently there were like fifty billion entrances to the Quad, and only one of them involved belly flopping the way down)—and then, without warning, she launched into a surprisingly cogent and articulate explanation of Squad History.

"The Squad program has been around, in various incarnations, for about fifty years," Lucy said, sounding strangely professional. "Originally, the program was geared toward recruitment and training. Playing on cheerleaders' natural abilities for subterfuge and athleticism . . ."

Subterfuge? Seriously?

". . . the program was designed to allow a select number of young women to complete the training necessary to become CIA operatives upon their high school graduation.

The cheerleader mystique ensured that the program remained sufficiently covert."

"Riiiiiight," I said. "Covert. Because no one in their right minds would suspect that the government was training cheerleaders for the CIA."

Lucy rewarded me with the perkiest of grins, either ignoring or failing to notice the sarcasm in my tone. "Exactly."

"By the late eighties," Lucy continued, "most of the remaining Squad programs had been disbanded due to various budget cuts, but ours remained operational. Over time, the Bayport High Squad Program evolved to be less and less about training and more about helping the government keep an eye on a very specific group of people."

"In other words," I started to say, and before I'd finished the sentence, Lucy was nodding.

"In other words," she said, "we're like totally special."

I would say that she'd stolen the words out of my mouth, but the *totally special* comment bore no resemblance whatsoever to what I'd intended to say.

"Okay," I said. "Let me get this straight. Once upon a time, the government—God knows why—started recruiting high school cheerleaders and training them to be spies, and somewhere along the way, it actually occurred to them that this wasn't the best use of the taxpayers' dollars, so they stopped with the cheer-spies thing, except here in Bayport, where the Squad went from being a cover-up for some sort of spy school to being an actual operative agency?"

Lucy nodded. "That about covers it."

"And these people that we're supposed to 'keep an eye' on?"

Lucy shrugged. "They're the bad guys."

How very illuminating.

I was going to ask more questions, but Lucy changed the subject with all the subterfuge her cheerleading mystique could muster. "What do you think—blow darts—in or out?"

I pictured myself blow-darting an evil football player. "In."

I had so many more questions about the Squad—what exactly did we do? How much training did we receive? How was this whole thing even legal? Despite Lucy's dumb act (and, overcaffeination aside, I was starting to suspect that it *was* an act), I had a feeling that she knew more than she was letting on. At the same time, though, she was holding a knife, and I didn't want to press her.

"So," I said, eyeing the knife nervously. "Have you always been into weapons?"

"Me?" Lucy asked, and then she laughed loudly. Given the insanely broad smile on her face and the extra-large knife in her hand, it was borderline freaky. "Gosh, no. A couple of years ago, I'd never even seen a slingshot. I just wanted to make the varsity squad, you know? I'd been cheerleading for like ever, and making varsity seemed to be like this huge challenge and stuff. It was just something I did, and I wanted to do it well, you know? Cheerleading and student council and school and riding classes and . . . well, you get the drift. Anyway, when they brought me onto the Squad, I had like no specialty whatsoever. I wasn't a transfer like you. I was just a regular old recruit, like April, but I wanted to be good at something, and their weapons person had just graduated . . ."

"Hold on there, Skippy . . . errr . . . Lucy, what do you mean 'a transfer' like me?"

Lucy shrugged. "Some of us are Bayport natives," she

said. "We grew up here, and when we were old enough, we started cheerleading. It's just what people do here, you know?"

I didn't interrupt her, but did concentrate on using my nonexistent mind-control powers to compel her to get to the point.

"When I was in fifth grade, everyone wanted to be a cheerleader. I mean, I think every single girl in our class tried out. They picked forty of us that year, and then the next year, it was thirty-five, and they kept getting rid of people. Tryouts kept getting more and more competitive. By the time I made JV, there were only twelve of us."

Lucy's voice took on a new tone as she talked about the lengths she'd gone to in her pursuit of making varsity.

"Lucy," I told her. "Transfer."

"Oh yeah," Lucy said. "Well, the way it works is like this. The Bayport Cheerleading Association runs the tryouts for JV and under, and they're like, a bunch of overinvolved parents and all of the coaches. And I guess maybe some of the coaches are government people or something, because by the time we reach JV, they have all kinds of reports on us. And every year, the Squad captain gets profiles on all the current members of JV, and any other 'people of interest' in the sophomore class, and the members do a little digging around. We read through the files we've been given, and we do a bunch of prescreening and whoever the current Zee is runs all her psycho-whatsits on them, and then if there are any open spots, we make our recommendations to the Boss Guys."

I raised an eyebrow.

"No idea who the Boss Guys are," Lucy said. "That's why

I just call them the Boss Guys. Or maybe you were wondering about the whole 'current Zee' thing? Because obviously, there's only one Zee, but I meant, you know, whoever has Zee's job. Because picking the new Squad is part of the current Squad's duty, and the current Squad is always changing and stuff, so . . ."

"Lucy?"

"Yeah?"

"Transfer." I tell you, keeping the Queen of Babbling on task was a full-time job.

"Oh yeah," Lucy said. "Well, you know how I said we fill in any extra spots with girls from JV?"

I nodded.

"Well, sometimes we don't have that many extra spots, because ever since the Squad went from being a training thingy to an action thingy, the Boss Guys have been bringing people in from outside the system."

"The system?"

Lucy nodded. "As in the school system," she said. "If they find someone they want on the Squad, they fix it so that they're transferred to Bayport. That's how we got you. They transferred your dad, and you moved here."

I tried to digest this information. I'd hacked into the Pentagon, and a month later, my dad had been transferred to Bayport. I'd never made the connection before, but now, it was undeniable. "Are you telling me that I moved to Bayport *because* somebody wanted me to eventually be Squad Girl?"

Lucy gave me a very meek smile. "Would that be a bad thing?"

Honestly, I wasn't sure. I didn't like the idea of the government playing puppet-master with my life, but it made me realize, maybe for the first time, that the Squad was very real, and that the Big Guys Upstairs, whoever they were, were very, very powerful.

"How many other transfers are there?" I asked.

Lucy, sensing that I wasn't going to maim the messenger, smiled broadly. "Most of the time, the Squad's about fifty-fifty. Half of us have been cheerleaders forever, and just happen to have an aptitude for the spy thing, and half of us are special skills peeps who are transferred in."

"Which half is which?" I asked.

"You, Chloe, Tara, and Zee were transfers," Lucy said happily. "Did you know that Zee has a PhD?"

"She has a *what*?"

"A PhD. In forensic psychology and stuff. She might have another one or something, but I'm not really sure."

"Lucy," I said patiently. "Zee's a senior in high school. And her claim to fame is the fact that she can tie a cherry stem in a knot with her tongue. Unless PhD stands for Pretty Hot Diva, I don't think—"

"She was a transfer," Lucy said stubbornly, like that explained it.

"So she got a PhD, and then a bunch of government guys said, 'Hey, want to become a high school cheerleader?' And she just said yes?"

Lucy nodded. "Pretty much," she said. "I guess the first time around, she graduated high school when she was like eight or nine, so it was pretty much no fun at all."

My mind was spinning. The government had transferred my parents to Bayport so that I would become a Bayport High varsity cheerleader, aka Double-0-Toby. These same government guys plucked Zee straight out of grad school and convinced her that high school would be more fun the second time around.

"And Tara and Chloe?" I asked.

"Tara's an exchange student," Lucy said. "You've probably noticed the British accent. It's real. She grew up in England, mostly, but traveled a lot. Her parents were really gung ho on the Squad thing. And Chloe got some patent thingy when she was like ten, and they got her here the next year."

"And the rest of you guys?" I asked. "One day, you were just cheerleaders, and the next—boom—you're secret agents?"

I could almost understand the idea behind using a cheerleading squad as a cover-up—after all, if you stick a girl in a cheerleading skirt, no one takes her seriously—but the idea that half of us had been handpicked by the government for our "special skills" and that the other half had been chosen from the current supply of cheerleaders was still a little mind-boggling.

"Cheerleaders and secret agents have more in common than you might think, Toby," Lucy said.

I think the word *incredulous* would probably be something of an understatement for the expression that came over my face at that pronouncement.

Lucy rolled her eyes. "Oh, Toby," she said, like we'd been friends for a million years and she just couldn't get over how very silly I was in the most endearing of ways. "Here," she said, picking a notebook up off the counter. "Read this. It's this Squad history thing that Brooke got somewhere. It's got all of the stuff I told you in it, but it probably explains it better."

I seriously doubted there was anything in that book that could make me believe that high school cheerleaders were somehow predisposed to being brilliant government operatives, but it would have taken someone with a far harder heart than my own to tell that to Lucy Wheeler.

"So," she said brightly. "We still have like twenty minutes before you have to report to the salon. Wanna blow stuff up?"

All things considered, that was the nicest thing anyone had said to me all day.

CHAPTER 10
Code Word: Makeover

Unfortunately, happy explosives time couldn't last forever, and sooner than later, I'd bid goodbye to Lucy's lab and said hello to the twins'.

"Copper frost for the skin?"

Brittany pursed her lips at her twin's question. "Only if we go dirrrrrrty blond on top."

That's the way she said it, too. Like it was from some idiotic Christina Aguilera song that was cool when we were younger.

"If we go blond, we may need to change the eyes, too."

"Crystal clear?"

"Here's an idea," I said from my seat between them. "How 'bout we leave my hair, skin tone, and eyes the same?"

"Brown, taupe, and brown? Puh-lease."

"My skin's not taupe."

Brittany and Tiffany remained suspiciously quiet.

"Hyperdye for the hair," Brittany said suddenly. "It's totally brill. Like who's gonna believe that she became

70

Hollywood blond overnight? Nobody. But if we hyperdye her, and she changes her hair color like all the time . . ."

"People will think she's just releasing her inner cool," Tiffany completed her twin's thought. "People are so dumb."

"Hyperdye?" I asked, trying not to let them push me past the breaking point.

"It's this totally cool stuff Chloe made for us," Tiff said. "It like changes colors when you do this thing to it with another one of Chloe's gadgetmathingies."

I groaned inwardly, because obviously that incomprehensible (not to mention ungrammatical) sentence cleared everything up. Like, totally.

"So my hair could be blue one day and red the next?" If I was going to have to dye my hair anyway, a punk look was the most I could hope for.

"Blue?"

"Red?"

The twins spoke with identical, horrified tones.

"Toby, you're a cheerleader. Cheerleaders do not have blue hair."

"You hyperdye it. I'll pick the colors." I wasn't entirely sure how hyperdye worked, but it seemed like a good compromise to me.

"Maybe hyperdye isn't such a great idea," Brittany said slowly, still twitching in horror at the idea of a varsity cheerleader sporting bright blue hair. "Chloe gets kind of mad when we use it recreationally."

A six-syllable word. Impressive from a twin.

"Can't we just leave my hair brown?" I asked. "It's either that or bright red. Your choice."

For a moment, the twins stared at me, homicide in their little cheerleader eyes, but then, the twin on the left perked up a bit.

"Chocolate brown?" she suggested.

"Or maybe mahogany?"

"Honeysuckle!"

"Ohhh . . . or we could do mahogany with honeysuckle highlights."

"Perfect," they both said at once.

I tried to follow their conversation. "So we're going with brown, then?"

The two of them stared at me like I was the stupid one. "Were you not listening at all, Toby? We're going to go with a mahogany base and then add some honeysuckle high-lights around your face to bring out those nonexistent cheekbones."

Tiffany softened her sister's words a little. "Don't worry," she said, patting me on the head like I was a small child. "We'll hyperdye you before a mission sometime. That way, if you get caught and have to run or something, you can change your hair color like that." Tiff snapped her fingers, and the sound, sharp as her manicured nails, echoed in my ears.

I glanced around the room nervously. Four walls, no visi-ble door, and I was pretty sure I couldn't "EXIT, OKAY!" under pressure. There was nowhere to run, nowhere to hide—just me, trapped alone in what looked like the world's most high-tech salon, with twin fashionistas who had been au-thorized to administer a Stage Six makeover.

At least I still had my combat boots.

Britt reached up and pushed me into a chair. Immediately, restraints locked down my arms and legs.

"Wha . . . ?"

Without a word, the twins spun the chair around and forced my head into a sink.

"Don't move," Brittany advised. "Most of our stuff is kind of . . . you know . . ."

"Killer strong? Illegal?" Tiffany suggested.

"Yeah," Brittany said. "That. Oh, and you should probably wear these sunglasses, too. Are you allergic to avocado?" Without waiting for a response, she slipped the glasses onto my face. I won't go into the ugly details of what happened next: the dye so potent that the Squad bought it on the black market, the electron wave accelerator that the twins had co-opted to properly blend the highlights with the rest of my hair, the tanning spray that totally got up my nose, and the superstraightening serum that was, and I quote, "completely supposed to be used in some bomb thingy." They plucked me. They waxed me. They exfoliated the crap out of me.

They put makeup on my face.

Worse, they tried to teach me how to do it and acted like I was completely intellectually delayed when I couldn't explain the difference between lip liner, lipstick, and lip gloss. When they sat me back up and turned my chair to face a wall-length mirror, I prepared myself for the worst. What I got was absolutely shocking.

I looked just like them. All of them. Perfect tan. Perfect nails. Silky soft skin, gloriously shiny and thick hair, brushed to perfection. Big, pouty lips, and huge doe-like eyes, which they'd actually left my original chocolatey brown. I still looked like me. Sort of. It was just like me, cheerlead-o-fied.

You know those movies I was talking about earlier, the ones where the popular crowd makes over the dorky, shy girl, and even though she's quirky and zany and a real individual, she can't help but become enamored with her new look, because deep down, she's always wanted to be pretty?

This is not one of those movies.

"What the hell did you do to me?" I asked, horrified. "Do you know what I look like?"

Brittany smiled. "A cheerleader?"

"I look like Barbie's brown-haired friend! I look like something out of a commercial for capri pants, and I don't even know what capri pants are." I raged on, but even raging, the mirror let me know that I looked what most of the school would have termed *fabulous*. "I look," I spat out, "like the brunette love child of Mandy Moore and Marcia Brady. If they made a TV movie of my life right now, do you know who they'd cast to play me? Do you?" I couldn't say the name out loud. I despised tween queen actresses with the passion of a thousand fiery burning suns, and now, one of them was going to be starring in *Toby: The Untold Story*.

Until this moment, it hadn't been entirely real. Sure, people were talking about me, and yeah, I'd worn pink sparkles for the first time in my life, but I'd still felt like me. Now, staring at my face covered in their makeup, I had no choice but to be honest with myself: I was becoming the thing I hated most in the world, one of *those girls*. You know them. Every school has them. They're the girls you love to hate, but it's okay to hate them, because they hate you, too. If they even know you're alive. They're the kind of girls who step on the little people with their kitten heels.

And I was one of them. Minus the heels, thank God.

"You look fabulous," Brittany told me, interrupting my inner rant.

Tiffany smiled and hooked her arm through Brittany's.

"We're brilliant," she said, beaming first at her twin and then at me.

I glowered back at them, but with my shiny lips and mascara-ed eyes, the effect just wasn't the same. Either that, or the two of them had the combined emotional intelligence of a walnut, and couldn't read the obvious distress in my now clearly heart-shaped face.

"Access granted." The computerized voice spoke, a previously invisible door slid open, and Tara walked in. She seemed serious. Poised. Dignified. For one of *those girls*, she wore the look well.

"Nice job," she told the twins, who were too busy congratulating themselves and giving me an impromptu lecture on cuticle management to hear her. Tara shrugged slightly, her dark hair falling behind her shoulder. "You'll get used to it," she told me softly. "We all did."

That made me think of my one-on-one time with Lucy, and everything she'd told me. The über-salon existed for a reason. I wasn't the only transfer, which meant that I probably wasn't the only person who'd had to be cheerlead-o-fied. I'd always pictured the God Squad as the kind of girls who were born in a tanning booth wearing a bikini and getting exfoliated. It was like being born royal: the Divine Right of Popularity. And maybe that was true for girls like Lucy and the twins. But what about the other transfers? I couldn't help but wonder—what had Zee looked like back when she was a child prodigy PhD? What about Chloe? And . . .

Tara took my elbow and gently led me out of the room. "You *will* get used to it, Toby," she said. "You'll find a way to make it work for you, and after a while, you won't notice so much anymore."

The day I didn't notice I looked like this was the day I

lost the majority of my senses. I looked different. I felt different. I even smelled different.

"It's necessary," Tara continued, her voice even and low, "to keep up appearances. Our anonymity in the real world is based on our complete domination of the high school one. It sounds harsh, but if we look like *those girls* no one will ever see us as anything else."

I was slightly mollified by the fact that she knew of the existence of *those girls*. I stuffed my hands into my teeny-tiny skirt pockets and glanced down at my shoes. "What's next?" I asked glumly.

"Training," she replied. "Espionage. World domination."

The corners of her mouth twitched, and I could see that she was trying not to smile.

"Seriously," I said. "I don't think I can take any more surprises right now. No more teal hands, no more secret shower passageways." I narrowed my eyes. "No more Brittany and Tiffany's beauty shop of horror and doom."

That got a full-fledged smile out of her.

"As a matter of fact," Tara said, "you've just been assigned your first mission."

I briefly forgot the fact that I looked like the female lead of a one-hour teen drama and pictured myself as the butt-kicking girl-in-power type. "A mission," I said slowly.

Tara nodded. Her silence made me somewhat suspicious.

"Tara," I said. "What's my first mission?"

Tara stared straight ahead as she answered. "We're going to the mall."

CHAPTER 11
Code Word: Abercrombie

"Explain to me again why I'm in Abercrombie and Fitch."

Personally, I firmly believed that there could be no suitable explanation for such an atrocity.

"You have to tag one of the salesguys." Tara's directive didn't sound any more reasonable the third time she said it than it had the first.

"Why?"

The cheerleading sophisticate sighed. I eyed her warily, because if she told me that information was classified one more time, I was going to have to reevaluate my position toward her as borderline tolerable. "Practice," she said. "It's protocol. Before we can move on to our actual mission, we're required to assess your skills and transmit the results for approval."

Once upon a time, the Squad had existed as a training program. Now, the closest I came to "training" before my first mission involved a salesguy at Abercrombie. It was official: the Big Guys Upstairs were severely unhinged.

"Come on, Toby. It's not that bad."

Tara had already given me a lightning-quick explanation

of tagging, and somehow, I totally didn't think the phrase *not that bad* applied. As Tara explained it, tagging someone involved identifying them as your target, and (a) putting some sort of homing device on him or his vehicle, (b) planting something on his person crucial to your mission, or (c) interacting with him in a way that alerted the rest of the group to his presence. For those unfamiliar with the whole notion of cheerleaders as spies, I'll give you three guesses on what the acceptable form of interaction is.

Flirting. When you identify a target, if you're going for a C tag, you flirt with him until your partner or whoever picks up on special flirt vibes and secret flirt code and begins an intricate, multiagent course of action against the tagged person.

Luckily, this wasn't a C tag. This was a B tag. I had a stick of bubble gum. It had to go into his back pocket. Don't ask me why. That information was classified. If this was the Big Guys' idea of training, no wonder the other Squad training programs had been shut down.

"How am I supposed to do this without him noticing?" I hissed in Tara's ear.

"You're a cheerleader," Tara said. "You figure it out."

"Flirt?" I asked uncertainly. That seemed to be their answer for everything.

Tara slung her arm around my shoulder. "Toby," she said with a wry grin, "it's called misdirection."

"It's Tara, isn't it?" A woman my mother's age with a too-tight face, wearing too-tight pants and an obviously fake smile, approached us.

Tara whispered something in my ear and giggled. I forced a giggle, too, and pretended that she'd said something about a boy instead of telling me to proceed with the tag as planned.

Ever obedient (I can't even say that with a straight face), I turned to leave the awkward "my daughter goes to your school" interaction that was already under way, but the woman's voice stopped me.

"And who is your little friend?"

Little friend? I bristled at the term.

"This is Toby," Tara said with all the poise in the world. "She's a sophomore."

I nodded, trying to appear as if this whole conversation wasn't nauseating. I have deep and abiding suspicions that my attempt was a failure.

"A sophomore at Bayport High," the mother said, as if that was some kind of phenomenal accomplishment. "Are you on the squad, too, Toby?"

And the conversation went from nauseating to shocking, just like that. The Squad? She knew about the Squad?

"What squad?" I asked, trying to put a vacant look in my eyes. Come on, I told myself silently, if Bubbles the contortionist can play clueless, you can, too. Though of course, in Bubbles's case, it wasn't exactly a brilliant facade.

Tara rolled her eyes. "The cheerleading squad," she told me in what I can only describe as a faux indulgent voice. "Toby just still can't believe it."

"Just can't believe it," I echoed, trying to suck a little less at not blowing our entire operation.

The woman patted me on the shoulder and then moved to squeeze me into a full-on hug. "These years are so precious," she said.

Personal space, I thought, I'd like you to meet Nauseatingly

Reminiscent Mom. NRM, this is my personal space. Please stop violating it.

"Well, you girls have fun." With one final squeeze, she was off and shopping. "And do let me know when you have another one of those bake sales."

I so didn't sign on for bake sales and touchy-feely, Botox-ed über-moms.

"Happens all the time," Tara said calmly as soon as the woman was out of hearing range. "It's like every football parent or every mother of a freshman girl who wants to be a cheerleader acts like they know and love each and every one of us."

"I feel violated," I said darkly.

Tara half grinned. "You'll get over it." She prodded me gently in the side and I got the message. I had a stick of gum and it had to go in the hot salesboy's back pocket. Such is the glorious life of a sixteen-year-old secret agent.

The way I saw it, I had a couple of options. I could do as Tara had suggested and flirt with him. I could try a drive-by approach in which I ran by, rammed the gum into his pocket, and left in a blur of honeysuckle highlights, but somehow, I thought that forcibly ramming gum into said mark's pocket was not what the Squad had in mind. I could somehow get him to remove his pants. . . .

"I'm going to have to flirt with him, aren't I?" I said, less than overjoyed at the prospect.

"It's not you flirting," Tara told me. "It's the cheerleader."

Right. My cover. Malibu Toby, varsity cheerleader.

I knew then that I had exactly two choices: barf all over Tara in a fit of self-loathing, or suck it up and take one for the team. I gracefully opted for option B and wondered how exactly one went about flirting. I knew it involved teasing and giggling and a lot of hair tossing, but beyond that, the only picture that jumped into my head was one of Hayley Hoffman pulling her evil girl mojo on some unsuspecting senior jock.

I briefly considered the barfing option one more time, but that would have been like accepting that Hayley Hoffman should have made the Squad instead of me. I am Toby, I thought. Fear my wrath.

I wasn't going down without a fight, and even though I was completely lost in the alternate dimension that was Abercrombie & Fitch, I decided to play to my strengths. Flirting might not have been one of them (understatement), but I don't think I'm bragging when I say that mocking the flirtations of the Hayley Hoffmans of the world was more than one of my strong points. It was a calling.

So that's what I did. I sashayed up to the salesguy and thrust out my chest in an Oscar-worthy parody of the flirt styles of the bitch and famous. "Do you have this in blue?" I asked, holding up a microscopic miniskirt. I pressed it against my body and posed. "Black is soooooo depressing."

I batted my eyelashes at him at a ridiculously high velocity. And he fell for it. It was completely and utterly disgusting, and yet . . . strangely empowering.

"I . . . uhhh . . . uhhh . . ."

Two seconds, and I had reduced him to a bumbling fool. Was it wrong that I liked this? All this time I'd been knocking guys out, when I could have just made them grovel at my girly feet. Who knew?

"Blue?" He finally managed a coherent word. I almost felt sorry for him, but I was in superspy femme fatale mode. Take no prisoners!

I reached my hand toward his jeans. "Blue," I repeated,

and even though the Toby inside was wishing we'd opted for tossing our cookies before stooping so low, I forced myself to let my hand graze over his belt loops. "Like maybe the color of your jeans."

"You mean a jean skirt?" the guy asked, coming back to his senses. "Sure, we have those."

And just like that, my spell was broken. Was the inner Toby showing in my face? Were my eyelash bats too slow? Were my boobs too small? That was it, wasn't it? My boobs were too small. I knew there was a reason I pummeled guys instead of flirting with them.

As the guy turned to show me the jean skirts, I lost my patience. Okay, okay, maybe I never had my patience. Long story short, I slipped the gum in his pocket, and when he turned around to look at me, I slapped him on the butt. There you have it. I'm not proud of it, but hey, it worked.

He turned a bright shade of pink, and I could feel my face turning much the same color.

"Sorry," I said, completely straight-faced. "There was a fly."

And then I did what any self-respecting pseudogirl would have done. I turned on my heels and walked as fast as I could out of the store. For Tara's benefit, I even put a little shake in my hips.

She caught up with me halfway to the food court.

"I cannot believe you just did that," she said quietly.

"Yeah, well, that makes two of us."

I couldn't tell whether she was fighting down anger or hysterical laughter. "What was that?" she asked.

"That," I said simply, "was misdirection."

CHAPTER 12
Code Word: Gel Bra

"So . . . where to now?"

Tara hadn't said a word about whether or not my butt-slapping performance, which she'd somehow "transmitted" to our superiors, had passed Squad scrutiny. This was my not-so-subtle attempt to see if we were ready for our real mission, or if I was about to be fired for sexual harassment.

Tara stirred her iced mocha (with caramel swirl) with one hand and looked down at her watch. "It's time," she said. She stood up, neatly tucked a wayward strand of dark hair behind her left ear, and picked up the mocha to leave.

"Time for what?" I kept my voice low. This was the mall, and who knew what kind of bizarre and twisted enemy forces were lurking around every corner.

Yeah, right.

Tara took another sip of her mocha and then threw it into the trash can, still half-full. I crumpled my empty cup into a ball and tossed it in after hers. She gave me a look, and I got the impression that cup crumpling wasn't a preapproved cheer girl course of action.

"Come on," Tara said. I followed her.

"Time for what?" I asked again.

Tara's eyes flitted to the side, and I got the distinct feeling that she was checking our surroundings.

"Time to get to work," she said, like *that* wasn't vague.

"Work," I repeated. By this time, we'd left the food court, and she was a girl on a mission. Literally.

When she stopped in front of a lingerie store, I gave her a look of my own.

"Victoria's Secret?" I asked dryly. "Really?"

Tara smiled, and her eyes told me not to argue. "Shop for underwear now," she told me. "Ask questions later."

"Blink once if there's a purpose to all of this."

I was expecting another look, but instead, I got a smile and a slow, deliberate blink.

"Okay then," I said. "Underwear shopping. Lucky me."

Five minutes later, I couldn't even manage a sarcastic yay. There are certain things that should never be stuck onto underclothes. The list (and believe me, it's extensive) includes, but is not limited to: bows, chains, rhinestones, ribbons, ruffles, feathers, and anything that spells out the words *kiss me*. Call me old-fashioned, but I like my underpants plain and simple. And sometimes I like to call them underpants, but that's beside the point.

My arms full of offending articles, I trudged toward the dressing room. As soon as we got back to the Quad, I was going to kill Tara.

"Cheer up, Tobe," the traitor in question said. The double meaning behind her words wasn't lost on me, but I wasn't exactly in the mood to put a little more pep in my step.

I'd no sooner shut myself into one of the dressing rooms

and unloaded my booty (no pun intended) when someone knocked on the door. "Is everything all right in there?"

I know the salesgirl was just trying to be helpful, but what did she think could have possibly gone wrong in the past five seconds?

"Everything's fitting? You don't need any other sizes? A consultation?"

Consultation? I thought. It was underwear, not rocket science.

Or was it? A little alarm bell went off in the back of my brain. What if "consultation" was code for "information transfer" or something?

"Actually . . . I could use a consultation. Hold on just a second, let me . . ."

I didn't get to finish the sentence before the salesgirl flung open the door and barged into the room. Before I could manage a single word, she'd whipped out a tape measure and was halfway to wrapping it around my chest.

I'd like to clarify for a moment that I do not have personal space issues. I interact with others normally on a day-to-day basis, and I'm not one of those people who gets huffy when someone stands a little too close, but she was actually touching my boobs, and call me crazy, but that wasn't exactly my idea of a good time.

"Thirty-two inches." She surveyed my breasts through my shirt. "And an A by the looks of it." She gave me a sympathetic look. It was like someone had died.

"Is that . . . bad?" I asked, thinking of my failed flirtation with Abercrombie boy.

"No, no, of course not." She was somewhat less than convincing.

"So, is the consultation over?" I asked. For a split second, I'd thought that maybe this was part of the mission, that the girl measuring my breasts was a fellow operative, out to do whatever secret agents did (I was still a little vague on that point), but clearly, my sixth sense, the spy sense, was completely deficient.

"Let me just grab you a few things real quick," the girl said brightly, as if I hadn't asked her a question at all. "Thirty-two A . . ."

I couldn't tell whether that last part was a musing or whether she was actually addressing me by my cup size. I didn't have any time to ponder the question, though, because she was back in record time with a half-dozen bras. For one horrifying moment, I thought she was going to demand to stay in the dressing room with me while I tried things on, but she demurely stepped back, allowing me to close the door.

"Found anything yet?" Tara called over the door.

"Dead girl," I called back, matching my tone to hers. "You're a dead girl."

I eschewed the underwear Tara had forced into my hands in favor of the bras the salesgirl had given me. I slipped off my own sports bra and reached blindly for a test subject. My hands closed around a flesh-colored bra, and I put it on, fastened it, and turned to the mirror. I moved back and forth, and the bra wiggled and jumped as I did.

"Tara," I said flatly. "It's moving." I poked it. "What is this thing?"

"I'm not certain, but I think you're probably wearing a gel bra."

I poked it again. Weird, and yet, as much as I hated to admit it, comfortable. Feeling a little less daunted by the task at hand, I threw the gel bra aside and picked up the next one. I slipped into it, but the moment I did, something poked into my skin. I eased back out of the bra. It looked perfectly normal, but when I ran my hand along the inside of the cup, my fingertips caught on a tiny, uneven bump. I prodded the bump with my fingers, and as if by magic, the fabric parted, and out came a tiny, round disk, no bigger than a nickel.

"Found anything yet?" Tara called over the door once more.

I stared at the disk. "Yeah," I called back. "I think I did."

"Gel bra?" Tara continued conversationally, like we weren't shouting over dressing room doors.

Still somewhat enchanted by the tiny disk, I nodded. "Sure," I said. "Gel bra. Whatever."

Fifteen minutes later, I was standing at the checkout, lingerie in hand, the minidisk hidden securely in my own sports bra. Tara surveyed my purchases: the befuddling gel bra, five pairs of multicolored, cotton bikini-style bottoms, and at her insistence, a turquoise thong with teeny-tiny sequins on it.

I didn't even care about the underwear. Thongs? Sure! Sequins? What could be wrong with a little sparkle? I'd found the disk. I was on top of the world.

"Next."

At the cashier's call, Tara stepped forward. She sat her selections on the counter and held up a lime-green bra. "Do you have this in pink?"

The cashier looked at the bra, glanced at Tara, and then took the green monstrosity with her into the back room. She emerged a moment later with an identical pink bra, and handed it to Tara. "Is that all?" she asked.

Tara nodded.

When her total appeared on the cash register, I came off my minidisk high. How could something composed of so little fabric be so expensive? Not wanting to blow things at this stage in the game, I slipped my wallet out of the purse the twins had forced me to carry, wondering if I had enough cash to cover an expenditure of this magnitude. I so didn't want to have to explain the appearance of a Victoria's Secret purchase on my emergency-only credit card.

When I flipped open the wallet, a completely foreign sight greeted me with sleek metallic sheen. I pulled it out, and my eyes bulged: a gold card. With my name on it. I tried to get Tara's attention, but failed.

"Next." The register next to Tara's opened up.

Going with the flow, I stepped forward, plopped my purchases down on the counter, and held out my card. My gold card. My hopefully government-funded gold card.

I avoided eye contact as the cashier rang up the turquoise thong, but the Mall Gods must have had it in for me, because a microsecond before the thong was in the bag and I was in the clear, the pushy mom from Abercrombie appeared out of nowhere, bounded to my side, and said, loudly enough for the entire store (and possibly a large portion of the rest of North America) to hear, "That is just adorable!"

I cringed.

"Look at those sequins, and that color!"

Please stop. I sent her a silent, telepathic message, but it did no good.

"Where did you get that, Toby? I just have to pick one up for myself."

I discovered in that moment that there was indeed something far worse than froofy underpants, and it involved someone my mother's age buying a sequined turquoise thong.

The attendant handed my card back. I stuffed it in my purse, gestured haphazardly across the store in response to the mom's question, and bolted.

"That woman is everywhere," I hissed the moment Tara caught up with me.

My partner shrugged, that carefree-yet-divine gesture I'd come to associate with her public persona. "At least you got some new things," she said, playing around with the last word. She grinned wickedly at me. At first, I thought she was talking about the underwear, but the minidisk took that moment to push against my chest and remind me that our shopping adventure had been about more than just lingerie.

As we slid into the car, I thought about the fact that today was definitely a day of firsts. I'd attended my first cheerleading practice. I'd been recruited to work for my first top-secret agency, I'd had my first makeover, and I'd slapped a hot guy's butt for the very first time. Add to that new lingerie and the spy sense that hadn't led me astray, and I was starting to feel like Toby in Wonderland. Or possibly, given the lingerie factor, Toby in Wonder*bra*land.

Tara started the engine, and I marveled again at its magnificent purr. I wasn't exactly a Beemer type, but this one was amazing.

"Is this your car?" I asked, thinking of my newly acquired credit card. "Or is it, you know . . ."

"Squad owned?" Tara supplied. "It's mine. The Big Guys Upstairs bought it, but people would totally get suspicious if someone else inherited my BMW when I graduate, so it's mine to keep."

"I can't believe you have a BMW," I said.

"I'm supposed to be the foreign sophisticate," Tara said. "They thought it fit the role." She turned onto the highway and floored it. "Not that I mind."

The car did fit her image, and her words confirmed exactly what I'd been thinking ever since I'd learned that like me, Tara wasn't a lifelong cheerleader. She was supposed to be the foreign sophisticate. It was a role she played, like I was learning to play Cheerleader Toby. I looked at her out of the corner of my eye and wondered if I'd ever get to see anything but the image.

Tara Leery—who are you really?

"Pop the digi-disk in, and we'll see what we've got," she said.

I filed away the term for future reference and tried to think of a way of retrieving the disk that didn't involve reaching my hand down into my bra in a very conspicuous manner.

Luckily for me, Tara pretended not to notice my hesitation and just kept talking. "We'll need my disk to decode yours," she said, "but we should be able to get some idea of what's on it without running through the decode."

"Yours?" I arched an eyebrow at her. "You have one too?"

Tara zipped into the next lane over. "But of course," she said. "Want to be a good little Squad trainee and tell me when you think I got it?"

I ran over the events in my mind, playing them back in my memory the way other people might have rewound a taped episode of the trashy reality show du jour.

"Please tell me it had something to do with the hideous pink bra," I said, taking a shot in the dark based on the fact that I sincerely hoped that I wasn't trapped in a car with the kind of psychotic person who would have actually wanted that travesty of an undergarment.

"Bingo," Tara said. "Most of the time, we don't even bother with disks, but with the frequency of leaks increasing, our superiors thought a handoff was more secure than a direct transfer. The fact that there are two disks is added security—though if they'd thought there was actually a threat of interception, they would have sent the disks to two different locations."

"So there was no threat of an enemy agent sweeping in and stealing our lingerie?" I asked, only half joking.

Tara offered me a small grin and an answer, in that order. "If they'd thought there was a real chance that the mission would be compromised," she said, "they probably wouldn't have given it to a rookie."

Had any of the other cheerleaders called me a rookie, I would have been offended, but coming from Tara, it sounded like a statement, not an insult. Plus, I had to admit that I was slightly mollified by the fact that our Victoria's Secret mission hadn't been a high-stakes operation, because saving the world one gel bra at a time wasn't exactly what I'd signed up for.

"Digi-disk," Tara reminded me. "Player."

I averted my eyes, highly aware of the tiny round disk digging into my right breast. Tara was waiting, and out of the goodness of my heart, I offered her an explanation for the delay. "Digging things out of my bra?" I snorted. "I haven't had much practice."

"You should get Bubbles to give you some tips," Tara advised, "because you will."

"Will what?"

"Get a lot of practice."

I ignored her prediction, fished quite unstealthily around in my bra, and held up the digi-disk triumphantly. "Where do I put it?" I asked.

"Media on."

This time, no cheer-voice was needed. The dashboard, impervious to my grumbling, rearranged itself, and a control panel popped out of the inner console.

"Insert digi-disk," a highly synthesized female voice commanded.

A small slit in the panel lit up, and I touched the disk to its surface. Immediately, the car swallowed it whole, and above the dashboard, between Tara and me, appeared some sort of 3-D diagram.

"Disk data analyzed," the computerized voice continued. "Video, audio, and digital data found. Decode needed. Index data available. Play first available index entry?"

Tara checked her rearview mirror and changed lanes. "Index data," she commanded. "Audio only."

Instantly, the holographic diagram disappeared, and the car began reading off a list of available files.

"Interaction logs, Peyton, Kaufman, and Gray. Updated client list (partial), Peyton, Kaufman, and Gray. September sixth audio, Peyton, Kaufman, and . . ."

"Sensing a pattern here," I said, drumming my fingers on my knees. "Who are Peyton, Kaufman, and Gray?"

I was asking Tara, but the car answered me instead.

"Peyton, Kaufman, and Gray, formerly Peyton, Peyton, and Gray, formerly Peyton and Peyton. Officially a civil, criminal, and corporate law firm, established in 1932."

"And unofficially?" I asked.

This time, it was Tara who answered my question. "Unofficially?" she said. "They're the bad guys. Their client list is a veritable who's who of über-criminal types. They represent everything from white-collar criminals and nefarious corporations to mobsters, terrorists, and the black market underground." Tara shook her head. "They all have one thing in common: a lot of money."

A law firm in Bayport whose clients had a lot of money? Shocking! That said, the whole evil part of the equation was a little more difficult to wrap my mind around. I thought about what Lucy had told me earlier. When the rest of the Squad programs across the country were axed, the Bayport program was expanded, helping the government to keep an eye on a very specific group of people: the bad guys.

"So Peyton, Whatever, and Whatever represent the enemy?" I asked, trying to work my way through it all.

Tara shook her head. "They *are* the enemy. The law firm is a convenient cover."

"Evil lawyers," I said. "Check." I nodded toward the digi-disk player. "And the disk?"

"Instructions for our Mission," Tara said, and her tone left no question that it was spelled with a capital M. Picking up the disk had been a baby mission. The instructions that were on the disk were for the real deal. "And, given that our superiors don't want to risk a direct data transfer from their database to ours, probably most of the information they think we'll need along the way."

"So," I said. "About this Mission."

"It's . . ."

"Classified," I finished for her. "I know, but I just pulled a disk out of my bra. Personally, I think that earns me some clearance."

Tara paused for a moment and then shrugged. "You'll get

the full scoop at the debriefing once Brooke's had a chance to go over the information on the disk, but from what I've been able to pick up, the gist of it is that the Big Guys have managed to trace the source of the recent hacks on their system to Bayport, and if someone in Bayport is doing it, then there's an extremely high likelihood that the Peyton firm is involved. Until a couple of days ago, the Big Guys had a man on the inside at Peyton." Tara very delicately did not mention what had happened to the man. "He managed to smuggle out some information that might be relevant before he was caught."

"Do people get . . . *caught* often?"

"If by people you mean the string of agents the Big Guys have sent to infiltrate the firm? Yes. If by people you mean cheerleaders at the local high school who could not possibly be involved in anything that could threaten the firm's security—no."

I remembered Brooke's words at that first meeting. *We're smart, we're pretty, we're in perfect physical condition, and best of all, we never get caught.*

Not to sound like a cheerleader, but go us.

"The Big Guys have a long history of trying to infiltrate Petyon, Kaufman, and Gray," Tara continued, "but their bugs never last more than a week or so, and their agents don't even last that long."

"And when you say they don't last that long, you mean . . ."

Tara's face showed absolutely no emotion as she answered my unasked question. "You don't want to know."

Well, that was certainly a sobering thought.

"So what do we do with all of this information?" I asked, half ready to throw myself into supersecret agent mode once more and half thinking that this whole thing had been some kind of giant mistake.

Tara pulled into the school parking lot and immediately into a primo spot. "Whatever they tell us to."

It was funny—in my mind, when I asked Tara what we were going to do with the information we'd acquired, her response had been "Whatever we want."

CHAPTER 13
Code Word: Cheer Shorts

"F-A-B-U! L-O-U-S! Bayport Lions, fab-u-lous!"

I heard the rest of the Squad before I saw them. As we wrapped around to the practice gym, their shouts echoed down the hallway. Tara pushed the door to the gym open, and I spent about five seconds devoutly praying that the cheering girls in front of me were a hologram. Because if they weren't . . .

"Last time," Brooke called out, meeting my eyes, and a few seconds later, all of the girls struck poses, cheesy grins plastered to their made-up faces.

Brooke pushed a stray piece of hair out of her face, and I noticed that she'd worked up a sweat. So much for my hologram theory, I thought. Somehow, I doubted cheerleader illusions had holographic sweat.

"You guys get what you were looking for?" Brooke asked Tara.

Tara nodded. "Totally."

Brooke smiled. "Awesome."

How many other times had I overheard the cheerleaders talking like this? Had they always been talking in cheer code? Like I'd assumed that they were talking about some guy or MAC lip gloss or an outfit at the mall, and they'd actually been communicating on a completely different level? I was supposed to be the hacker. I broke codes without even meaning to, but all it had taken was one too many *awesomes* from them, and I'd assumed they were idiots.

Such was the brilliance of the Squad.

"Ready for practice?" Brooke asked.

I wonder what we would be practicing. Martial arts? Disguise and surprise strategies? Misdirection?

"You guys get changed. We're getting ready to go over Saturday's halftime routine."

I opened my mouth to tell her that I seriously hoped she wasn't talking about what I thought she was talking about, but Tara reached over and pressed gently on my chin, forcing it back up.

"Come on," she directed. "Let's get changed."

And then before I could so much as audibly lament my dismal situation, she dragged me into the girls' locker room.

"You have to learn to cheer eventually," Tara told me. "The sooner, the better, and side note, Brooke can get kind of ugly when she's mad, so trust me when I say it's not worth arguing with her over this."

"I could take her," I grumbled. Part of me wanted a rematch with Brooke on solid ground.

"Maybe you could," Tara said, "but I couldn't, and you're my partner, which means . . ."

"I'm your responsibility?" I asked.

Tara shrugged. "Something like that."

I whistled under my breath. "Man, they must really hate you."

"Nah." Tara shook her head as she stripped off her shirt

97

and slipped into a sports bra. "It was either Chloe or me, and Chlo . . ."

"Hates me," I finished.

"She doesn't hate you," Tara said. "She just doesn't like what you represent." Tara opened a locker and tossed me an extra set of workout clothes. I took one look at the teeny-tiny gym shorts, which had the word CHEER written across the butt, and gave Tara a look.

"It's all part of the game," she reminded me, and because I liked Tara and felt bad that she'd gotten the short end of the spirit stick and ended up with permanent Toby Duty, I changed clothes with only a minor level of grumbling.

"So what do I represent to Chloe?" I asked.

Tara bent down to tie her shoes, and she didn't look at me as she answered. "What she used to be."

"You're kidding me." Lucy had said that Chloe was a transfer—that she'd registered her first patent when she was ten, and it had occurred to me that the average child inventor wasn't exactly Chloe-esque, but still . . . I had a hard time picturing a younger Chloe as me. In fact, I was more apt to believe that she'd been a watermelon in a former life than that we'd ever been anything alike.

"You ready?" Tara asked. I got the message: she was done talking about Chloe.

I deliberately took my time tying the sneakers she'd given me.

"Toby."

"Fine." I pulled my hair back into a ponytail. "Ready." As we walked toward the door, I stopped. "Remind me again why we have to do this instead of downloading all of the information on the disks." I paused. "And where are the disks?"

"We have a game on Saturday," Tara said, answering the

first part of my question. "If we don't take ourselves seriously as cheerleaders, no one else will either. Hence, practice."

I considered emphasizing the fact that the very phrase *taking cheerleaders seriously* was somewhat oxymoronic, but Tara didn't give me the chance.

"As for the disks, I gave them to Brooke. She's in direct contact with our superiors—she'd know if it was urgent, and if she says we practice first, then we practice first." Tara didn't wait for me to ask how she'd managed to give both disks to Brooke without me seeing it. Instead, she walked out the door, and I had no choice but to follow.

I don't particularly care to relive that practice, but I'll tell you one thing: cheerleading is hard, and not just because it should be illegal to be that happy about anything. It's actually, physically hard. Everything hurts. You kick your leg up high next to your face, and even if you're used to kicking karate-style, that doesn't do much for you when you're high-kicking like the freaking Energizer Bunny on uppers. Then there's all these little nuances that the cheerleading Gestapo expect you to get right the first time. Point your toes! Pop your motions! Straighten your legs! Donut holes are bad, and hyperextension is good. It's like they speak a whole other language.

By the time we took a water break, my voice was hoarse, my legs were killing me, and I felt like a complete and utter imbecile because I kept switching the words *win* and *again* in the halftime cheer.

"You're not nearly as horrendous as we thought you were going to be," one of the twins told me brightly.

I was too busy chugging water like a desert camel to respond.

"So," another voice said. "You're Toby Klein."

I looked up from the water fountain. "Yeah," I said. "And you're April."

I was the transfer. She was the regular recruit. I was a life-long hacker. She was a lifelong cheerleader. For me, this whole cheer gig was a cover. For her, it was a way of life.

"There's a party at my place on Saturday after the game," April said, snapping me out of my thoughts. "Daddy's out of town, and we'll have the whole house to ourselves."

I remembered Zee's analysis of April: independent, charming, intelligent, rich.

At least she wasn't Hayley Hoffman.

"So I see you two have met." Her tone of voice was so very Chloe that I recognized it right away.

"Yup," I said.

April shrugged.

"Come on, April," Chloe said, placing herself between the two of us. "I want to show you some of our more advanced cheers."

Chloe spared me a single look as she said the phrase *more advanced*. Apparently, I wasn't the only one who had noticed that I belonged in the remedial cheer class.

April leaned around Chloe. "See you on Saturday?

I was about to say no, but Tara answered for me. "Of course," she said.

Before either of us newbies could say another word, Chloe dragged April away.

"Let me guess," I said evenly. "Chloe's April's partner?"

Tara nodded.

"We're only going to have to do a Stage One on April, I think," Brittany piped up suddenly. "Her highlights are gorgeous, but I want to even out her skin tone a little."

I nodded. As awkward as I'd felt during our little mall

100

mission, this was a million times worse. Now it wasn't just me trying to adjust to the Squad: it was me and April. April, who could cheer. April, who Chloe had selected as her Mini-Me. April, who barely needed a makeover at all.

And then, as if things weren't already bad enough, the torture started back up again. We went through the routine time after time, until I was the only one messing it up.

"That's it for today," Brooke said. "Let's hit the showers."

"Finally," I groaned under my breath to Tara as we headed into the locker room. "I feel like my legs are going to secede and wage war on the rest of my body. All I want is to go home, and . . ."

I recognized the look on Tara's face.

"I don't get to go home, do I?"

Tara shook her head.

"Are we really hitting the showers?" I asked.

Tara bit her bottom lip and then nodded.

"Is this going to be anything like when we hit the showers this morning?" I asked.

Instead of answering, Tara walked from the gym into the locker room, and after casting a single sheepish look over her shoulder, she walked into one of the shower stalls, reached out, and twisted the shower knob. Left, right, and then left again, 180 degrees this time.

When the shower wall rotated and gave way to a staircase, I wasn't all that surprised.

At least, I thought as the shower wall closed behind us, no one is going to tell me to point my toes in the Quad.

CHAPTER 14
Code Word: Party!

I didn't see Brooke place the digi-disk into any kind of player, but before I could say "Go Lion(esse)s," the index was up on the screen, and the other girls, sweaty from practice, were taking their seats at the table. Stiff and drenched in the fruits of my cheery labor, I slipped into the last available seat at the table, in between Tara and Zee.

"Chlo, can you decode?" Brooke asked. "Here's the second disk."

As soon as I heard the word *decode*, I leaned forward in my seat. I was new to this, but wasn't decoding supposed to be my area of expertise?

Chloe tossed her ponytail over her shoulder and held my eyes with her own. "No problem," she said, reaching forward to take the disk Tara had acquired from Brooke. She pulled something that looked like a makeup compact out of one of her shoes (how had she high-kicked with that in there? how?), and a split second later, she flipped it open, inserted the disk, and lifted a powder puff to reveal a tiny circular keyboard.

"Chloe's compact has some basic decoding formulas programmed in. When she puts in the decoder disk, it runs the specifics through the formula and decodes the file," Tara said.

"All of that in a makeup thingy?" I could feel my eyebrows rise as I asked the question. Tara might not have realized how complex the type of program she had described was, but believe me, I did, and the very fact that it was programmed into a unit that came with a powder puff was the equivalent of technological blasphemy.

"*Voilà.*" Chloe leaned back in her seat, and after another hair flip and another oh-so-pointed look in my general direction, she turned back to Brooke. "Looks like we have something we can work with."

In response, Brooke hit a few keys on the arm of her chair, and a thin green line appeared on the middle of the screen. "Play audio," she said, her voice loud and clear.

The lights dimmed slightly, and as a voice filled the room, the green line on the screen began to move in sync with the words. I could only infer that whoever our bosses were, they were even bigger drama queens than the girls in this room—which, as you might have guessed, was *really* saying something.

"Hello, girls," the voice said. I had an incredible urge to respond with "Good morning, Charlie," but somehow, given the sudden seriousness that had settled over my teammates, I doubted anyone would appreciate the reference.

"As you know, the CIA databases have been accessed by an unknown entity twice in the past week. While neither of the hacks lasted more than thirty seconds, we have reason to believe that the limited window of time allowed the hackers to access highly classified information."

The voice didn't expand on what that information was. I was beginning to hate the word *classified*.

"We've managed to track the source of the breach to somewhere in Bayport, and have therefore included our most up-to-date analyses of the Peyton firm's activities this month: financial records, interaction logs, and limited audio surveillance. You'll want to go over it all with a fine-tooth comb. For the duration of this mission, you should refrain from using your database to access ours. Since there's no link between the two and no mention of the Squad program in any of our files, your system should be secure."

Somehow, I was less than shocked that the CIA didn't have an electronic paper trail detailing its use of teenage cheerleaders as secret agents. This whole operation had top-secret written all over it.

Without warning, the green line on the screen was replaced with a picture of a guy I vaguely recognized as an international playboy who had recently broken up with a celebutante heiress who shall remain nameless.

"Girls, this is Heath Shannon."

There were a couple of girly sighs in the room, and my resultant eye roll was nothing short of reflexive.

"According to our surveillance, his contact with Peyton, Kaufman, and Gray has increased significantly since the first leak earlier this week. Whatever information the firm has managed to acquire, they'll be looking for a buyer, and right now, Heath Shannon is our best lead. We have reason to believe that he has contacts on the information black market who would be more than willing to pay for the kind of information accessed during the leaks."

The picture changed, this time to reveal an office building nestled in between a Starbucks and a bookstore. It could have been anywhere, but I was going to go out on a limb and guess it was in Bayport.

"This is the office building for Infotech Limited," the voice continued. "A privately owned technology company, specializing in internet security, virus protection, and advanced TWD."

"Technological weapons defense." Tara whispered the clarification in my left ear.

"Infotech's Pentagon contract was terminated in 2004. Our systems have changed some since then, but of all of Peyton's clients, they're the most likely suspects in the breach."

Everyone seemed awfully sure that these leaks were tied to the law firm. It made me wonder just how evil these lawyers were.

A third picture flashed up on the screen—a map. As the voice continued talking, bright dots of light appeared all over the map, which covered most of the globe. "The illuminated points on this map represent our operatives worldwide," the voice said. "Take a good, long look at the numbers here, girls. This is what's at stake. Our latest analysis of the leaks suggests that the information accessed includes the names and aliases of some of our overseas operatives. We don't know which ones, and we don't know how many, but we do know that Peyton has started the ball rolling on brokering a deal with Heath Shannon's terrorist contacts. This must not come to pass. The lives of these operatives—and our national security—are in your hands."

Again, I thought, with the melodrama. But then I glanced at Tara, who was sitting beside me, and I noticed how very pale she'd gone. I found myself staring at my partner instead of the screen. I didn't know much about Tara, but I did know she was a professional. Tara was cool, calm, and collected. So why did she look like she'd been hit in the face with a very large, very heavy fish?

I wasn't a profiler like Zee. I wasn't even a people person, but I could tell, just by looking at her, that something was wrong. To Tara, this wasn't just a case. This was personal.

I looked back at the thousands and thousands of dots on the map and thought about the way that operatives caught at Peyton, Kaufman, and Gray had a tendency to disappear. Somehow, I couldn't imagine foreign governments or terrorist organizations being any more forgiving. Maybe Tara had it right. Life and death, even represented by dots on a map, *had* to be personal. And just like that, this Mission was real, and everything I'd thought and joked about at the mall seemed a thousand miles away.

"Your mission is threefold," the voice said, leaving the map on the screen so that not one of us could forget what was at stake. "First and foremost, we have to shut down the leaks. Peyton, Kaufman, and Gray cannot be allowed to access any more of our operatives' locations. Penetrate Infotech's system, disable it, and acquire any and all files that relate to information they may have already forwarded on to the firm. That leads me to your second initiative. We need to know what information Peyton has access to and how much—if any—of it has already been sold. To do that, you'll need to reinstate our surveillance inside Peyton, Kaufman, and Gray. Our organization is not in a position to send another agent in unnoticed, so we're going to have to go with a stealth bug, and one of you is going to have to plant it."

My mind organized the information that the voice was imparting, even as I sat there, pinned to my seat with some kind of horrific fascination. The gears in my mind turned and spun, coming to the logical conclusions, as if this whole situation were just another piece of code to be puzzled out in the nooks and crannies of my brain.

The government had a leak. Like a person with a nasty virus, it was sick, and we were the lucky ones who got to play doctor. First, we had to attack the metaphorical virus, which meant eliminating the leak before it could wreak any more havoc on our national security. And then, we had to assess the damage that had already been done. To do that, we needed to bug the nefarious law firm. As my mind processed all of this, in the span of seconds, I knew exactly what our third task was going to be. You stop the virus, you assess the damage, and then you do what you can to treat the symptoms that already exist.

"Finally, we need you to put a tail on Heath Shannon. You girls can blend in a way that our agents can't, and sooner or later, Shannon is going to go back to Peyton to finalize the deal for whatever information they've already acquired."

And by *information*, he meant sensitive data that could and would be deadly if we didn't stop its transfer. Finding out what the leak entailed wasn't enough. That was damage control; it wasn't a solution.

"We believe that the information trade will be physical, rather than electronic, so your orders are to wait until after Shannon leaves the firm to take him down and retrieve the data before it falls into enemy hands."

Just listening to the instructions made my heart pound a little faster. Hacking into secured systems and messing with their files? Taking down an international playboy who doubled as a freelance baddie? Even with the seriousness of the situation, I couldn't push down the thought that this was the stuff that dreams were made of.

"And girls?" the voice added.

Yes, Charlie? I thought.

I expected him to tell us to be careful, but instead, he said, "Good luck at your game on Saturday. I'm sure you'll be great."

And then just like that, the audio feed switched off, and the screen flashed back to the index that Tara and I had examined in the car. For a split second, there was silence, and then, I just couldn't restrain myself.

"Is it always like this?" I asked. "With the messages and the melodrama and a faceless voice telling us what to do?"

"Actually," Chloe said brightly, her voice somehow sugary sweet and acerbic at the same time, "usually, our superiors tell Brooke what to do, and she tells us." Chloe paused. "Which leads me to wonder . . ." She brought her eyes to meet Brooke's. "What do you know that we don't?"

I didn't need Zee's PhD to figure out that Chloe won the Most Likely to Start a Cheer Coup title hands down.

Brooke met Chloe's eyes, her voice equally pleasant. "Chlo," she said, "I couldn't begin to tell you."

"Can we concentrate here?" Tara bit in, and the tone of her voice surprised me. I'd been under the impression that as far as cheerleaders went, she was relatively docile. When Brooke told her to do a cheer jump, Tara asked how high. So why was my partner suddenly Miss Dominant? And what exactly did her personality transplant have to do with the information we'd just learned? I filed these questions alongside others in my mind, namely, when exactly I'd wake up from this crazy dream and why it was the CIA felt that it was too dangerous to send an agent to infiltrate the Law Firm of Doom, but somehow expected a bunch of varsity cheerleaders to do the same.

"I mean it," Tara said. "We've got a job to do. There are lives at stake. Some things are just more important than your petty rivalries." Tara's words and demeanor pierced the Brooke/Chloe tension bubble, and almost instantly, Chloe began to look vaguely like she'd been hit in the face with a Kate Whatshername purse. Brooke, in contrast, didn't visibly respond, but when she spoke again, her voice was softer than I'd ever heard it. Not exactly how I would have predicted her responding to direct insubordination.

"We'll get this thing, Tare," our captain promised. "We'll knock out the Infotech hack, we'll figure out what damage has already been done, and we'll bring Heath Shannon down before he has a chance to do any more. Nobody is going to get hurt." She narrowed her eyes, her voice still soft and gentle, with just the slightest traces of something scarier. "Nobody is going to get hurt," she repeated, "and everybody is going to follow orders. Am I clear?"

Contrary to common belief among my cheerleading cohorts, I wasn't an idiot. Or if I was, I was definitely an idiot savant, what with the near-photographic memory and intuitive understanding of all things encrypted. So why was it that the subtext between these girls was a complete mystery to me? I could follow Brooke's game plan and see the logic in the three tiers of our mission without a problem, but the sympathy in her eyes even as she laid down the cheer law and the way Tara was responding were, quite simply, beyond my grasp.

"So," Brooke said, switching modes without waiting for

Tara's response, her voice louder and full of perky authority. "As far as planning goes, let's start with the easy one. We need to infiltrate Peyton, Kaufman, and Gray."

That was the easy one?

"You know what that means," Zee said, and I waited for our expert profiler to impart some kind of psychological wisdom. Instead, the twins squealed in unison.

"Party!"

CHAPTER 15
Code Word: Hottie

"Help me out here," I said to the room at large. "We need to place surveillance on an evil law firm that probably has so much security that we couldn't sneeze in front of their building without someone handcuffing us to a large metal object, and we're throwing a party because why?"

Brittany leaned forward, her lips spreading into the smile of a girl who was about to spread a particularly juicy bit of gossip. "Jack."

"Jack?"

"Oooohhhhh! Jack!" Lucy clapped her hands in front of her face.

"Jack Peyton," April said, and again, I felt like the dumb stepcousin or something. April turned to Chloe. "Are you telling me that Jack Peyton, Mr. Tall-Dark-and-Good-Looking himself, is somehow tied up in this?"

"His name's actually John Peyton," Brooke said. "John Peyton the Fourth. His great-grandfather was John, his grandfather was Johnny, his father is John-John, and he's Jack."

"Let me guess," I said, doing the mental math. "John,

Johnny, and John-John, they're the Peyton in Peyton, Kaufman, and Gray?"

"John was the founder, Johnny was his first partner, and now that they're gone, John-John is the senior partner."

So Jack Peyton (whoever that was) was the son of the Big Kahuna of the evil law firm.

"And we're throwing a party because why?" This time, I asked the question louder, like that would get me an answer. Codes and numbers made sense to me. The Squad way of life did not.

"The easiest way to Peyton is through Jack," Brooke said. "Trust me."

Little warning bells went off in the back of my head at the tone of Brooke's voice. The bells sounded suspiciously like they were saying "stay away from Brooke's ex-boyfriend; go near Jack Peyton and die!"

"Jack never misses a party," Chloe said. "If one of us is going to use him to get into Peyton, we'll just have to throw one." She gave me another special Chloe look before turning to smile at April, her perfect little protégée. "Can we move Saturday's party up to tomorrow night?"

April nodded. "Daddy's out of town, the pool house is always open, and besides, I have it on very good authority that Thursday is the new Friday."

"Great," Chloe said, and she turned back to Brooke. "You think you can get Jack to take you to Peyton?" It sounded more like a challenge than a question.

Brooke returned Chloe's smile. "Do you think you can?" she asked sweetly.

Whoa. I might not have been cheerliterate, but I could read between the lines. Somewhere along the way, this Jack guy had dated both Brooke and Chloe. What a player. And, for that matter, what an idiot. You couldn't pay me enough money to spend time alone with either one of them, and some guy had actually voluntarily dated them both? Clearly, this Jack character had emotional, if not *mental*, problems.

"Guys, this is serious." Tara's voice was louder this time, and sharp enough to cut the silence between Chloe and Brooke. "We don't have time for some infantile spitting contest."

Wow. Chalk another one up for the British girl.

In one motion, Brooke and Chloe turned to glare at Tara.

"You know as well as I do that Jack doesn't like cheerleaders," Tara said, her voice nice and calm again, despite the fact that I could still actually see the tension in her neck. "He won't take either of you to Peyton."

"Classic operant conditioning," Zee piped up. "He associates cheerleaders with pain and heartache and physical discomfort. He views us as an ontological kind and extends properties freely from one exemplar to another."

Hmmm. Maybe Jack wasn't as dumb as I'd thought. We seemed to have the same kinds of beliefs about cheerleaders as a species.

"In short, he hates all of us equally." Zee diffused the tension between Chloe and Brooke with a single flip of her hair. "I don't think he can even tell most of us apart."

I couldn't help but wonder why exactly Zee kept glancing at me as she spoke.

"If he hates us so much, why does he hang out with us?" Bubbles asked, knotting up her pretty little forehead in what appeared to be genuine and profound confusion.

"Status quo," Zee said. "Jack was born to rule. It's been ingrained in him since childhood, and at Bayport, we, my friends, are the ruling class."

"So he'll hang out with us, but he won't date us?" one of the twins asked. "That is like so totally wrong."

"He has textbook Conditioned Cheerleader Aversion," Zee said.

He and I both.

And that's when I got why Zee kept looking at me. Feeling paranoid, I glanced around the room. Brooke and Chloe were looking at Zee looking at me. Tara had her eyes fixed on mine. One by one, the rest of the girls followed suit.

"He likes you," Zee said frankly. "He thinks you're different."

"Yeah," Brittany said, "if by *different* you mean bizarre and freakish."

"Zee's right." Brooke spoke slowly. "Jack's been so anti lately, but today at lunch, he actually talked to Toby."

Today at lunch? I played the whole ordeal over in my head: Noah's celebration, Hayley's threats, Lucy saving me, Brooke instructing me to flirt with Chip, me resolving to get some blackmail material on the arrogant guy with dark hair . . .

It occurred to me then that April had referred to Jack Peyton as Mr. Tall-Dark-and-Good-Looking. As much as I hated to admit it, Smirky Boy had been tall. He'd had dark hair. He'd known that he was good-looking.

"*That's* Jack Peyton?" I asked. I'd fully intended to cut smarmy smirk boy down to size and wipe the cocky expression off his perfectly symmetrical face. And now a bunch of cheerleaders were telling me I was supposed to suck up to the guy? Make him like me? Have him take me back to Daddy Dearest's office so I could plant some kind of cheer bug there?

"No way," I said. "I hate that guy."

"That's why you're perfect," Zee said, highly satisfied with her analysis of the situation. "Everyone else thinks he's good-looking; you couldn't care less. Everyone else would like their lips plastered to his; you'd just as soon kick him in the crotch."

I had to admit it—Miss PhD Zee was right on target, about the crotch-kicking, at least.

"You are exactly what Jack is looking for. He just doesn't know it yet."

I tried to imagine myself seducing Jack, and it wouldn't be an exaggeration to say that I was genuinely concerned that the very thought might make me throw up in my own mouth.

"Toby." It was Tara, her eyes still on mine. "Please."

I'd wondered earlier in the day what the real Tara was like, who she was when the cheerleading cover went away and her guard came down. Now she was looking at me, and for the first time, she didn't seem poised. She didn't seem sophisticated.

She seemed lost, and I had no idea why.

"Okay," I said. Tara was my partner. And yeah, she'd only been my partner for like a day, but that was enough. Black belt and "attitude problems" aside, I was turning into a verifiable softy.

"If Jack's going to be your mark," Tiffany mused, "you're probably going to need some new shoes."

That's where I drew the line. If I was going to be putting the moves on one of *those guys* (you know, the guys who date *those girls*), I was damn well going to do it in combat boots.

"Did you get her a gel bra today?" Brittany asked Tara, eyeing my boobs. I folded my arms over my chest and glared at her. Silently, Tara nodded.

"Can we discuss something other than my chest?" I asked, my voice dangerously pleasant. "Like the other two parts of the Mission?"

"Chloe, you'll take lead on the Infotech hack," Brooke said, and I wondered how much of that decision was based on the fact that Chloe was Brooke's second-in-command and the most capable of running a large tech-based operation, and how much of it was basic cheer politics. "I'll handle the Heath Shannon end of things. Chlo, you've got Toby. Let me know who else you need."

Wait a second. Had Brooke just given me to Chloe? Had she seriously just loaned me out like a tube of flavored lip gloss? And what about Tara? The two of us were supposed to be partners.

Just as these thoughts were flying through my head, Lucy piped up with a suggestion of her own.

"Let's talk about who's going to go through the files on the disk," she said brightly. "Not it!"

Not it? What was she, five?

"Not it!" Seven other voices said in unison.

Damn.

April and I stared at each other, and then April spoke up. "Toby and I can't do it alone," she said. "We don't know what to look for."

"I'll do it." Chloe's offer surprised me. "We should start working on a game plan for hacking Infotech's system anyway. We can listen to the audio files and strategize at the same time."

Who was this mysterious *we* she was speaking of?

"I'll stay, too," Tara said.

"No." Brooke didn't provide a reason, but her voice was strong and final.

Tara opened her mouth and then closed it again. Then, after a moment's deliberation, she spoke calmly and clearly. "Toby's my partner. If she's going to be here with Chloe making plans for the Infotech hack, I should be here."

"Tara," Brooke said evenly. "Go home. Zee and I will tail Heath Shannon tonight, and by tomorrow, we'll have a plan of attack on that front. Chloe and Toby can handle the Infotech strategizing on their own. And just for good measure, Bubbles and Lucy will case Infotech tonight, on the off chance that the Big Guys are wrong and Heath Shannon interacts directly with the source, rather than using Peyton as a middleman."

"I'll go with you and Zee, or Bubbles and Lucy," Tara said. "I can't just do nothing."

"Yes," Brooke said, "you can. And you will."

The only thing about that discussion that wasn't slipping straight over my head was the fact that Brooke was even bossier than I'd previously thought, and that somehow, I'd been drafted not only to pick up Jack Peyton at April's party the following night, but also to coordinate with Chloe on breaking into Infotech's system while scanning the rest of the digi-disk for files that might shed some more light on our current situation.

The way the Squad worked was becoming clearer to me by the moment. Apparently, the Big Guys Upstairs issued orders to Brooke, Brooke issued orders to the rest of us, Brittany and Tiffany did makeovers, all of the girls did halftime routines, some of them went on low-key stakeouts, and I did everything else. I glanced at my watch. It was five-thirty at night. I'd been a member of the Squad for exactly twelve hours, and in that time, I'd slapped a guy's ass, bought a gel bra, successfully obtained a disk that contained classified information, learned that the lives of nameless foreign operatives were in the hands of fewer than a dozen high school cheerleaders, and quite possibly torn every muscle in my entire body doing bouncy little jumps with names like *toe touch* and *spread eagle*. And now . . .

"You might want to call your parents, To-bee," Chloe advised me, condescension dripping from her tone. "You're not going to be home for dinner."

CHAPTER 16
Code Word: Pizzazz

Five minutes later, I added two additional firsts to my list of things I'd never done before (and desperately hoped never to do again). First, I became the owner of a limited-edition hot-pink cell phone identical to one owned by innumerable vacuous celebrities. Mine, of course, came equipped with a variety of special features, ranging from my very own electron wave accelerator to the world's teeny-tiniest hard-core hard drive, but that didn't make it any less pink. Secondly, for the first (and I hope only) time in my life, I did exactly what Chloe Larson had advised me to do. I picked up my nauseatingly pink cell phone and called home.

"Noah's Love Haven, Noah speaking." My brother answered the phone.

"Noah," I said calmly, "I'm going to forget this ever happened. Please never answer our phone again. In fact, the whole talking thing? Not your forte, so . . ."

"Toby!" Noah had never sounded so happy to hear from me. "Where are you? Did they take you to their secret lair in room 117? Are you doing secret cheerleader things? Did anyone mention me?" He lowered his voice. "Are they wearing those shorts that say CHEER on the butt?"

I couldn't help but glance down at the back of my own shorts.

"Noah, put Mom on the phone."

"Answer the question," Noah said, completely impervious to what should have been a very clear and demanding order. "Does it say CHEER? On their butts?"

"Tell Mom I won't be home for dinner," I said. "We're doing this . . . uhhhh . . . this initiation thing tonight."

That, apparently, was the wrong lie to tell Noah.

"Initiation?" he asked. "Does it involve whipped cream? Please tell me it involves whipped cream. . . ."

"Noah."

"Yeah?" He stopped talking long enough for me to say a single word.

"Goodbye." I flipped the phone closed and shuddered again at its freakishly bright color. Still, I knew that I'd be facing something far, far worse as soon as I looked up from the pink.

"Well, are you going to stand there, or are you going to help me?" Chloe had the amazing ability to somehow cram a different insulting undertone into every single word she spoke.

"Hello?" Chloe said, hands on her hips.

"Fine," I grumbled. "Let's just get this over with."

At Brooke's orders, Tara had abandoned me, leaving me alone with Chloe as the others went on their merry way to do whatever mentally stimulating activities cheer-spies did in their off time. The only bright side was that Chloe had been forced to let me into her lab, and the tech geek in me was practically salivating over the wall-to-wall, floor-to-floor technohaven workshop.

"Once I get the audio set up, we'll talk hacking," she said.

Part of me wanted to tell her that I didn't "talk hacking" with anyone. I just did it. Toby Klein worked alone. The other part of me was way too curious as to what exactly was involved with setting up the audio and whether or not the four computers set up in the lab had government access.

Chloe popped the digi-disk into a player that looked surprisingly like an actual CD player. After getting a look at her powder puff decoder, I'd expected something with a bit more pizzazz.

I stopped myself. Had I actually just thought the word *pizzazz*? Clearly I'd passed the point of no return a few handsprings back. My pizzazz instincts, as completely mortifying as they may have been, weren't entirely wrong, because the next instant, Chloe picked up a couple of sparkly picture frames (glam shots of Chloe and Brooke inside both) and arranged them on either side of the player.

I raised an eyebrow at her in question.

"Filter," she said. "Each frame has its own program, and they're linked wirelessly to the player. The pink one filters out white noise. The purple one focuses in on human voices."

"How . . ." I stopped myself from asking the question the second it tried to leave my mouth, and Chloe immediately and without pause made me devoutly wish I'd stopped any of it from escaping in the first place.

"My lab," she said sharply. "My secrets." She smiled Brooke's patented no-teeth nonsmile. "Your job is hacking: codes, firewalls, security systems. That's all you. Technology and equipment design? That's me."

And the line was thus drawn in the sand.

Daintily, Chloe pressed a button on the player, adjusted the volume, and then turned to face me again. "So," she said. "Infotech."

In the background, I could hear a conversation on the disk, as clear as if the people were standing in the room with us. "Good morning, Mr. Hayes. Coffee, black." The sound of a ceramic coffee cup set down on a wooden desk.

"Most of the audio is garbage," Chloe said. "If and when we hit something good, I'll know it."

And you won't, her tone taunted me.

"So," I said, forcing myself not to physically assault her; I had a feeling that would be frowned upon. "Infotech."

"I pulled up the basic file," Chloe said, and she literally tossed a pile of papers at me. "They've got almost nothing uploaded to the internet. If you can get within their wireless range and access the company password, you can file share, but you probably won't find anything of interest unless you dig around a little, and you probably won't be able to dig around unseen. These guys secure websites for a living. They developed the beta version of the program the government uses to safeguard their databases."

I shrugged. "And look how well that's turning out for the government," I said. "Infotech's system can't be half as secure as the CIA's—they can't possibly have the funding. If these guys can find a way into the government's files, I can find a way into theirs."

"Without them noticing?" Chloe was nothing if not skeptical.

"I'll ghost it," I said, not caring if she knew what I meant by the term or not. I hadn't learned computers by the books. I didn't spend much time talking to other hackers. Every piece of terminology I used was my own, completely made up in the mind o' Toby. "I'll piggyback on a few of their usernames simultaneously and use their traffic to mask my own. Then I'll set up a new username, and use its traffic to divert attention away from what I'm doing."

"And what will you be doing?"

"Other than accessing their files and looking for the program they're using to hack us?"

Was it weird that I was suddenly referring to the U.S. government as "us"?

"Finding the program won't fix everything," Chloe said.

"Tell you what," I said. "I'll find the program. You worry about the rest. I do the hacking and break the codes. The technological innovations, those are yours, right?" I couldn't help it—I tried a no-teeth smile of my own.

Chloe opened her mouth to say something, and given the look on her freakishly symmetrical face, it probably would have been something I would have been forced to make her regret, but the audio track had picked up again, and we both stopped to listen.

"Mr. Gray here to see you, sir."

Gray. As in Peyton, Kaufman, and Gray.

"I understand you're meeting with one of our clients this afternoon," the voice I identified as Gray said. "He's concerned about the settlement we've drawn up. Most of his concerns with the settlement can be easily assuaged by putting him in contact with our claims department. The officer in charge is working out of his home today, but if you could tell the client that he can be reached at this number, that would be wonderful."

There was a faint sound then. Paper being handed from one man to the next? Immediately, I began practically salivating for that paper. I wanted to know what it said. Was it actually a phone number? Was it a message that Mr. Gray, as a partner in a nefarious law firm, had known better than to speak out loud? Which "client" were they talking about? Heath Shannon, perhaps?

For a long moment, there was silence. Then the secretary-type person offered Gray a coffee, and as he declined, I could hear someone flip open a cell phone and type in a number—presumably the one Gray had just handed his cohort. So much for my secret message theory.

For about fifteen seconds after the interaction ended and miscellaneous office noises filled the tape, Chloe and I just stared at each other.

"Your pores are the size of land mines," she said finally. "The twins must be slipping."

I gathered the papers she'd thrown at me. I could look at them just as well at home as here.

"We aren't done here," she said. "There's still more audio, and you have no idea where Infotech is, let alone how you're going to get close enough to enter into their wireless system. You don't even know what kind of program you're looking for, and we're going in first thing tomorrow."

I waved the papers in front of her face. "My pores and I will figure it out." With all the dignity I could muster, I grabbed my pink cell phone, pulled down my cheer shorts (which had inched their way up my freshly waxed thighs), and asked Chloe one final question.

"Which way's the exit?"

CHAPTER 17
Code Word: Gossip

The Quad was a frigging labyrinth. Even after Chloe haughtily pointed out the exit, I'd still somehow managed to get turned around. But I was not, repeat NOT, going to go back and ask for a clarification of her directions. I wasn't an idiot, and I wasn't about to risk feeding Chloe's obvious superiority complex any more than I already had.

"You're pissed at Chloe. And lost."

Years of training had me whirling around to face the owner of the voice. As I turned, I shifted my weight back on my heels, sinking into a ready position.

Zee lifted her hands up and arched an eyebrow at me. "I come in peace."

Feeling more than a little stupid, I rose out of my position and shifted my weight to the balls of my feet. "I'm not lost," I grumbled. "Chloe just gives really crappy directions."

"Which brings me back to my original point," Zee said. "You're pissed at Chloe. What'd she do this time?"

I narrowed my eyes. "Are you asking as a PhD or as the resident Gossip Girl?"

Zee shrugged delicately. "Little bit of column A, little bit of column B."

I was less than amused. "Aren't you supposed to be on a stakeout?"

Zee shrugged. "Brooke decided I should stay here and work on profiling Heath Shannon. She took April with her instead."

It just figured—I was here listening to audio clips with Chloe, and April got to go on a stakeout at the evil law firm.

Zee put her hand lightly on my shoulder. "Come on," she said. "I've got some stuff you should probably see."

I didn't move.

"Seriously, Toby. I swear that it has nothing whatsoever to do with lipstick, pore-reducing cleanser, or whatever else has your panties in a twist."

"Panties in a twist," I said. "Is that a technical term?"

Zee rolled her eyes. "So what? Just because I have a PhD, I have to be smart all the time? A person can be more than one thing, Toby. I can be smart and a cheerleader and incredibly knowledgeable about celebrity marriages, all at the same time."

"A girl of many talents," I said.

Zee grinned. "Damn straight. Now, are you coming or aren't you?"

She turned around and started walking off. Since I had exactly two options, Chloe or Zee, I chose Zee. Chloe was predictable (or, at least, predictably witchy). Zee was something of an enigma.

I followed her up a staircase, and after two security checkpoints (one that scanned our fingerprints, and one that scanned our retinas), found myself in a small room with a desk, a large filing cabinet, a computer, and a television.

"Your office?" I guessed. Zee nodded. It occurred to me that I should probably demand my own computer lab/office setup—Lucy and Chloe had labs; the twins had the salon; Zee had an office. Judging from her demeanor, I could only guess that Brooke probably ruled over a small country somewhere in the Quad. The least they could give me was an office with the world's fastest computer.

"I'm sure it can be arranged," Zee said, making me wonder if she was psychic. "But give it a few weeks. The rest of the girls are still adjusting to the new group dynamics."

The way Zee switched from one mode to another, sounding like one of *those girls* one minute and full of psychobabble the next, freaked me out. Then again, wasn't that what the Squad was all about?

"So what did you want to show me?"

The sooner she showed it to me, the sooner I could go home, eat, shower, and pass out. In that order.

"Have a seat." Zee gestured, and I sat. Post–herkie torture, my body was fundamentally opposed to standing for any extended period of time.

When Zee sat down behind her desk, her eyes watched me carefully, and I frowned. "I am so not in the mood to be psychoanalyzed," I told her.

Zee flipped her glossy black ponytail over her shoulder. "Been there," she said. "Done that. You're not that interesting."

I folded my arms across my chest and waited.

"Actually, I thought you might want the rundown on everyone else."

"Say what?"

"Let's face it. You're not exactly Miss Sociable. You didn't know any of the girls this time last week, and I'm pretty sure you hated all of us anyway. Now you're a part of the Squad, and, correct me if I'm wrong, you've decided that Tara is tolerable, and you're trying awfully hard not to like Lucy. You still haven't forgiven the twins for the Stage Six, you're mildly threatened by April, you think Bubbles has the IQ of a doorstop, you've already created a mental list of dictators whose personalities resemble Brooke's, you can't understand what Chloe's problem is, and my PhD freaks the hell out of you."

It was like she had me in some kind of freaky cheerleading mind meld!

With another hair flip, Zee crossed her arms over her chest, matching her posture to my own. "How'd I do?"

I didn't answer.

"I take it that means I did well? Know you better than you know yourself, et cetera, et cetera?"

"Didn't you have something to show me?" I asked.

"Sure," Zee said. She pushed a folder across the desk, and I picked it up. Not sure what to expect, I opened it.

The first thing I saw was the numbers. I got numbers. They were comfort food for my brain. I read the labels, examined the axes of the graphs, and flipped through the pages.

"What's this?" I asked.

"Ideal profile for an operative," Zee said. "Aptitude tests, IQ, EI, personality diagnostics. The works."

Then Zee slid another folder across the desk.

I opened it, and as I digested the data in front of me, Zee explained.

"That's the breakdown for the Squad," she said. "I didn't

label the different individuals, but you get the drift. There's some EI/IQ tradeoff, and the personalities vary, but they're all good at keeping secrets, they all know how to command a situation, they're all incredibly intuitive about the strengths and weaknesses of others, and they're all extraordinarily loyal."

Without a word, Zee slid another folder across the table. Unable to help myself, I opened it.

A little girl with dark hair, glasses, and a serious expression on her face stared back at me.

"That was taken the day I graduated from high school," Zee said. "I was eight." She shuddered. "I know, I know, the bangs are hideous, and it's more than obvious that my mother was still picking out my clothes. . . ."

She trailed off. "I didn't start picking out my own clothes until grad school, you know? And I never hung out with people my own age. I think that's why I was so into psychology. I always thought that if I could understand what it meant to be normal, I could just sort of fake it. And then one day, someone comes along and offers to pay me to do it all over again. They styled my hair, they made me over, they gave me a car, and they put me on a cheerleading squad with nine other teenage girls."

Zee paused. "And those nine other girls? They would have died for me. A couple of times, some of them almost have."

I didn't know what to say.

Without a word, Zee handed me another folder. I opened it, and Lucy stared back at me.

"She's a perfectionist," Zee said. "She's got this really incredible drive to be good and nice and sweet and happy, and she doesn't do anything unless she can be the best at it. She

129

had an older sister, but the sister died in a car wreck when she was nine. Lucy being Lucy is pretty much the only thing that kept her family together."

Zee pushed another folder across the desk. I didn't open it.

"That one's Chloe," Zee said. "You gonna open it?"

I thought about it and then shook my head. "You going to give me the Cliff's Notes anyway?"

"But of course." Zee twirled her hair absentmindedly as she spoke. "Chloe was, in layman's terms, the world's biggest dork. Kind of chubby, socially awkward, really into *Star Wars*."

As Zee dished, I couldn't help but think that maybe the Gossip Girl/profiler pairing made sense. I mean, wasn't a profiler just someone who knew everything about everyone to the point that they could practically see inside their heads? And wasn't a gossip queen pretty much the exact same thing?

"*Star Wars*?" I couldn't help but ask.

"She'd kill me if she knew I was telling you this, but yeah. *Star Wars*. She spent the majority of fourth grade building a functioning light saber."

The next time Chloe made a computer geek comment, she was so incredibly toast.

"Chloe moved to Bayport when she was eleven," Zee continued, "and she was drafted to the program immediately."

"She joined the Squad when she was *eleven*?"

"No," Zee said. "She was befriended by a cheerleader who more or less Stage Sixed her all by herself. This girl strong-armed Chloe into joining the cheerleading squad and molded her into the Chloe we all know and love. Four years later, both girls made varsity. Now they have this sibling love/hate thing going on."

Zee paused then, and I got the feeling that she was waiting for me to catch up.

"Brooke?" I guessed.

Zee nodded. "Brooke. She's been in the program longer than anyone. She was raised for it, and she's been slated for Squad captain since she was like nine. Brooke turned Chloe into her own little Brookeling, and ever since the whole Jack Peyton thing, Chlo's been gunning for the captain spot."

This was, in some horrible, sick way, fascinating. I think the way I felt listening to Zee was the way most people feel watching soap operas. You know, on some level at least, that you shouldn't want to watch it, but you just can't help yourself.

"And then you come along," Zee said. "And all of a sudden, there's another techie girl on the scene, and Chloe's feeling a little bit threatened. Add to that the fact that your makeover reminds Chloe of what Brooke did for her, and the fact that you're the only one Jack is currently interested in, and voilà, you've got Chloe."

When Zee put it that way, it all made sense: what Tara had said about me reminding Chloe of who she used to be, the cheer-coup vibes I'd caught Chloe shooting in Brooke's direction, the way Brooke was Captain with a capital C.

"You can go now," Zee said. "If you want to. I just thought you should know. Chloe can be a bitch, but she's not a bad person. The twins may be shallow, but they're not idiots. And Brooke's bossiness personified, but she really can't help it." Zee paused. "And whether you believe it or not, they'd all risk their lives for you. You're part of the

Squad now, Toby, and that means something." She gestured at the first folder she'd handed me. "One of the traits we look for is a sense of loyalty, an ability to put the good of the Squad before your own interest. All of us have it, and whether you know it yet or not, I'd be willing to bet a lot of money that you'd risk your life for them, too."

I opened my mouth to argue, but Zee stopped me.

"If someone made Lucy cry," she said, "what would you do?"

My answer? Odd, but probably the same thing I did when someone threatened Noah.

"When Tara asked you to seduce Jack, what did you say?"

I'd said yes.

"And if you heard gunshots in Chloe's lab right now, what would you do?"

I looked away. "Point taken."

Zee stood up. "Come on. I'll walk you out. And ooohhh, by the way, did you hear that Mary Pierce and Bronson Lenning were caught all horizontal in the girls' bathroom?"

From zero to gossipmonger in point-two seconds.

And yet, thinking of Zee, the eight-year-old prodigy with bad bangs and a mom-chosen outfit, I couldn't hold it against her.

"As in . . . *completely* horizontal?"

CHAPTER 18

Code Word: Bee-yotch

By the time I got home, all I wanted to do was inhale fifteen pounds of edible matter while submerging myself in steaming hot water. My mind was full of Zee's psychobabble and gossip and thoughts about stakeouts and evil law firms and plans of action so complex that there was a distinct chance that my eyeballs were going to explode from the sheer number of unanswered questions in my mind. Plus my shoulders were killing me. My back was killing me. My legs were pretty much already dead, and there was a distinct chance that I'd dislocated my crotch.

Unfortunately, I didn't get to make good on my gorge-myself-and-shower plan, because the second I stepped into my house, three freshman-shaped blobs popped out of nowhere and screamed, "Surprise!"

I'll hand it to Noah—I was surprised. And, I might add, not amused. I counted slowly backward from ten in my mind and tried to appraise the situation without losing my temper. There was a handwritten banner hung across the sofa that screamed "Congratulations, Toby!" in bright pink letters. Bubblegum pop blared from the living room speakers, and someone had baked a cake and decorated it with what appeared to be a stick figure doing a high kick.

About a microsecond before I destroyed my brother, his partners in crime, and what was left of their manhood, Noah thrust a gift sack into my hand.

"We got you something," he said, giving me his most adorable puppy-dog smile.

I looked down at the gift sack and then back up at the boys. They were wearing party hats. As I stared humorlessly at the three of them, Noah's friend Brad actually threw confetti into the air.

"Where's Mom?" I demanded.

"What? You don't like? The boys and I wanted to do something to mark the occasion. . . ."

"C-c-congrats, Toby." Chuck Percy was sweating and stuttering, and let me tell you, it was a winning combination. He'd been that way in my precheerleading days. It was a miracle the poor kid had managed to say anything without spontaneously combusting given my current postmakeover state.

"Wow." Noah appraised my appearance. "You're wearing the shorts!"

I smacked him in the side with the gift bag, sat it calmly on the ground, and walked up the stairs toward my room, literally growling under my breath. It figured—I made the cheerleading squad, and the freshman goof brigade threw a party celebrating their own good fortune. From the sound the bag had made as it connected lightly with Noah's body, I was going to go out on a limb and guess it was a can of whipped cream.

I didn't even want to know what Noah expected the God Squad to do with a can of whipped cream.

I couldn't decide which part of this experience was more mortifying: the fact that Noah had accepted this cheerleading thing no questions asked, or the fact that my butt said CHEER on it in big blue letters.

"Toby. You're home." My mom gave me the once-over: mahogany hair with honeysuckle highlights, perfectly tanned skin, plucked eyebrows, cheer shorts. "Did you have a good day at school?"

Nothing fazed my mom. Nothing.

I stomped toward my room. "I don't want to talk about it."

I closed the door behind me, walked over to my bed, and screamed into my pillow for approximately thirty-seven seconds. I threw down the ginormous purse I had carried home under protest. While I'd been having fun one-on-one time with Chloe, one of the twins had swiped my backpack and upgraded it to some kind of designer purse big enough to carry a small country in the side pouch. I took out the papers Chloe had given me, glared at them, and threw them on my floor. I then ripped off the cheer shorts, and they joined the papers.

Two minutes later, I was standing there in nothing but my underwear (no sequins—thank God). I wrapped a towel around my body and headed for the shower, where I turned the water on and let the entire room steam up.

Malibu Toby watched me from the mirror, her hair miraculously perfect even after the hissy fit I'd just thrown in my room.

Looking at the stranger in the mirror, I had to remind myself—this was me now. I was a perfect-bodied, perfect-haired, perfectly tanned cheerleader. I carried a designer bag, wore designer clothes, and had a limited-edition designer phone. And somewhere, on the other side of the globe, nameless, faceless government operatives were counting on me to hack into a system I didn't know the first thing about. There was only one thing to do at a time like this.

I climbed into the shower and curled into a small ball on the floor, letting the water hit my perfect hair. Droplets dripped down my face and into my eyes, but I just sat there, my body aching and my skin rebelling against the heat of the water.

I breathed in and out, thinking back on my day, watching as scenes flashed one after another in my mind and things I'd heard repeated themselves on a loop. More often than not, showering brought me answers. In fact, had water heaters of today's caliber been invented way back when, I would have placed a large amount of money on a wager that Einstein's theory of relativity had first come to him while he was doing what I was now. But today, the steam wasn't giving me any answers, and I just kept coming back to the same questions, over and over again.

Had Chloe and I missed something on those tapes? Was there something we were supposed to find?

Who was the "Charlie" who'd given us our instructions and then gone on to wish us good luck for our game? Would I hear his voice again? Five years from now, or ten, or twenty, would I be a Charlie, handing out orders to a squadron of teenage girls? Was that what the Squad prepared you for? And if not, where did our "superiors" come from, anyway?

Why had Tara reacted so violently to this mission? Did she take every life-and-death situation with that same clammy, forced calm?

Sitting perfectly still, I turned my mind from questions and let it wander freely again. This time, I surpassed scenes and spoken words and went into the zone. Numbers flitted in and out—codes I'd broken, patterns I'd noticed in everything from the daily paper to the rhyme scheme of our half-time routine.

"Hmmm hmmm hmmm hmmm hmm hum."

The tune came to me: six tones strung together at an even pace.

"Hmmm hmmm hmmm hmmm hmm hum."

Why did that sound so familiar? I tilted my head back and came dangerously close to getting water up my nose.

"The audio." As soon as I said the words, I knew where I'd heard that particular series of notes before. When the lawyer at Peyton had programmed the number into his phone, I'd written it off as inconsequential, but here, with water beating at my body and my mind free to wander, I conjured up the sound it had made as he'd entered the number.

I tore myself away from the water and forced myself to stand up. "Hmmm hmmm hmmm hmmm hmm hum."

Part of our objective in listening to the audio had been to figure out who Infotech was passing the information along to. A phone number wasn't exactly the guy's name and Social Security number, but it was a start, right?

I finished my shower in record time considering my limbs weren't really cooperating with the rest of my body. I wrapped the towel back around my body and headed straight for my room, or more specifically, straight for the designer bag on my floor.

Straight for my hot pink, limited-edition cell phone.

Too physically and emotionally drained to think angry thoughts about its color and trendy nature, I picked the phone up, flipped it open, and started playing with the keys. Systematically, I pressed each number, listening carefully to its tone.

"Hmmm hmmm hmmm hmmm hmm hum."

I hummed the first tone, and hit each of the keys. It wasn't a two. It wasn't a six.

It was a slow, painful process, but bit by bit, I sorted it out.

024106.

Wait a minute. "Hmmm hmmm hmmm hmmm hmm hum."

I went over the rhythm again and again in my head, but it stayed exactly the same. There were only six numbers. This wasn't a phone number, and if it wasn't a phone number . . .

"024106." I ran over the numbers again and again in my head. I scrambled them, rearranged them into every possible permutation. Did they stand for letters? Maybe it was a payment amount. I tried to remember everything the lawyer guys had said. Gray had realized that the younger lawyer had a meeting with an anonymous client, and he'd delivered a phone number with only six digits, in case the client was running late.

I considered calling someone with the information, but then I realized that (a) the last thing I wanted to do right now was talk to anyone who'd even once said the phrase *Go Lions/Lionesses* and (b) all I had was six numbers. Six lousy numbers and a body that was killing me.

And yet, I had to know. I'd always been that way with

numbers. Give me a six-digit phone number, or one of those puzzles where numbers stood for letters, or a mathematical sequence whose pattern was a mystery, and it would eat my brain from the inside out until I'd unraveled it. For that reason (and that reason alone), I did the unthinkable. I sucked it up and scrolled through the address book in my peppy little phone. After I'd passed the numbers for Abercrombie & Fitch, Barney's, and a couple of others that had for some unfathomable reason been programmed in, I found Chloe's number.

She answered on the third ring.

"This is Chloe."

"The phone number only has six digits." I laid it out there, no preamble.

"Say what?" To her credit, she didn't waste time insulting me.

"The phone number that Gray gave to Hayes. It only has six digits." I paused and stated the obvious. "It's not a phone number."

Chloe sighed. "You couldn't have noticed this an hour ago?"

"Can you just get me the files? If there are any more of these numbers, I need them."

I don't know what made me ask for the files, or what made me think there might be more to the number set than I already had. Maybe it was the sixth sense that always came into play when there was a code to break, or maybe it was the fact that I knew asking for the data would annoy Chloe, and annoying Chloe was quite possibly one of the only pleasures I could still wring out of my pathetic existence on this planet.

"If you give me a few minutes, I can scan for phone tones on the tape. I'll isolate two minutes on either side of every tone sequence, and send it to you when I'm done."

What was this? Chloe . . . being helpful? Chloe having a civil conversation with me? For that matter, the fact that Chloe Larson could scan audio tracks for a particular sound and isolate the relevant areas all in a matter of minutes was almost as remarkable as the fact that she'd gone off auto-bitch to do it for me. I thought of everything Zee had told me: chubby little Chloe, the *Star Wars* fanatic. Brooke saving her from her own dorkdom. The two of them fighting over Jack. Me representing everything that Chloe wanted to forget. It was times like this that I really didn't appreciate having a profiler take it upon herself to enlighten me. This was exactly what Zee had been aiming for. I couldn't just disregard Chloe as Chloe. She was an actual person.

"Chloe," I said, knowing I was going to regret it. "Thanks."

No response. I made a face at the phone, and when a few more seconds of silence went by, I rolled my eyes. "It's customary to say you're welcome," I said dryly.

No response.

"Chloe?"

As quick as I'd been to figure out the six-digit telephone number thing, it took me an embarrassingly long time to realize that Chloe had hung up on me. Gritting my teeth, I redialed her number and got sent immediately to voice mail.

"Hey, this is Chloe. I'm probably screening your call, and I probably won't call you back. Isn't life a bitch?" Beeeeeeeep.

To my credit (and possibly because of my little psycho-session with Zee), there wasn't a single obscenity in the message I left in response. "Hey, this is Toby. You're probably screening my call, and you probably won't call me back."

As this was an exercise in complete futility, I hung up the phone. I opened my mouth to curse Chloe, but then I thought of the whole hopeless dork/light saber thing, and couldn't quite bring myself to do it. Darn Zee.

CHAPTER 19
Code Word: Bubbles

Checking your email every fifteen seconds isn't a healthy habit. I know this, and usually the only reason I check my email is to activate new user accounts through which I can mask my own internet activity, but Chloe had said she'd send the files my way, and as much as she wasn't exactly the Honest Abe of the cheerleading world, I didn't think she cared enough about what I thought to lie to my face. At least not about this.

I refreshed my inbox.

"Wow. You get like totally no email."

I physically jumped in my seat, and Bubbles tilted her head to the side.

"Bubbles," I said slowly.

"Uh-huh?"

"What are you doing in my room?"

"Watching you check your email." She tilted her head in the other direction. "You don't have any."

I was tempted to thank her for the clarification, but became incredibly distracted when, without any warning, she hooked her hand around one of her ankles and lifted her leg straight up until it nearly hit her ear. To top it off, she just stood there, looking at me, bright-eyed and bushy-tailed, like she hadn't just contorted herself into a position that was painful to even look at.

"Stop doing that," I told her.

"Doing what?"

The sad thing was, she was serious.

I gestured to her foot with my head, and when she turned and saw her ankle an inch away from her face, she blinked several times, surprise etched thoroughly into her baby-faced features.

I stared at her, refusing to say another word as she lowered her leg.

"Sometimes I do that without realizing I'm doing it," she clarified needlessly.

"Bubbles."

"Uh-huh?"

"What are you doing in my room?"

I could practically see déjà vu replacing the surprise on her face. I swore to myself that if she said a single word about my email, I was going to toss her out of my second-story window.

"I was on my way back from the stakeout thingy," Bubbles said. "Chloe called, so I went to her house, and she said to give you this." She thrust out a pink square box.

What was with these girls and pink?

It took me about a second to realize that pink or not, this box in all likelihood held the information I'd asked for. Chloe just hadn't sent it via email. She'd sent it Ditz Delivery instead.

I opened the box, and inside there was an old-school Britney Spears CD.

"If this doesn't have phone tones on it," I told Bubbles, "Chloe is a dead girl."

Bubbles tilted her head to the side.

I popped the CD into my computer, and prepared myself to immediately turn it off if "Baby One More Time" blared from the speakers. Instead, a password protection window popped up on the screen. Chloe hadn't included the password in the package.

I smiled. My fingers flew across the keys, trying different combinations. I did some hard-core googling, and within minutes, I'd tried every combination of Chloe's address, her cell phone number, her birthday, and the words to our half-time cheer.

Bubbles watched, fascinated, until the urge to do a back bend overcame her, and then she bent over backward and out of my peripheral vision.

After about five minutes, I hit on the right password, and logged in.

"Wow," Bubbles said, standing up straight again.

I shook my head. As much as I would have liked to revel in my own hacking prowess, I had to admit that Chloe was tech-savvy enough that she never would have picked a guessable password unless she'd meant for me to guess it. "No big deal," I told Bubbles.

"Uh-huh," Bubbles said. "But I usually just use my phone."

"Your phone?"

She pulled a hot pink phone identical to mine out of a purple suede purse and gestured. "You just plug this thing into that thing, and then it does its thing."

Nobody had told me our cells were equipped with decoding technology. As brightly colored as it was, I had a feeling that my fashiony flip phone was going to be my new best friend. Forget shoes or flowers or chocolate. The way to a girl's heart was through code-breaking technology, and if my phone had that kind of program, I was officially in love.

"Anything else about this phone I should know?" I asked.

Bubbles thought for a moment. "If you want," she said seriously, "you can get *American Idol* ringtones."

I didn't have the heart (or the stomach) to respond. I turned back to the computer screen, found the audio files, and plugged in a set of headphones. I didn't want to chance someone overhearing the audio, and after years of living in the same house with Noah "Su-Underwear-Drawer-Es-Mi-Casa" Klein, I had accepted the fact that privacy was a fictional concept that didn't exist in real life.

Reluctantly, I held off on opening the files and played hostess to Bubbles. "Anything else?" I grunted. I'd never been a particularly good hostess.

"Chloe also said to give you these," Bubbles said, and she pulled two more items out of her purple purse. The first appeared to be an iPod of some type (not pink, for once), and the second was a small, unmarked bottle. She handed me the iPod.

"You're supposed to listen to the playlist tonight while you sleep," she said.

As I tried to process that information, I turned my attention to the bottle. "What's that?" I asked. The truth serum I'd been promised, but never gotten? Some form of mild explosive from Lucy? A magnetic-based lotion that would scramble any hard drive it came in contact with?

"It's an aloe-based avocado mask," Bubbles said. "Chloe said to tell you it's good for your pores."

Touché, Chloe, I thought. Touché.

"Thanks, Bubbles."

If Bubbles caught the dry note in my voice, her face didn't give it away. I tried to remind myself that based on the test scores Zee had shown me, there had to be more to Bubbles than surface appearances. After all, if the biggest partier in the senior class had a PhD in forensic psychology, anything was possible. Besides, looking at Bubbles, I almost couldn't believe that anyone could be that clueless.

"What's your real name?" I asked her curiously.

"Bubbles," she said immediately. "Why?"

"Is it a . . . uhhhh . . . family name?"

"No," Bubbles said, mystified as to why I considered her name even the least bit odd. "It's Bubbles. You know, like bubbles?"

"Uh-huh," I said. Zee might have technically been Dr. Zee, Tara might not have been one-hundred-percent foreign sophisticate, and Chloe might have secretly been more tech than chic, but Bubbles, the contortionist, was just . . . Bubbles. You know, like bubbles.

Thinking of Tara made me want to quit wasting time and give in to the seductive lure of the numbers in my mind. The faux Britney CD held the rest of a code, and even though Tara had only begged me to do the Jack thing, everything Squad-related, including seducing Jack Peyton and breaking this code, had gotten tied up in one giant neural ball labeled *cheerspionage* in my mind.

As all of this passed through my mind, Bubbles passed through my room and was halfway out my window before I realized she'd moved at all. She might not have been a rocket scientist, but she was fast. And stealthy. No wonder I hadn't heard her come in.

"Hey, Bubbles?" I stopped her before she'd disappeared entirely.

"Yeah-huh?" Only the top half of her body was still visible, but she turned back to look at me.

I asked one of the questions I'd stopped dwelling on once I'd started concentrating on the numbers. "Why does Tara care so much about this case?"

I don't know if I asked the question because I was thinking about Tara, or because I had a feeling that Bubbles would answer me more honestly than anyone else on the Squad.

"I dunno," Bubbles said thoughtfully. "I mean, there are what? About a bazillion foreign agents? And her parents are only like two of them." Bubbles shrugged. "Maybe she's homesick."

I sat there, frozen to my seat. Tara was British, and yet somehow, she'd ended up at an American high school. She spoke nine languages fluently, and her cover act was so perfect that even after having seen her this afternoon, I still bought it. When Lucy had explained Tara's transfer status to me, she'd mentioned that Tara's parents were "really into the Squad thing," and Tara had started freaking out the moment she'd realized that the information leaks had involved the aliases and locations of individual foreign operatives, to the point that Brooke had taken her off the case altogether.

I'd barely gotten over the fact that people's lives were in our hands, and now I had to deal with the fact that the people in question might be Tara's parents. And I'd bitched and moaned about having to hit on Jack Peyton. Tara's parents could already be dead, and I'd felt sorry for myself because my butt said *CHEER* and my hair was picture perfect.

"Toby?" Bubbles brought me out of my guiltfest. "Can I go now?"

Since she had the answer to one of my remaining shower questions, I decided to ask the other. "You know the guy who gave us our orders today?"

"Yeah-huh."

"Who is he?"

Bubbles looked at me like I was very simple. "He's the guy who sometimes gives us our orders," she said sagely.

"Yeah, I get that, but who is he?"

Bubbles was one-hundred-percent solemnity when she answered. "Nobody knows." I almost expected eerie mood music to start playing in the background as she continued, but her next sentence entirely ruined the effect. "I call him Bob."

"Bob?"

"Yup." If Bubbles found it at all ridiculous that she called the mysterious voice, the head of our operations, Bob, she didn't show any signs of it. Instead, she shifted her weight and tilted her head to one side. "Hey, Toby? Can I go now?"

I nodded, and just as she was about to descend from my window, the door to my bedroom flew open.

"I knew I heard girls in here," Noah said triumphantly.

Bubbles flashed him a grin, and a second later, maneuvered down the side of the house and out of sight.

Noah stared at me, a tortured look on his face.

I turned back to my computer and put my headphones on, but he just came to stand closer, his expression almost comically anguished.

I sighed. "What is it?" I asked, leaving the headphones in place.

"You had Bubbles Lane in your room and you didn't even tell me," he said.

Woe is Noah, I thought, but I knew from experience that talking could do no good at a time like this.

"If you loved me, you would have told me," Noah said. "And you would have loaned her your whipped cream."

I searched my desk for projectiles. I was way too tired to get up and chase after him, but I had a hell of an arm, and as soon as I found something worthy of throwing . . .

Noah read the look on my face perfectly and made quick work of ducking out of range, but on his way out the door, he turned back to play the Hormone Martyr one more time. "Life is so not fair," he said. "If either of us is going to have cheerleaders sneaking in the window, it should be me."

CHAPTER 20
Code Word: Bayport

Thanks to Chloe's audio-editing skills, it only took me three hours to listen to all of the phone sequences and decode the tones into numbers. We'd caught thirteen other dialing instances on tape, which was impressive considering the secretary's cubicle was outside the range of the bug. Of the thirteen, one was the tone from my head, exactly as I'd remembered it. Just to be safe, I compared the number I'd ended up with and the sound of the number on the tape.

"024106," I sang the number in tune with the tones, and it matched up exactly. I paused the audio just long enough to type the number into my pink phone again, checking and double-checking that I'd recorded it right.

Of the other twelve phone tone sequences on the CD, eleven had either seven digits (local number), ten digits (long distance), or eleven digits (given the fact that Mr. Hayes sounded somewhat sexually frustrated, probably a 1-900 number). The single remaining number had six digits.

"Hmmm hmmm hem hmm hmmm hem."

I could tell from the sound that it was a different number

than before, and this time, my fingers flew across the phone pad at warp speed as I sounded out the number. 023243.

I listened to the entire CD again. And again. And two hours later, I still had nothing except two six-digit numbers: 024106 and 023243. They both started with zero and contained a four and at least one two. They both had more even than odd digits. Neither of them was prime.

I tried translating the numbers to letters. Using the phone keys as a guide, 2 was either A, B, or C. 4 was G, H, or I. 1 and 0 didn't have corresponding letters, and 6 was either M, N, or O. I closed my eyes and let the different combinations play over the backs of my eyelids. *ABC/GHI/MNO.* Bin. Ago. Bio. Cho.

Cho. That was a name, wasn't it?

I tried the other number. *ABC/DEF/ABC/GHI/DEF.* More letters this time meant more combinations, and more nonsense. Ceche. Adaif. Beaid.

In other words, a whole lot of nothing.

I scrambled the letters in the second word set, looking for new combinations and still came up absolutely blank.

023243. 024106.

I sat there until my eyes watered. My foot fell asleep beneath me. My butt was as numb as the endless strings of possible decodes had made my mind. I was tempted to take another shower, thinking the steam might loosen up something inside my brain, but when I looked at my watch, it was already two in the morning.

Just another half hour, I promised myself. If I don't get it in another half hour, I'll sleep on it. Sleeping was almost as good as steam for unlocking an answer dormant in my own mind. As I sat there, staring straight ahead and willing the answer to come to me, I reached absentmindedly for the iPod Bubbles had given me. I traded my computer headphones for the iPod ones, and the iPod in question immediately began playing a preselected playlist, and I couldn't get it to go back to the main menu.

"Ready, OKAY! B to the A to the Y to the Port, Bayport Lions take the court! L to the I to the O-N-S; when we leave, you'll be a mess. Go, fight, win. You'll see us again. BAYPORT!"

Oh no.

"Bay-port Li-ons! (clap clap, clap-clap-clap) Bay-port Li-ons! (clap clap, clap-clap-clap) . . ."

Please, for the love of all things good and right in this world, I thought, please don't let them have made MP3s of their cheers.

"B to the A to the Y to the Port . . ."

No wonder Bubbles had instructed me to listen to this while I slept. I'd be cheering in my sleep—literally. As the very thought of this made my skin crawl, I turned the iPod off. I couldn't think about numbers and cheers at the same time. It was scientifically impossible.

My phone picked that moment to ring (not anything from *American Idol*, thank God), and for a moment, the hairs on the back of my neck stood on end. Did the others have me under constant surveillance? Did they know I'd turned the iPod off? I picked up the phone, but when I flipped it open, it turned out to be a text message, which was (all things considered) both a good thing and a bad thing.

It was a good thing because it meant that I didn't have to talk to anyone whose voice I'd just heard on the "Best of Bayport Spirit Squad" mix.

It was a bad thing because it meant that my regular ring

(and not just the text message sound) might still be one of any number of pop songs I abhorred. It was also a bad thing because although the text message did not in any way suggest that I was under constant Squad surveillance, it did inform me of a rather unfortunate circumstance.

Practice gym. 5:30. Tomorrow morning.

It didn't take me long to do the quick mental math. If I crawled into bed this second, and if I actually managed to fall asleep and not, for instance, spend the next three hours trying to get the chorus of "Bay-port Li-ons" out of my head, then I'd get a full three hours of sleep before my whole torturous existence began again the next morning. And that was assuming that I could actually tear myself away from the code long enough to concentrate on the whole going-to-sleep thing.

As it turned out, after I made it to my bed (minor miracle #1), I didn't fall straight to sleep, but I didn't lie there staring up at the ceiling and thinking about numbers or cheers, either (minor miracle #2). Instead, I thought about Tara and the foreign operatives who probably weren't Tara's parents. Even if they weren't, the operatives weren't nearly as anonymous and unreal as they'd been before I'd found out that in my partner's case, a tendency toward espionage was as hereditary as good skin.

Superslowly, my body still aching with the day's cheer-capades, I fell asleep.

024106. 02-41-06. 0-24-10-6. 0-23-24-3.

I stand in front of my locker, turning the dial. Left, then right, then left again. My body turns sideways, and I turn the dial up and down, then down and up. 0-24-10-6. 0-23-24-3.

The lock opens, and with sweaty palms, I rip it off the locker. This is it. This is the answer. Somewhere in the background, a dark-haired boy floats by. And then a giant slice of cheese.

But I'm concentrating on the locker. My hands are so sweaty, and the latch keeps slipping. I don't have time. I have to open it. My fingernails are growing as I'm groping at the locker door. The nails grow longer and longer, until even my sweaty fingertips aren't touching the locker latch. I fumble with it again, my long nails (hot pink, of course) doing the dirty work, and finally, it pops open.

Bubbles is sitting inside my locker, her feet behind her head. "Surprise!"

I bolted straight up in bed. Talk about nightmares. The sad thing was, Bubbles ending up in my locker wasn't completely outside the realm of possibility. From what they'd said in our original meeting, fitting into tiny spaces was more or less her forte.

"Surprise!"

"AAAAGGGGK!"

Someone slapped a hand over my mouth and I stopped screaming. Tiffany (I was getting better at telling the twins apart) leaned forward. "Shhhh," she said. "It's like five in the morning. You don't want to wake your brother and parents up."

I glanced past Tiffany, because I'd yet to see one of the twins without the other, and sure enough, Brittany was on the other side of the room, rifling through my closet. She had an enormous trash bag (suspiciously full), and even from this distance, I could see that my closet was now home to an obscene number of sparkly items and a disproportionate amount of pink and superbright blue.

"We totally forgot about the rest of your wardrobe

yesterday," Tiffany said. "And, hello! It's called Stage Six for a reason, right?"

Only one thing kept me from screaming then, and it wasn't the fact that Tiffany had very wisely kept her hand over my mouth. I quite simply could not risk waking Noah. If he'd freaked out about Bubbles hanging out my window, I somehow doubted he'd be okay with the twins reorganizing my closet, especially since they were wearing what appeared to be a combined total of eighteen square inches of clothing apiece.

"What time is it?" I asked, but since Tiffany's hand was still firmly in place over my mouth, it came out sounding more like a meow/lawn mower hybrid than actual English words.

"I can't understand you," Tiffany said.

I removed her hand from my mouth—and there's a slight chance that I used more brute force than was entirely necessary, but, hey, I never claimed to be a morning person.

"I asked what time it was," I said.

Tiffany rubbed her hand. "Sheesh. Touchy much?" she huffed.

I didn't dignify that comment with a response.

"It's five-oh-five," Brittany said, answering my question in a voice that can only be described as chipper. "And if you touch my sister again, I'll make Lucy lend me one of her Tasers."

Until that moment, I'd forgotten about Lucy and the Tasers, and though I wasn't the least bit intimidated by Brittany's threat, I was (despite all of Zee's test-score mumbo jumbo) disturbed all over again that either twin had access to anything with more voltage than a hair dryer.

"Here," Brittany continued, keeping her voice low. "Wear this."

I didn't intend to make puking sounds when she shoved the outfit at me, but again—not a morning person.

"You know, for someone as fashion delayed as you are, this room isn't bad," Tiffany said. She'd finally gotten over pouting about her hand.

Tiffany meant the comment as a compliment, but I took it as an indication that letting my mom decorate my room because I was too lazy to deal with yet another new room in yet another new house was a big mistake.

"We don't have all day," Brittany told me, crossing her arms over her chest. "Put on the outfit. I'll even let you choose the accessories."

"Accessories?" I asked darkly. She nodded toward my desk, which now appeared to be housing a very large item which may or may not have been called a Caboodle in some circles. I'm not exactly up to speed on my Caboodle knowledge.

"Toby? Accessories?" Tiffany prodded me on her twin's behalf, and I wished that I hadn't woken up. I mean, having Bubbles in my locker wasn't exactly my idea of a great time, but it beat having to pick out accessories at five in the morning.

"Do any of them have sonar?" I asked. I didn't mean the question seriously, but Brittany, impervious to sarcasm, daintily handed me a silver necklace with a blue-green butterfly charm.

"Sonar?" I asked. "Really?"

The twins nodded in unison.

I opened my mouth and closed it again, not wanting to

admit to Buffy and Muffy, the social scene twins, that I had no idea how to use sonar or what I'd go about using it for.

Five minutes later, I was dressed (a denim miniskirt, a white tank top trimmed with silver rhinestones, and high-heeled boots the color of the butterfly charm) and only feeling slightly homicidal.

"Kate Spade or Louis Vuitton?" Brittany asked Tiffany. Somehow, I got the feeling that they weren't talking about enemy agents, and my suspicions were confirmed when they handed me another oversized designer purse.

I might have at least registered a complaint, but when Tiff handed me my phone to put in the purse, I thought of the code, and of Tara's parents, and of my realization that maybe my transformation into Suzy High School was by some freakish twist of fate for the greater good. With that in mind, I walked over to my desk and picked up my notes on the numbers I'd pulled off of the audio track the night before, as well as the papers Chloe had given me on Infotech.

Unfortunately, the whole "greater good" thing didn't make walking in blue-green high-heeled boots any easier, and on my way back across the room, I fell flat on my face. To their credit, the twins said absolutely nothing. I got back to my feet and threw the few schoolbooks I'd actually brought home back into my bag.

"What are those?" Brittany asked, looking at the books the way that normal people looked at dog feces.

"Books," I said. "For school." The twins stared at me blankly. "Homework. Ring any bells?"

"You actually do your homework?" Brittany asked.

Actually, doing my homework wasn't exactly one of my strong suits, but she didn't need to know that.

"Yeah, with your GPA, we figured . . ." Tiffany broke off when Brittany elbowed her in the middle of her exposed midriff.

"Well, I definitely didn't get any homework done last night," I said. "I was too busy messing with this code, and—"

"Code shmode." Britt dismissed it with a wave of one highly manicured hand. "And don't stress about the homework—we'll just put in an order with HWA this morning."

Dare I even ask? I wondered.

"HWA?" I dared.

"Homework Assistance. They keep a database of our assignments, and if we're too busy doing Squad stuff, we just put in an order, and they print it out for us."

" 'They' as in the Big Guys Upstairs?" I asked, marveling at this new development. "And isn't that cheating?"

" 'They' as in the Big Guys who give Brooke her orders and the rest of us our supplies," Tiffany confirmed.

"C'mon," Brittany said, deftly eluding my "cheating" question. "We'd better get going. Brooke hates it when we're late."

I slung my bag over my shoulder and followed her out of the room, my attention divided equally between hoping I didn't fall and praying that Noah wouldn't wake up to see the twins leaving my room.

It was 5:17 a.m., and sonar necklace and HWA aside, I was still not a morning person.

CHAPTER 21
Code Word: Warm-up

When we got to the gym, everyone else was stretching, and Brooke was staring at her watch.

"Sorry!" the twins chirped together.

Brooke turned to look at me.

I returned the favor. "I stayed up almost all night working on a code," I said, "my feet may have to be amputated because of these boots, and quite frankly, I don't give a flying buttkiss about whether you glare at me or not."

There was absolute silence, and even though I didn't show any visible signs of it, I tensed my body, preparing myself in case Brooke should launch some sort of physical attack.

Instead, she flipped her hair. "Whatever," she said.

I glanced around the room, trying to figure out from the others' responses whether or not I'd won this battle of wills. I was, in fact, so busy looking around that I didn't notice when the floor began moving under us, and I wasn't exactly ready to drop three stories onto the trampoline. I managed to land on my feet, but it wasn't pretty. Or graceful. And it definitely didn't involve any flipping whatsoever.

This time, I maneuvered my way off the trampoline ASAP, and soon, all ten of us were seated at the conference table at the center of the Quad. For a few seconds, there was silence, and then Lucy started babbling.

"Bubbles and I hung out at the coffee shop across the street from Infotech for like six hours, and logged every person who came into the buildings into our phones. Then I came back here and cross-referenced the pictures we'd taken and our timetables with the system's files on Peyton's operatives, and came up with nothing."

Brooke nodded. "Anything else?"

"I got three phone numbers," Bubbles volunteered.

"Four," Lucy corrected.

"Oh yeah. Four."

Brooke nodded again, as if this, too, was the kind of information she expected us to report. "April and I staked out Peyton, and luckily for us, we weren't the only ones doing it. Heath Shannon—"

The twins sighed identical girly sighs at the thought of the international playboy.

"—cased out the place, but kept his distance. We took video feed and Zee analyzed. Zee?"

"He's careful," she said. "And on the surface, very calm, but he's getting a buzz from this. I analyzed the video on a frame-by-frame basis, and even though he's good at concealing his emotions, when you break facial expressions down to small enough units of time, something comes through. He's anxious, which tells me that the Big Guys were at least partially right—whatever deal he's brokering hasn't gone down yet, but there's a level of self-satisfied smugness there that makes me think he's well on his way. If

I was to *guess*"—she stressed the word—"I would guess that at his earlier meetings with Peyton, he acquired some information from them to pass on to his client or clients. He's probably received a beginning payment, but not his full commission, which means that Peyton still has information that Heath Shannon and whatever terrorist organization he's working for do not."

"Add to that the fact that he was casing the firm, looking for potential escapes, drawing up mental plans . . ." Brooke left it to us to fill in the blank, and I obliged.

"The meeting the Voice talked about is going to happen soon," I said. Everyone stared at me. "What? I can't connect the dots?" I asked. I felt oddly compelled to start defending my dot-connecting ability, but refrained.

"There's going to be a meeting soon," Brooke confirmed. "Our best time estimates place it at four this afternoon."

I opened my mouth to ask how exactly they'd made that estimate based on facial expressions and a very limited amount of video footage, but I didn't get the chance, because Brooke turned the tables on me.

"What have you got?" she asked.

With all the talk of stakeouts and meetings and international playboys who doubled as terrorist liaisons, I'd forgotten that I had anything at all.

"Chloe said you found a code," Tara prodded me, good partner that she was.

I nodded. "Yeah," I said. "Two six-digit numbers. One of the senior partners gave it to another lawyer in preparation for some meeting a couple of days ago."

More silence.

"I pulled the numbers off of an audio track containing phone tones," I said. "Since six digits won't do you any good as a phone number, there has to be something more to it." I dug around in my bag and pulled out the slip of paper on which I'd written the numbers. "Here they are. I tried looking for a number-to-letter code, but couldn't come up with anything. I worked the numbers over, looking for patterns, and came up with nothing. I tried running them through a few search engines—nada."

"Six digits," Zee mused. "What has six digits?"

"Locker combinations." I didn't realize I'd spoken out loud until after I heard and processed my own words. "If you break the numbers up into a sequence of three two-digit numbers, it could be a locker combination."

"And Peyton would be dealing with lockers why?" With a tone like that, I didn't need to see her glossy lips moving to know that Chloe was the one speaking. "They're passing on top-secret information. And if this is actually the information, and not some random payment scheme, then chances are it's either the names of the operatives' aliases, or their locations."

"The only name I could get out of the numbers was Cho," I said. "I've got some other combinations, but nothing that looked familiar." I slid them across to her. "If you think you can do better, knock yourself out."

Tara touched my arm softly, Zee cleared her throat, and I shut my mouth.

"Locations," Lucy mused. "So we're talking what? City names? Addresses? Map coordinates?"

An image of the map the Big Guys had shown us during our debriefing popped into my mind, and I wondered why I hadn't thought of the possibility that the numbers were coordinates before now.

"Map coordinates." Our mighty captain latched onto the last possibility immediately—apparently, I wasn't the only one who saw the logic. "Computer," she said loudly, "locate 02-32-43." She paused for a moment. "North, south, west, or east?" she wondered.

"We're talking Europe, Asia, or Africa," Tara said. "Possibly South America, but more likely not."

"Show grid for 02-32-43 east," Brooke said.

I paid no attention to her words, as I was caught halfway between berating myself for not thinking of the map coordinates thing (I mean location, duh) and giving in to the itchy feeling in my brain. As a map popped up on the plasma TV, with a vertical region highlighted, I gave in to the itch and let my mind go where it wanted to go.

023243. 024106. I didn't like that both numbers started with a zero. Why "02" instead of just "2"? I mentally scratched the zeros off the end as Brooke ran a cross-reference analysis of the highlighted portion of the map with the information that may have been compromised on the (not so) secure CIA database.

(0)23243. (0)24106.

I shook my head, completely dissatisfied. It just felt wrong. Going on a whim (I like even numbers better than odd), I threw out the last digits as well, making the numbers (0)2324(3) and (0)2410(6).

"Two degrees, thirty-two minutes, and forty-three seconds east . . . no matches found." The computer sounded distinctly peppy, but I barely noticed. Somewhere, in my subconscious, I registered the fact that the coordinates

Brooke had tried hadn't worked. There was no 02-32-43 east, at least not one that mattered.

East. The word echoed in my head, complete with peppy computer voice. *East. East. E.*

E = 3.

It came to me more like a splash of water in the face than a lightning bolt. On the telephone, the letter *E* was on the number 3, and the number 6 was the letters *M*, *N*, and *O*.

0-23-24 E, 0-24-10 N.

I scribbled the numbers down and handed them to Brooke. "Try these," I said. Miracle of miracles, she did, and even more remarkably, it actually worked.

"Al Jawf, Libya."

My eyes went immediately to Tara's, but she gave no sign of whether this was good news or bad news.

"How many operatives in Al Jawf?" I asked, hoping the answer would be "none" even though I knew in the pit of my stomach that we'd gotten the code right.

"I don't know," Brooke admitted, "but I'm getting ready to find out." She picked up her cell phone and dialed. We couldn't risk uploading anything to our superiors' breached database, but a secure phone call was a different beast altogether.

On the other end of the phone line, someone answered, and Brooke didn't spend any significant amount of time beating around the bush.

"Al Jawf, Libya," she said clearly. Then she paused, and about fifteen seconds later, she hung up.

"There are three operatives in the area. They're alerting two of them. The third is in too deep." Brooke tilted her head slightly and her hair (pulled into a high, glossy ponytail) fell to one side. "The primary assessment is that younger operatives will stand a better chance of moving in un-detected, especially since our covers aren't at risk from the leak." She paused. "We've been authorized to send in a team of post-eighteens." From her demeanor, she might as well have been talking about a sale on capri pants (still no idea what those were) at the mall.

"I'll go." Tara spoke immediately.

"Guess that means I'm in, too," I said. I wasn't sure, but I was going to go out on a limb and guess that going to Libya would get me out of Mr. Corkin's class and cheerleading practice. If I was lucky, it might even get me out of Satur-day's halftime performance. Besides, there was such a thing as loyalty. I wasn't about to let Tara go it alone.

"No and hell no," Brooke said, responding to us in or-der. "Tara, you're too close to it, and Toby, (a) you're not eighteen yet and therefore not eligible for any mission des-ignated post-eighteen, and (b) you're a mess. No offense."

Why was it that girls like Brooke always said some-thing offensive, and then followed it with the phrase *no offense?* And what was up with having to wait until I was eighteen to go on any of the really cool missions? I vaguely recalled Brooke saying that at age eighteen we had the option of being promoted to full CIA status, and yeah, I could see the legal benefits to only letting the older, more trained girls go international, but that didn't mean that I had to be happy about it, and it didn't mean that I planned to wait another two years before I got in on the action.

"Zee, you're in," Brooke said. "So am I. Lucy, we'll need complete weapons hookup in less than an hour. The Big Guys will have their fastest jet here within the hour, but it'll still be a ten-hour flight, minimum. Chloe—"

Chloe waited, her arms crossed over her chest.

"—I need you here. Getting this agent out is only half of our problem. If I know Peyton—and believe me, I do—this is only the beginning. I think there's a very real chance that this was the freebie, a show of good faith that they gave Heath Shannon to prove that they've got legitimate information. Once Shannon's clients manage to verify the information, they'll want more, and one guess as to when that particular exchange will be going down."

Bubbles waved her hand madly in the air.

"Yes, Bubbles?" Brooke said.

"Four o'clock today," Bubbles said brightly, proud of her inference skills.

"Okay," Chloe said. "I get it. We need to send a team in to intercept the data Shannon's collecting from Peyton." She paused. "And we need to hack Infotech ASAP, crash their system, and make sure they can't get any more of our intel."

It seemed simple enough. One trip to Infotech to shut down the leak, and one trip to Peyton to take down Heath Shannon and keep him from passing on any more information to his terrorist contacts. Personally, I was liking this plan a lot better than the one that involved me seducing Jack Peyton.

Unfortunately, fate (and Brooke) was against me. "Getting into Peyton and bugging their offices is still important, but right now, the most important thing is stopping this transfer and containing the leak. After that, you can do your . . . thing with Jack."

I wanted to go on the record that Jack and I would not be doing any thinging, but didn't have the chance.

"Does that mean we're moving the party back?" April asked glumly.

The twins looked absolutely scandalized by the very idea.

"Don't be ridiculous," Brooke said. "Chloe will take a team to Infotech this morning. You guys should plan to be back by lunch so you can spread the word about the party, and then head over to Peyton during seventh period. The party won't start until nine or ten tonight— that should give everyone plenty of time to get ready, even if Zee and I will have to play hooky because of the whole Libya thing."

I glanced around the room and verified that, yes, I was the only one who seemed to be thinking that this time frame and Brooke's priorities qualified her for the loony bin.

"You think you can get the agent out with only two people?" Tara asked.

Brooke gave her a look that made me think a "no offense" statement was forthcoming, but in the end, all she did was smile and nod.

"Zee, you'll handle our covers?" Brooke's voice rose at the end of the sentence, but everyone (including Zee) knew that it was an order, not a request. Brooke Camden didn't make requests.

Zee ran her tongue over her lip as she thought. "Let me download some information on Al Jawf," she said, "but we'll probably go with either visiting schoolgirls or actresses there for an on-location shoot, unless antifemale sentiment is too high, in which case we'll go with a blender."

"Blender?" I mouthed at Tara.

"Blending in," she said.

I looked at Brooke and then at Zee. Boobaliciousness and blending didn't exactly go together.

Brooke turned to the twins. "Prepare wardrobes for all three scenarios," she told them. "And get ready to hyper-dye us."

Our great and mighty captain stopped talking then, and without being told, the rest of the Squad began to disperse. Lucy skipped off to prepare "goody bags" filled with firepower, bulletproof bras, and stun guns; the twins sauntered toward the salon; Zee whipped a laptop out of her designer bag; and Brooke disappeared through an unmarked door without another word.

Bubbles, Chloe, April, Tara, and I stayed at the table, staring at each other. The second Brooke was out of sight, Chloe sat up a little straighter, tossed her perfect hair over one shoulder, and took the bull by the balls (or, in cheerleading terms, took the pom by its handle).

"If the actual exchange is taking place inside the firm, I think we can assume that we're not getting in, which means that our best bet to stop the transaction from going through is to take Heath Shannon out after he picks up the data, but before he can send it to his clients."

"What if it's an online transaction?" I said. "I know the Big Guys seem to think it's going to be a physical exchange, but what if Heath delivers the money and then Peyton just sends the info electronically?" With the speed of modern internet connections, we wouldn't stand a chance at intercepting the information before it made its way into enemy hands.

"Peyton's system is secure," Chloe said. "Annoyingly so, but one of the reasons we haven't been able to pin anything on them over the years is that they don't leave a paper trail of any kind. Witnesses disappear. Data self-destructs, and when it comes to stuff like this, they don't risk exposure online."

"So we're looking for what? A flash drive?"

Chloe nodded. "Something like that." She pursed her lips, thinking. "We'll want to keep our numbers down," she said. "Sending agents anywhere near Peyton, Kaufman, and Gray is risky, and we can't take the chance of exposure. We'll go in undercover."

"Define *we*," Tara said. I noticed a marked change in her. Ever since Libya had come up, most of the tension in her body had melted away until all that was left was the cool exterior the school knew and loved. I didn't need Zee's PhD to infer that Tara's parents were probably not stationed in Al Jawf.

"You're in on this one, Tare," Chloe said. "I'm going, obviously, and Lucy, since we might need some weapons analysis." Chloe stopped talking and had to actually force herself to continue. "And I guess you." She was absolutely thrilled to be talking to me, but since we were talking about a mission that involved data technology and hand-to-hand interaction with a very dangerous guy, the black belt/ hacker of the group was an obvious choice. So obvious that even Chloe had to make it, despite how much it obviously pained her to do so. "I'll have the specifics by seventh period." Chloe tossed her hair over her shoulder, a motion I interpreted as indicative of how drunk on power she currently was. "For now, we need to concentrate on the Infotech hack.

"I got some basic surveillance reports on Infotech off

the disk our superiors sent," she said. "According to the reports, Infotech operates under two different wireless units. The first is broader range and could feasibly be accessed from the street in front of the building. The second is confined to the executive wing, and the general wireless more or less serves to insulate that area from outside interference."

Translation: to hack into the executive database, I didn't just need to be inside the building; I needed to be inside the executive wing.

"Security?" Tara asked.

"Lax on the rest of the building, tight on the executive wing," Chloe replied.

"Methinks I sense a pattern," I said.

"You thinks?" Chloe asked. I didn't know which was more deadly: her smile, or her tone.

"Our best bet into their system is to plant a device that magnifies the wireless signal and transmits it to our receiver," Chloe said.

"Can you do that?" I asked.

"Duh," Bubbles said. "Chloe can do anything."

"Unwhelmable," Tara coughed under her breath, and I smiled.

"So how do we get the device thingy into the executive whatever?" Bubbles asked.

My mind produced no sarcastic reply to this comment. It was just too easy.

"I think our best bet is to Doublemint it," Chloe said. "We send one of the twins in as a decoy, and the other can plant the device."

"That works?" I asked.

Chloe smirked. "It has the last eight times we used it," she said. "Brittany can be very distracting." Chloe let the word hang in the air a moment before continuing. "As long as security doesn't figure out there are two of them, we can sneak the second one in without anyone noticing.

"And if that doesn't work, we'll Plan B it," Chloe said.

I refused to ask her to clarify.

"Ohhhhh!" Bubbles said. "If we Plan B it can I plant the thingamawhatsit?"

Tara scrawled a quick note on a piece of paper and slid it toward me without anyone noticing. I read it, and understood within seconds what Plan B was. If twin # 2 couldn't get in unnoticed, she joined her sister at distracting the guards while a third, slightly more stealthy operative did the dirty work.

If one of the twins was distracting, two was more or less a three-ring (four-breasted) circus. After having gone to school with Brittany and Tiffany for a year and a half, I'd gotten a firm hold on the mathematical property known only as the Exponential Hotness of Twinness. Each twin, by virtue of the fact that there were two of them, became infinitely more attractive to the average male than either of them would have been on their own. Since neither of the twins was exactly a dog to begin with, the resulting attention when they were together was usually astronomical in proportions.

"After we plant the device," Chloe said, looking slightly to my left as she addressed me, "it'll be up to you to break through their safeguards and find what we're looking for. Locate the program they're using to hack, download any files pertaining to information that they've already acquired or sold, and fry their system."

Even for someone with as much recreational hacking under her belt as me, that was a pretty tall order. I was practically giddy with techie anticipation. Or maybe that wasn't giddiness—maybe it was dizziness, pure and simple, based on the fact that my mind was swimming with dictates and schedules and master plans. This morning: hack Infotech. This afternoon: take down Heath Shannon. Tonight: plant a bug in the evil law firm.

Tomorrow: the world.

"So," I said, "are we ready to move out?"

Chloe rolled her eyes, like she didn't use jargon like "move out" all the time. "No," she said. "We're ready to go upstairs and hang out with everyone else in the cafeteria before first period. We have to make up for the fact that we're going to be missing half of the school day. Appearance is everything, and making appearances is key."

"Besides," Tara said, "somebody's going to have to explain to the vice-principal why Brooke and Zee won't be at school today, and why the rest of us are skipping our first four classes."

"Like that's going to be hard," Bubbles said, rolling her eyes and bringing her feet into the chair next to her so that she could hook her elbows under her knees.

"Spirit conference, do you think?" Tara asked, arching one eyebrow.

"Nah," Chloe said. "We used that one last time. Mental health day?"

"Didn't we use that for the, like, thing with the thing?" Bubbles asked.

Chloe and Tara nodded contemplatively. Apparently, they weren't having any of my difficulties understanding Bubbles's meaning.

Chloe smiled then. "I know," she said. "I'll tell him it's initiation, and that you guys have to, like . . . sign the spirit book and take the spirit oath and receive your Bayport Code training."

Spirit book? Oaths and training?

"You actually think Mr. J is going to buy that?" I asked. "Are we talking about the same guy here? Vice-principal? Loves handing out detention so much that he does it with a smile on his face?"

I had nothing against Mr. J—after all, he'd gotten me out of Corkin's detention the day before, but still, the guy was the high school's disciplinarian. It was what he did for a living. There was no way he was going to buy "cheerleader initiation" as an excuse for missing class.

"Mr. J," Tara said, her voice quite serious, "would buy anything, so long as a varsity cheerleader says it."

"Totally," Bubbles agreed. "He loves us!"

I thought of the fact that Mr. J had excused me from detention just so that I could attend a cheerleading meeting.

"Seriously?" I asked.

"Seriously," the others said, all in one voice.

"Okay," Chloe said, back in vice-captain or cocaptain or whatever mode. "I'll go make nice with the administration. The rest of you guys put in an appearance at the cafeteria. Come down here as soon as first period starts. Hopefully, by then, Lucy and the twins will be ready to go for the hack, and we can move out." Chloe paused, just slightly, when none of us moved. "Dismissed."

She actually said it that way, like she was some army colonel and we were her soldiers. For the first time, I found myself grateful that Brooke was the cheerleading captain.

"You ready for this?" Tara asked me as we made our way out of the Quad.

"Toby?" Tara nudged me.

173

"I'm ready," I said, even though secretly, I wasn't so sure. Yesterday, I'd been dealing with hot guys and Victoria's Secret, and today, I was dealing with secured databases and freelance agents known to be deadly.

Talk about a baptism by fire.

CHAPTER 22
Code Word: A-list

On the way to the cafeteria, we stopped in the locker room to give ourselves a once-over in the mirror. Or, at least, Tara, April, Bubbles, and Chloe gave themselves once-overs. Since the twins were busy preparing outfits for Brooke and Zee's mission, I took the opportunity to tug on the end of my skirt, forcing it to cover at least a small portion of my upper thigh, and I meticulously plucked the rhinestones off my tank top.

Tara watched me. "Ten-to-one odds it's back in your closet, re-jeweled, tomorrow," she said.

I frowned.

"And double or nothing says that next time, the jewels are pink," Tara added.

I continued de-jeweling my shirt. I would have ditched the necklace, too, but even I had to admit the sonar thing was cool. "You seem to be feeling better," I told Tara. She turned her face away from me slightly. I kept going. I'd had too many years of practice resisting subtle snubs to be put off by something as benign as a head turn. "The people in Al Jawf, they're not your parents, are they?"

If Tara was surprised that I knew about her parents being foreign operatives, she didn't show it. "I don't know, actually," she said, her accent crisper than I'd heard it in a while. "Their contact information is classified—even from me, but my mother's very fair-skinned, and my father doesn't speak any of the relevant languages terribly well."

That was as close as Tara would come to saying that the chances that either of her parents was stationed in Al Jawf were slim to none.

"Are they the reason that you do this?" I asked, gesturing to the locker room and its contents (a half-dozen cheerleaders, plus me). "Did you join the Squad because you're a legacy?"

Tara turned back to look at me. "I'm not a legacy," she said, her mouth pulling into a half smile at the thought. "I'm just an intelligence brat."

"There's a difference?" I asked.

Tara lowered her voice. "Brooke is a legacy," she said, the other half of her mouth completing the smile. "Her mom was on one of the original Squads. There's a big, big difference." Then she pressed her lips together, and I knew as well as if she'd told me that I wasn't going to get another piece of information out of her.

"HWAs, anyone?" Bubbles popped out of nowhere to stand by my side. Tara reached past me to grab some papers from the tiny, peppy one, who then turned to me. "Here are yours," she said. "History, math, chemistry, Spanish, and computer science." She paused. "Didn't you do any homework last night?" she asked.

It was freaky—Bubbles Lane, two parts contortionist, one part professional airhead, sounded bizarrely like my mother.

"I was busy," I replied, pulling the last rhinestone off my shirt with my free hand. Then I thumbed through the papers she'd handed me. "Number three's wrong," I said, scanning over my math homework. "And how in the world did they match my handwriting so well?" Even the chicken scratch in the margins was identical to my own.

"You have a ninety-seven in math," Tara said (did everyone on the Squad know my GPA?), and then she nodded toward the papers in my hand. "Number three is wrong because if you get number three wrong, you'll get a ninety-seven on that assignment."

I wondered if this meant my history homework was going to be yet another C-.

"The HWA program is designed to let you keep your current average. It doesn't help you or hurt you. It keeps things the same."

I gave Tara a look of mock dismay. "Are you trying to tell me I'm not going to be on the honor roll?"

Tara rolled her eyes back at me. The exchange felt normal—more normal than I would ever have imagined any Toby–God Squad exchange capable of being, and definitely more normal than my interactions with Tara before she'd worked it out in her mind that the agents in danger probably weren't her parents.

But, I reminded myself, the operatives were still someone's family, and their lives were in the hands of Brooke Camden and Zee Kim. I had to work to remind myself that Zee was more or less a teen prodigy when it came to the human mind, and that Brooke, according to what Tara had just told me, was a legacy. She was born for this, she was bred for this, she was raised for this. She *was* this.

"Come on, people," Chloe said. "Need I rehash my 'appearance is everything, appearances are important' speech? Cafeteria. Now."

"Power trip," I coughed into my hands. Tara stifled a smile and elbowed me in the stomach.

"Come on," she said. "Let's head up." Bubbles and April followed. Less than a minute later, the four of us were in the high school cafeteria, which, for reasons that continue to elude me to this day, was *the* place to hang out before first period, assuming you weren't otherwise occupied with "cheerleading practice." The moment we walked into the room, the entire school turned to look at us. It was like they'd choreographed it or something. In deference to our superior social status, a few of the wiser and more observant JV cheerleaders excused themselves from the central table.

Our table.

I hung back as the others went to take their seats. How much did I want to be skulking in the shadows right now? A lot.

"Well, I heard that she's totally loaded, and before she came here, she dated Paris Hilton's ex."

At least in the shadows, I might have had a chance at avoiding the rumors that were still making their way through the student body detailing the supposed reasons I'd been chosen for the varsity cheerleading squad.

"Really? Which ex?"

When no one answered this question, I was overcome with an insane urge to say "That information is classified."

"Well, I heard that she's a complete lezbo who's sleeping with one of the other girls on the squad. Can you say *casting couch*?"

I had to hand it to Hayley Hoffman. She was creative,

and she must have had an excellent command of acoustics, because she pitched her voice just loud enough so that I could hear her, but not loud enough that Tara, Bubbles, or April could. I thought about just sucking it up and taking my place at the center table, but I couldn't quite bring myself to turn the other cheek, because the fact that Hayley was using that particular term as an insult meant that her words weren't just insulting me. With that in mind, I walked toward the JV table, ready to draw blood, metaphorically speaking. Probably.

I leaned toward the mass of chattering girls. "Well," I said. "I heard that April Manning's having a party and that people who start small-minded rumors about the other girls on the Squad aren't invited."

I've never seen mouths snap shut that quickly.

"Then again, April's your friend, so you already knew that, right, Hayley?"

I could tell from the look on her face that she'd known nothing about the party. I should have felt sorry for her then—she and April had been friends for years, and the moment April had made varsity cheerleading, she had quite willingly left Hayley in the dust. Yup, I should have felt sorry for Hayley, at least a little.

Oh well.

"Toby," one of the other girls said. "I love your boots. You always have the best boots."

I purposely didn't look down at the blue-green atrocities on my feet, half because my feet hurt more when I paid attention to them, and half because I couldn't stomach the idea that anyone would compare my combat boots to something with a heel this high. Driven by my desire to get off my feet, I turned and walked back toward the central table, and with one last deep breath, I sat down, taking my place between Bubbles and Tara.

I retreated inside my head, careful to keep a smile on my lips and a vacant expression in my eyes. In less than half an hour, I'd be well on my way to my first official Squad-sponsored hack. Chloe would provide the technology, the twins and Bubbles would plant it, and I would do my thang.

I snapped out of it like that. I'd been on the Squad for just over twenty-four hours, and I'd actually thought the word *thang*. That was worse than *pizzazz*. It was even worse than *Caboodle*. At that exact moment, a handful of guys joined us, and I remembered that Infotech was only one-third of this mission. Another third of the mission had just sat down at my table. He was six foot three, his hair was a deep chocolatey brown, and it fell in his face just enough to give his chiseled features something of an edge.

Jack Peyton. School heartthrob. Former boyfriend to not one, but two cheerleaders. Fourth-generation scumbag.

"Well, if it isn't Everybody-Knows-Toby."

Well, I thought, if it isn't Smirky McJerkface.

Out loud, I censored myself. A little. "Well, if it isn't . . . you."

"It is indeed me," he said.

I couldn't stand the look on his face. "Congratulations," I said, sarcasm dripping from my voice. "It must be a great honor."

He broke into a grin then, and it changed his face in a way that I had to admit wasn't entirely unpleasant.

Jack milked that gorgeous smile for all it was worth. "You going to the God Squad party tonight, Ev?"

Ev. Short, I had to assume, for Everybody-Knows-Toby.

"Of course she's going," Lucy answered on my behalf, her voice as bright and bubbly as ever. "She's on the squad."

"I'll be there," I said, and the thought of the party—loud music, low-cut jeans and lower-cut tops, alcoholic beverages served from large and suspect containers that I wouldn't touch with an eighty-foot pole—made me physically grimace.

"You'll be there under protest." Jack interpreted my scowl.

"Why would I protest?" I asked dryly. "I'm a cheerleader, aren't I?"

Jack raked his eyes up and down my body. "That shirt used to have sparkly things on it, didn't it?" he asked, amusement playing around the corners of his mouth.

Postmakeover, I might have looked like Malibu Toby, but Jack Peyton saw straight through it.

At least somebody did.

Jack took my silence as an admission of guilt, and he grinned again. "You know, Ev," he said, "a little sparkle never hurt a girl."

"Bite me, Peyton."

"Love to," he said. "Does that mean we're on for tonight?"

The other girls gawked at me. I'd done more or less nothing but insult him, and he'd asked me out. I was a little suspicious that my new look might have had something to do with it—I'd been insulting (not to mention physically assaulting) guys my entire life, and none of them had ever asked me out, with the not-so-notable exception of Noah's friend Chuck.

I was too busy pondering this turn of events to answer Jack, and someone (my money was on one of the twins, who'd arrived just in time to put in an appearance and pick up on the fact that I'd defaced my shirt) kicked me sharply under the table.

"Ow!" I shrieked.

"I'll take that as a yes, then," Jack said. "Pick you up at seven."

With that, he stood up and ambled away from our table. As soon as he was gone, four other guys leaned in my direction, and one of them moved his hand toward me. Given the look on his face and the current trajectory of the aforementioned hand, I inferred that for some incomprehensible reason, he was moving to rest his hand on my thigh.

Calmly, I reached for a fork someone must have left on the table the day before and held it, poised for action, as I met Thigh Guy's eyes. "Word of advice," I told him. "Don't go there."

He must have read the intention to draw blood in my eyes, because he quickly pulled his hand back.

"Everybody-Knows-Toby," Thigh Guy said, giving me an awed look without ever completely removing his gaze from the deadly fork in my hand. "No wonder."

And that was the exact moment when threatening bodily harm became acceptable flirting practice at Bayport High. Overnight, I had become one of *those girls*, and the rest of the girls at our school had begun taking their cues from me.

"Chip, if you try to look down my shirt one more time, I'm going to have to hurt you."

Chip, student body president and generic hottie, grinned. "Would you please?" he asked. The rest of the guys grinned lecherously at Chip's wit.

What was a girl to do? I kicked him in the shin, and not one of the other cheerleaders glared at me. They were too busy trying to figure out how I'd managed to get a date with Jack "Unattainable" Peyton in under two minutes.

Chip grabbed his smarting shin, the rest of the guys started laughing, and I grinned. As much as I hated to admit it, a girl could get used to this.

CHAPTER 23
Code Word: Footsie

Less than an hour after I'd actually agreed to go on a date with our school's most eligible and broody bachelor, I was in Chloe's car, along with Bubbles, the twins, Chloe, and Lucy. Tara and April had agreed to stay behind to prepare for our mission that afternoon, and equally importantly, for our party that night.

"So when you kick them, do you like kick them hard, or do you just sort of play footsie with their shins?"

Brittany and Tiffany were very interested in what they had termed my FT (flirting technique). I got the distinct feeling that it wasn't so much that they had trouble garnering male attention on their own as it was that they considered themselves to be connoisseurs of the art of flirtation. That there was any FT in existence that they had yet to master was a matter of grave concern.

"Toby." Brittany said my name again. "Hello, focus! Footsie?"

"Do I look like I play footsie to you?"

Tiffany nibbled on her bottom lip in concentration. "Well, you didn't before the Stage Six, but . . ."

I considered introducing Tiff to the concept of the rhetorical question, but ultimately decided that there were better uses for my time. The twins and I were sitting in the backseat of Chloe's car, a chic little red number that totally wasn't big enough for six people. Luckily, Bubbles and Lucy were so tiny that they only counted as two-thirds of a person each, and neither of them seemed to be the least bit put out that they were sharing the shotgun seat. Bubbles was equally unbothered by the freakishly bizarre angle at which her upper body was twisted and the fact that her positioning relative to the stick shift had to have been giving her a horrible wedgie.

"Do you kick them like this?" Brittany asked, and the toe of her foot made contact with my shin.

"No," I said. "More like this."

"Ow!"

In the front seat, Lucy started laughing, and Bubbles, always up for a good giggle, joined in. In a momentous lack of twin solidarity, Tiffany commenced giggling, and even Chloe Thrill-Driver Larson let out a short laugh. Was it possible? Was this a bona fide bonding moment? As I was pondering that question, Chloe took a sharp right, and my head banged against the window. As the resounding thunk filled the car, Lucy broke into another bout of high-pitched tee-hees.

I was about to tell Chloe in somewhat unpleasant terms to slow down when she whipped the car into a parking space and twisted around. "You ready?" she asked the twins.

Brittany and Tiffany immediately turned to each other. Britt smoothed her sister's hair, and in return, Tiffany touched up her twin's lip gloss.

"Ready," they said, speaking in unison. It was strangely

unnerving—I'd never seen them dressed identically before, and postsmooth/postgloss, they were more than identical. They were like the same person, which was, all things considered, more or less the point.

"You memorized the maps?" Chloe prodded. "You know your way to the executive wing? You've got a cover for each stage of security?"

The twins nodded.

Chloe took a deep breath. It was enough to make me wonder if she was actually nervous. Just how much did Chloe feel like she had to prove here?

"Here's the magnifier," Chloe said, handing them a small, wood-colored square. "Don't lose it."

As Chloe continued to rattle off directives, Tiffany slipped the magnifier into her bra like it was the most natural thing in the world. She was like a kangaroo with a freaking pouch.

"Activate your minicams, and you're good to go."

The twins, still moving in synchrony, fiddled expertly with their identical necklaces. Chloe adjusted one of the car's cup holders, pulled out a keyboard, and typed some form of command in. Instantly, a large screen came down from the ceiling, and with some more nimble finger aerobics on Chloe's part, the feed from the twins' necklaces showed up on the screen.

"Audio." I was unsure at first whether Chloe was giving an audio command to the car, or issuing an order to the twins.

"It should be on," Britt said, ever the spokesperson for her twin. "We'll do a quick check on our way to the building."

Since we'd parked a good two blocks away, that seemed safe.

Chloe nodded. "Proceed as planned," she said. "If any alterations need to be made in this initiative, I'll make them from here."

Alterations in the initiative . . . It wasn't that I'd expected gadget guru Chloe to have a ditz-sized vocabulary, but still, it was an incredible jump from "Beat the Bobcats!"

"Ready?" Chloe asked.

"Ready," the twins answered.

"Ready," Bubbles and Lucy chorused from the front seat, where Bubbles, for some unfathomable reason, had placed her feet behind her head.

Chloe cleared her throat and turned around to give me a pointed look.

"Oh," I said, my brain still dedicated to wondering how a person would go about contorting themselves into a pretzel shape and why exactly they might feel compelled to do so. "Ready."

"Ready," all of the others said again, and I recognized the cheer-tone in their voices. "Okay!"

Unfortunately, my mind took that as a cue to launch into a mental rendition of our halftime routine as Tiffany and Brittany slipped out of the car and Bubbles (feet now a safe distance from her head) wiggled her way into the backseat.

A few minutes later, the twins' audio clicked on. "Bangs."

"Out."

"Pointy-toed boots."

"Depends on the color."

"Designers whose last names are hard to spell."

"In."

"Heiresses."

"Out."

"Celebrity children."

"In. When Angelina Jolie's little boy grows up, he's going to be a total babe."

"Guys, we have audio." Chloe took that moment to cut in on their game of "In or Out," for which I was grateful. "When you get within a quarter-block of the building, hold back, Tiff. Give Brittany a ninety-second head start."

"Uh-huh," Tiffany said.

"Awesome," her twin agreed.

I watched the plasma screen as the two visual feeds split. From the one on the left, I could see the back of Brittany's head as Tiffany fell back, giving her sister a lead. On the right side of the screen, the other feed showed us a clear image of the building as Brittany approached.

As Chloe's surveillance reports had predicted, security on the bottom level was relatively lax. There was a single guard, and if it hadn't been for the length (or lack thereof) of Brittany's skirt, he probably wouldn't have looked up from his computer, which I was about eighty percent certain he was using to look at a website whose name I totally didn't want to know.

When a flash of real, live cheerleader leg caught his eye, he turned his full attention to Brittany. "Can I help you?" he asked, the question coming out noticeably too fast.

Brittany leaned forward. "I'm looking for a bathroom," she said.

"Tiffany, move to flank position," Chloe said. "Brittany, you're a go."

Tiffany approached the building and held her position just outside the double-door entrance.

After the security guard stuttered out directions to the nearest bathroom, Brittany flounced off. Two minutes later,

Tiffany made her way to the desk. "Which way did you say that bathroom was?" she asked. "I get lost really easily."

This time, the guard just pointed.

They hit the stairs then, Brittany taking the lead. If I hadn't been forced to endure the Cheerleading Practice from Hell the day before, I would have been surprised at their stamina, but now I knew better. To someone who could do two hours of kicking, jumping, and shouting out annoying rhymes without ever losing her larger-than-life cheer-smile, eight flights of stairs was nothing.

The door at the top of the stairs was locked, and for the first time, it occurred to me that April, who'd stayed back with Tara to party plan, might have actually come in handy. After all, her "special skill" was lock-picking.

As it turned out, though, the twins didn't need April.

"Tell them to use the grape-flavored one," Lucy said brightly. Chloe nodded.

"Guys? Use the grape-flavored one."

From Brittany's video feed, I could see Tiffany reach into her bra and pull out what appeared to be a single piece of bubble gum. All business, Tiff unwrapped it and folded it in two. Then she bent down and smushed it between the door and the wall, even with the doorknob.

"Stand clear," Chloe said, and the twins backed up a few steps.

The next thing I saw from the video feeds was a small spark of light, a single tendril of smoke, and an open door.

"Bubble-gum bombs?" I asked.

Lucy nodded. "Coolies, huh?"

Coolies wasn't the word I would have chosen to describe that particular explosive, but if I had one soft spot on the

Squad outside of my partner, it was Lucy, so I let it slide. Without so much as a single sarcastic comment, I turned my attention back to the screen. The twins were no longer together, and Brittany was approaching a second security desk. There were two guards at the desk, and a quick infrared scan of the building, courtesy of Chloe's cell phone, showed two more around the perimeter of the offices Chloe had identified as our primary target.

I expected Chloe to dish out some more directions, but instead, she just let Brittany do her thing.

Britt slinked toward the security desk. To their credit, these security guys weren't looking at porn on their computers, but they were just as fascinated with Brittany as the guy on the first floor had been.

"Hi," Brittany said, shooting them a slow, sultry smile. "This isn't the bathroom."

"Hell-lo," one of the guards said. The other one gave her a stern look.

"No, miss," he said. "This isn't the bathroom. This is a secured wing, and I'm afraid I'm going to have to ask you to leave."

Brittany stuck her lower lip out slightly. "Leave? But I haven't gone to the bathroom yet." She leaned forward and grabbed a piece of candy out of a bowl on their desk. She unwrapped it and put it slowly in her mouth. "Can't you two help me?"

The first guard dissolved into a puddle of testosterone on the floor.

The second guard trembled noticeably, but held firm. "There's a bathroom on the first floor, Miss . . ."

"Bunny," Brittany said. "My name is Bunny."

I rolled my eyes. She was already practically oozing sexuality out of her pores. The name Bunny was probably overkill.

"Miss Bunny." Apparently, the guards didn't share my reservations about the name.

With security suitably distracted, Tiffany snuck out of the stairwell and positioned herself out of sight, behind a pillar.

"First-floor bathrooms are always so icky," Brittany said. She let a single finger trail along her chest and down toward her cleavage. "And I've got such sensitive skin."

"Bud, she's got sensitive skin," the puddle on the floor begged. "Just let me show her to the bathroom."

"Please, Bud?" Brittany wheedled.

Poor Bud caved. "Fine," he grumbled. "But, Jimmy, you wait for her right outside that door, and if anyone sees you, tell them she's somebody's niece."

Jimmy, thanking his lucky stars, hit a button behind the security desk, unlocking the main entrance to the secured wing. Trying desperately to look debonair, he escorted Brittany inside.

Chloe watched carefully, and the second Brittany was in the bathroom, she cued Tiffany. "Go for it," she said. "Guard at the desk is named Bud."

"Bud?" Tiffany approached the desk.

He looked at her. "What are you doing back so soon?" he asked. "And where's Jimmy?"

Tiffany stuck out her bottom lip. "Jimmy left me," she said. "And I never found the bathroom." She batted her eyelashes at him. "I thought maybe you could show me."

Bud stood straight up, and I got the sense that when he

escorted Tiffany toward the bathroom, it was more to ream out Jimmy than because of Tiff's feminine wiles.

"Lose something?" Bud asked Jimmy darkly.

Jimmy did a double take. "But you're in there," he said.

Tiffany subtly pulled her shirt down and her skirt up. "I got lost," she said, and poor Jimmy melted into another puddle on the floor.

"I'll take it from here, Jimmy," Bud said.

Jimmy looked from Tiffany back to the bathroom door. "But . . . but . . ."

"Now, Jimmy."

Jimmy, looking strikingly like a heartbroken puppy in a security guard uniform, started walking back toward the front desk. Bud gestured toward the bathroom door.

"I'll tell you a secret," Tiffany said. "I didn't get lost. I just thought you were cuter."

And then, while Bud, who was easily forty years old and forty pounds overweight, stared at her, she popped into the bathroom.

After straightening each other's hair and reapplying lip gloss, the twins flushed one of the toilets, and then Brittany exited the bathroom, leaving Tiffany inside, undetected. From the feeds, I could see a newly confident and swaggering Bud escorting Brittany out of the secured area, and once both guards were back at the desk, Tiffany exited the bathroom.

"Doublemint complete," she said under her breath.

"Good job, Tiff. Now go into the corner office and place the magnifier under the desk." Chloe checked the satellite feed from the infrared scanner. Either that, or she was reading her text messages. From the backseat, it was kind of hard to tell. "One of the guards is in the kitchenette. The other is making his loop. He just passed the southmost corner office. Give it five seconds, and then head in. You should have about two minutes before he loops back by."

Tiffany headed for the office. It was predictably locked, but another piece of gum (cherry this time) fixed that little problem, and Tiffany slipped the magnifier out of her bra and placed it on the bottom of the desk with the stealth of someone well used to sticking (nonexplosive) bubble gum to the bottom of the tables in chemistry lab.

With a murmur to Chloe indicating her success, Tiff slipped back out of the office, closed the door behind her, and practically skipped back down the hallway.

"Hey!"

I heard the voice from the audio feed, but didn't see its owner until Tiffany turned around.

"You're not supposed to be in here," the guard said.

"Cohoon," Chloe hissed. I had no idea what she was talking about, but luckily, Tiffany spoke fluent Chloe.

"Mr. Cohoon told me to meet him here," she said. "I'm Jill. I temp downstairs, and Mr. Cohoon wanted to . . ." Tiffany gave the guard a look. "Go over some briefs."

The guard apologized, and Tiff managed to sneak out without Bud or Jimmy noticing, because Brittany was showing them how she could "totally do a back bend."

"Britt, Tiff is clear. Move out."

With no warning, Brittany popped up from the back bend, blew kisses to the security guys, and breezed out the door.

I didn't need Chloe to tell me that this stage of the operation was officially complete. The twins, who had spent a good twenty minutes impressing upon me the Ten Commandments of Cuticle Management the day before, had just managed to infiltrate a secured site and plant a high-tech device on an executive's computer with no one the wiser. Maybe there was more to Zee's statistical tests and profiles than even I'd thought possible.

"Who's Cohoon?" I asked, not even bothering to sound unimpressed.

"One of their executives," Chloe said. "He often conducts 'special meetings' with interns. It seemed like a plausible excuse." She rolled her eyes at the way my jaw dropped open. "And, hello! Shouldn't you be doing the hacker spaz thing right about now? Because there's no telling what they'll do when they discover the lock on the office was blown. Wasting time? Not a luxury we have right now, To-bee."

I opened my Squad-issued laptop (which was, by the way, somewhat glittery—complete technology sacrilege), booted up, accessed the now-magnified wireless signal, and set about showing nose-in-the-air, pain-in-the-ass Chloe that when it came to hacking, I was anything but a spaz.

CHAPTER 24
Code Word: Evil

You know when you were five or six, and you went to a new playground for the first time, and it turned out that they had a twisty slide, a tire swing, *and* a merry-go-round? That's sort of what I'm like the first time I access a new system. The adrenaline starts pumping, my heart jumps with joy at the technological twisty slides: firewalls, encryption, passwords, security blockers, antihacker detection programs . . . just thinking about it made me giddy, and there I was, fingers flying across the laptop keys, working my way around this barrier and that with the grace and artistic precision of an Olympic figure skater.

Of all the things I've ever done, hacking is seriously the only one that could even possibly make me think in skating metaphors.

"What's that do?" Bubbles asked, leaning toward me and scrunching her nose up at the screen.

"That" was my refiguring the security settings on the wireless network. They'd set it up with double-sided protection—you weren't supposed to be able to file share, and you definitely weren't supposed to be able to poke around some-one else's hard drive, but after I'd convinced the system that I, and not someone whose username was GSeymor5, was the network administrator, those settings were easily changed. I turned on some quality one-way file sharing, meaning that all of the computers could share information with me, but I couldn't share with any of the others, and none of them could share with each other.

I could tell you how I did this, but then I'd have to kill you.

Honestly, though, I lie—I probably couldn't tell you how I did this. I just did. I was in the zone. I was unstoppable. I ran a scan on each of the four hard drives belonging to Infotech executives, searching for encrypted files and the type of program they would have needed to hack a secure government database. Not that I was intimately familiar with that kind of program or anything. I certainly hadn't written several of my own.

I concentrated on what I had to do. I'd had it banged into my head over and over again—first by the Big Guys, then by Brooke, and at least five times by Chloe on the way here: find the program Infotech had used to implement the hacks, confirming the Big Guys' hypothesis that they were the guilty party; get copies of any and all files they'd man-aged to steal; and then do everything I could to completely and utterly cripple their system. It was a three-pronged at-tack, and in my own special Toby way, I was multitasking and laying the groundwork for all three prongs at once. I could have done it faster with my own computer, but de-spite the fact that it had a glittery finish, the Squad-issued laptop came equipped with a variety of hacking programs almost as good as ones I'd written myself.

Apparently, the previous hacker, whoever she was, hadn't been a complete imbecile.

The computer made a happy beeping sound as it located a program that fit the parameters I'd been searching for. It was impossible to tell anything about it at first glance, but based on file size and the basic configuration, all of my hacker instincts were telling me that this was the evidence I'd been looking for. I convinced the computer to scan for encrypted files tagged with the program-specific document tag, and a few minutes later, the results came absolutely pouring in.

"Bingo." As the names of the encrypted files started popping up on my computer, I couldn't help but gloat audibly.

Find the program used to initiate the hack? Check.

Locate any and all files related to the information acquired in the hacks? Check.

Download those files? It would take some time, but I was willing to give myself a preemptive check on that one, too.

"Bingo!" Lucy echoed my victory cry. Then she turned around and cocked her head to one side. "What bingo?"

"Encrypted files," I said. "Tons of them, actually."

I paused. I hadn't counted on there being this many. As the file names piled up, I bit the inside of my lip. Depending on whether or not they used a different encryption on each file, this could take some serious time to go through. What if I was wrong? What if the program I'd identified had nothing to do with the hack? What if . . .

"Problem?" Chloe asked.

Normally, I might have taken offense at the tone, but I was still in hacker mode. My mind was racing to find solutions, not paying any mind to Chloe's bitquo.

"There could be a problem," I said. "But I've got it covered.

I'm widening my download to include all of the encrypted files, on the assumption that if these guys have been stealing classified information, they're not going to leave it in their system unprotected."

Unfortunately, from what I was reading on the screen, it looked like nearly all of the system's files were encrypted. Not surprising given that these guys secured websites for a living, but still a pain in my butt. "There are hundreds of files here," I said.

Faster now, more and more names appeared on the list.

"Maybe thousands."

"Can you tell if any of them are the files we're looking for?"

"I could start decoding," I said. "Maybe screen for files that include imported data or encrypted applications, but . . ."

"But with that many files, decryption would still take forever and a day."

Unfortunately, yes. My mind buzzed, working the problem over and over again. I typed in some parameters and narrowed down the possible files of interest, and looking at them made me salivate to start decoding, but . . .

ACCESS DENIED.

I stared at the words.

USERNAME/PASSWORD INVALID.

"Problem?" Chloe asked.

My mouth responded while the rest of me went into hyperdrive. "They've switched the security settings. They might use a roaming administrator or . . ." I hit five keys in quick succession. "Or," I continued, "they might know I'm here."

"Do you have the files?" Chloe asked.

"Some of them. The downloading process wasn't complete."

Besides, even assuming that the information we needed was in the files I'd managed to download, Infotech's system was still up and running, and that meant that my job here wasn't done. I'd been given three very specific instructions, and so far, all I'd done was locate the program and begin downloading the files.

I still had to crash their system.

ACCESS GRANTED.

"Was that a happy beep?" Bubbles asked cautiously.

"Back door," I said. "A second way in. I created it when I was controlling the system. If they're looking for me, they'll find it sooner or later, but it should give me enough time to boggle their files, insert a couple of viruses, and convince their programs they want to stealthily self-destruct if anyone tries to access them."

The twins said something in response to my words, but I barely heard them. I searched my laptop for programs that would wreak a suitable amount of havoc on the Infotech system. Given more time, I could have come up with something a little more elegant, but the program I'd located would eat their system from the inside out, and if they tried to transfer any data at all, they'd just end up transferring the virus, which would devour any hard drive it came in contact with.

DOWNLOAD COMPLETE.

If the Squad's technology hadn't been remarkably fast, I might not have finished in time.

If the programs I was working with hadn't been written by someone almost as good as I was, I might not have finished in time.

If I hadn't been totally and completely, one-hundred percent brilliant, I might not have finished in time.

NO WIRELESS NETWORK AVAILABLE.

This was it—no more back doors, no Plan C. They'd turned off the wireless network. All of the hacking in the world wouldn't get me back into those files.

Luckily, that didn't matter.

"Done," I said, as out of breath as a marathon runner after the last leg of a race. "We've got everything they've got, including a copy of what I'm about ninety-nine percent sure is the application they were using to assist with their hacks, and in about another hour or so, their system will be technological dog meat."

Chloe's facial expression never changed, but her body shed just enough tension that I considered the possibility that the stick typically wedged in her butt might have been dislodged.

"Well," Chloe said, putting the car into drive and tearing back onto the road, causing my head to come dangerously close to rethunking itself on the window to my left. "Maybe you're not a complete imbecile after all." She shifted lanes, and I held on for dear life. "Now that we've shut down the leak, we should be in the clear to send these files on to the Big Guys. They'll put a team on it and find what we're looking for ASAP."

As much as I hated handing over the files, I was drained, and decided that a little manpower never hurt anyone.

Of course, the entire question of whether or not my pride should have been insulted by the idea of getting help from the Big Guys was going to be moot if Chloe's driving managed to kill us all before we got back to school.

As Chloe "merged" onto the highway, there was a moment of silence in the car. I, for one, was praying for my survival, as some people who shall remain nameless seemed to think *merge* meant "cause other cars to start swerving." The twins were probably thinking synchronized thoughts about lip gloss. Lucy was in all likelihood in perky perfectionist overdrive—either doing mental herkies or thinking up new flavors of explosive chewing gum. Chloe was concentrating on her need for speed, and Bubbles . . .

Bubbles was doing the freaky pretzel thing again.

After having seen Brittany, Tiffany, and even Lucy in action, I didn't view Bubbles' freakish stretching the same way. Was it twisted that all I could think was that if we ever needed someone to hide in a kitchen cabinet or ride in the overhead baggage compartment on an airplane, she'd be our girl?

"Toby."

Brittany's voice was murderous, and I turned a wary glance her way.

"I know you have to do the hacking stuff and everything, but do you have to hit the keys so hard?" she asked, her eyes narrowed into slits. "You totally chipped your nails."

Tiffany, ever the kinder of the two, reached over to pat me consolingly on the shoulder. "Don't worry," she said. "We'll fix them for you when we get back."

Like hell, I thought, but I didn't say it out loud. Evil or not, cheerleaders or not, I thought that just this once, I'd give the fashionista two a break.

CHAPTER 25
Code Word: Stud

By the time Chloe pulled a sharp right into a parking spot in front of the school, I had only two thoughts on my mind.

The first was that miraculously, we'd all survived.

The second was that if I could get twenty minutes alone with the laptop, I might be able to figure something out before we handed the data off.

Unfortunately, Chloe had other plans. Without my realizing it, she had managed to lift the laptop from the backseat. All that lovely encryption was now in her possession, not mine.

Double unfortunately, however, what with the sizeable drive to and from Infotech, the amount of time it had taken the twins to pull off the Doublemint, the time I'd spent hacking, and the half hour that I had been informed it would take to redo my nails, it didn't look like I was going to be getting much rest in before lunch.

I half expected the others to go their separate ways when we got back, but instead, Bubbles and Lucy followed me to the twins' salon, chattering happily away about some topic of conversation that I couldn't quite follow. Chloe didn't join us—she was too busy orchestrating a drop-off of the information on the laptop and coordinating our afternoon mission, which Lucy randomly decided to name "Operation Playboy."

"Why is it that evil guys are always so hot?" Tiffany wondered out loud as she focused on the index finger on my right hand.

"Tell me about it," Brittany said, buffing one of the nails on my left hand. "Heath Shannon? Hot. That guy we had to take out who'd stolen that nuclear laser thing? So hot."

"And Jack Peyton?" Tiffany continued.

"Hot." I surprised myself by finishing Tiffany's train of thought. Had I really just said that out loud? More importantly, since when had I become the type of girl who gossiped about the hotness of boys?

And was Jack Peyton, he of the ironically detached smirk, really *evil*?

"Jack isn't evil per se," Tara said, coming into the room just in time to answer my unasked question, and save me from the mortification of the others commenting on my slip of tongue. "He can hardly help who his father is."

"Okay," Brittany agreed affably. "So maybe he isn't evil, but he could be evil someday. And he *is* hot. Even Toby thinks so."

And that was my cue to leave. Except, unfortunately, each twin had me by one hand, and neither of them was done with the buff, polish, repair routine they had their hearts set on.

I had no choice but to change the subject—and fast. "How goes the party planning?" I asked April and Tara. It wasn't exactly a deep question, but it worked.

"We managed to get Rocksha to DJ, and April found a great caterer," Tara said.

203

"Caterer? DJ?"

April shrugged. "Major party."

"So no cheap beer in sketchy kegs?" I asked.

Tara leaned over and tweaked my ponytail. "Toby, it's a high school party. There's always beer in sketchy kegs. It will probably just be very expensive beer."

Lucy wrinkled her nose.

"Not a fan of beer?" I asked her.

"No," she said. "It doesn't ignite as well as vodka."

It didn't surprise me that when Lucy thought about alcohol, her main concern was flammability. For some reason, I couldn't see her as much of a drinker of anything stronger than orange soda.

"Done!"

"Done!"

The twins finished one after another, and finally, my hands were my own again.

"Lunch?" Tara asked, looking at her watch.

I nodded. "Lunch."

"Lunch!" the others chorused in unison. I rolled my eyes, but somehow, a smile found its way onto my face. It was amazing what a high-stakes hacking adventure with other people could do for team bonding. On principle, I refused to give any of the credit to our girl talk in the salon.

The moment we walked into the cafeteria, I was treated to three sights. The first was almost an exact replica of what had happened when we'd walked into the caf that morning. All eyes swung our way, and the sea of people parted for the seven of us. The second thing I noticed was that Jack Peyton was already sitting at the central table, his eyes locked on mine.

The third thing I noticed was that my younger brother

had just sat down with a bunch of senior girls, all of whom were staring at him like he was some kind of alien species.

Maybe they were right.

Even from this distance, I could tell that Noah's mouth was moving, and my sisterly instinct (and my unfortunate familiarity with his favorite pickup lines) cued me in to the fact that he was, in all likelihood, saying something along the lines of "Hey, baby, you're looking a little lonely, but don't worry, there's enough Noah to go around."

And then, right on cue, an enormous football player walked up to the table, slammed his tray down, and reached for Noah's shoulder.

Here we go again, I thought. I took a step forward, but before I could so much as take a flying leap at the buffoon who was about to decapitate my brother with a fist roughly the size and shape of a cinder block, the rest of the girls beat me to it. Granted, there wasn't actually any pummeling involved.

"Hi, Marcy! Hi, Jeff!" Lucy bounded over to the table, the rest of the girls on her heels. "Hi, Noah." Lucy smiled at him. Noah, ever the one to take the least bit of encouragement in any shape or form as a come-on, turned his "charm" on Lucy.

"Well, hello there," he said, his voice pitched lower than usual in an attempt to seem more manly.

While Lucy distracted Noah and pulled his attention away from the girl he'd been trying to hit on, the others worked on defusing the threat that was Cinder-Blocks-for-Fists Jeff. And somehow, they did it without a single menacing look, punch to the gut, or kick to the groin. In fact, as far as I could tell, they didn't do anything but flutter their eyelashes.

The girls lured Noah away from the senior table and deposited him back among the other freshman boys, who then stared at my brother with reverent awe. Noah looked at the cheerleaders, looked at the boys, and then arched one eyebrow freakishly high, a devilish look on his face, and took a bow.

"I'll see *you* later," he told Lucy.

Lucy actually giggled, and then, in one coordinated motion, all of the girls headed for our table, leaving my brother to milk the experience for all it was worth among his freshman cohorts.

Note to self, I thought. Tell Lucy not to encourage him.

I joined the other girls with every intention of telling them just that—and asking them why in the world they'd felt compelled to move my little brother out of harm's way—but when I got there, the twins had matching wicked smiles on their faces.

"You know, Toby," Brittany said, "your brother is awfully cute."

I think it's safe to say that hearing the words leave her mouth had a catastrophic physical effect on my being. I shuddered and almost lost my lunch—even though I hadn't eaten it yet.

Tiffany poked me in the side. "Yeah," she said. "He's adorable."

I frowned at them.

"They're just teasing you," Tara whispered.

"What? You don't like it when we talk about your brother?" Tiffany asked innocently. "But what if we wanted to ask him out? He's such a *stud*."

Okay, that was taking it way, way too far. If Noah heard any part of this conversation, he would become unbearable.

He already thought he was a ladies' man. He didn't need the twins giving him ideas.

"Stay away from my brother," I growled.

The twins just laughed, and as we sat down at our table—a safe distance away from Noah's—everyone else joined in.

"What's so funny?" Jack asked, never taking his eyes off my face.

"Nothing," I said, giving the twins a look that promised serious repercussions if they said anything else about my brother, the "stud."

"We still on for tonight, Ev?" Jack asked me, an amused smile playing around the corners of his lips at the look I was shooting the twins.

Before I had a chance to formulate a properly sarcastic response, the others answered on my behalf.

"Yes," Tara said.

"You are," Lucy finished.

I opened my mouth to object, but one of the twins grinned at me, and I got the distinct feeling that if I said so much as another word, they'd launch into a long, traumatizing, and detailed account of how much they'd just love fooling around with my younger brother.

Needless to say, I kept my mouth closed.

CHAPTER 26

Code Word: Taser

By seventh period, my high from Operation Doublemint had started to fade—in part because adrenaline had finally stopped doing the tango in my bloodstream, and in part because I'd had to spend most of the day focused on keeping the other cheerleaders away from my brother. Once they'd figured out that it was the easiest way to get under my skin, the girls were relentless, and even though I knew that Tara was right—they were teasing me, in a twisted and shockingly friendly way—I was determined to find a way to put a stop to it.

Unfortunately, I hadn't exactly succeeded. Fortunately, however, the twins—who were far and away the worst offenders—weren't going to have much opportunity to "tease" me for the next few hours. Operation Playboy was about to commence, and Tara, Lucy, Chloe, and I were the only operatives involved. The rest of the girls were under strict orders to finalize the details for April's party, check up on Brooke and Zee, and paint some kind of banner for the football players to run through at the beginning of the Saturday game.

Needless to say, getting away from the twins and their "Noah Is Hot" propaganda wasn't the only reason I was glad that I was going on this mission instead of staying behind.

"We're going to try to keep this as simple as possible," Chloe said, looking at me, Lucy, and Tara in turn. "We're all going in armed, but weapons are a last resort. Ideally, we'd be able to pull this off without engaging the enemy at all. The goal is to get whatever information Peyton has given him. It might be a CD, a portable hard drive, possibly even something similar to the digi-disks we use. Whatever it is, we need it. That's where you come in, Tara."

I arched one eyebrow at my partner in an open-ended question, and she gave me an impish look.

"I may or may not have some skill at picking pockets," she said delicately.

"Don't let her fool you," Lucy told me. "She's the best!"

"If Tara can't get the data unnoticed, no one can," Chloe concurred. "In which case, we move on to Plan B."

I couldn't help but hope that Plan B involved kicking some international playboy booty. Was that really so much to ask?

"If Tara isn't successful, we're going to move on to a Flirt and Flick," Chloe said.

"A Flirt and Flick?" I was nothing if not skeptical.

"We can't afford to actually physically engage a Peyton client within a two-block radius of the firm," Chloe said. "Peyton has surveillance of its own, and the last thing we need is for them to ID one of us. So if Tara can't steal the data, we're going to have to find a way to get Heath Shannon a suitable distance away from Peyton before we try anything else. Since we can't risk him handing off or transferring the data before we intercept it, one of us is going to have to stay with him at all times. Hence the Flirt and Flick."

As much as I hated to admit it, the flirting logistics of this equation made perfect sense to me. That said . . .

"What's a flick?" I asked.

"Female Liason Indemnifying Against the Possibility of Contact," Chloe said.

That sounded like a FLIAPC to me, but I wasn't about to argue the point, because Chloe's answer still hadn't cleared things up in my mind. "Translation?" I asked. "Preferably in English."

I sensed the eye roll coming before I saw it.

"Basically, one of us goes in and interacts with Heath Shannon in a way that makes it impossible for him to immediately contact someone else," Chloe said. "In this case, it means following him back to his car and convincing him that he wants to take me for a ride more than he wants to transfer the data."

"You're going to get into a car with this guy?" I asked. What was next, taking candy from strangers? Running with scissors?

"Worried about me?" Chloe asked.

Was I?

"I'm touched. Really."

Okay, I most definitely was not worried about her—especially now.

"So what's Plan C?" Tara interjected, coming in between the two of us.

I latched onto her question. "Plan A is Tara doing the pickpocket thing, Plan B involves you doing a Flirt and FLIAPC. . . ." I changed the acronym just to get under her skin. "If he won't take you with him, what's Plan C?"

"Plan C involves the fact that Heath Shannon's smart enough to know that working with Peyton is dangerous, which means that he won't be using their parking garage, which means that we stand a slight chance of being able to take advantage of the one weak spot in Peyton's security coverage of the area."

Lucy smiled broadly. "Yay! That's next to the tanning place, right?"

Chloe nodded. "If you can disable him and get him into SunTanz without moving outside the four-foot radius of Peyton's blind spot, we can drop him off in one of the tanning booths, and the Big Guys will send someone to pick him up later."

"And we're supposed to carry an unconscious and internationally infamous playboy into a tanning salon without anyone noticing how?" I asked.

"What? No questions about how to disarm him and knock him out?"

I gave her a look.

"Trust me, Toby," Chloe said, "if you can take him out, Lucy can handle the rest."

Lucy smiled serenely, which, given the circumstances, was just a wee bit creepy.

"And there's a slight chance that we may have some contacts inside the tanning salon. Hopefully, though, it won't come to that. Like I said before, physically engaging the enemy is a last resort, as are weapons."

Lucy sighed then, as if it would pain her greatly to holster her weapon of choice. That made me wonder what exactly the weapon of choice was, so I voiced the question.

"We just want to disable him," Lucy said. "We don't want to hurt him, so we should probably each take a Taser and some knockout patches. If things get sticky, one of us should have a gun."

Lucy and Chloe looked at Tara, who inclined her head slightly. I, for one, was grateful that if any varsity cheerleader was going to be packing, it was Tara. Despite Lucy's expertise, she was just bouncy enough that the idea of her holding a firearm was a little bit scary, and needless to say, I wasn't exactly keen on the idea of giving Chloe any literal ammunition. As for me, I didn't want a gun. I'd never been a fan of weapons—I preferred to fight hand to hand.

"Are the Tasers in the guidepost?" Chloe asked Lucy.

Lucy nodded. "They look like those teeny-tiny iPods," she said, "but if you use the scrolling function, the pointy things will pop out, and all you have to do to activate the charge is press the central button once the pointy things, you know, puncture the skin and stuff."

Lucy smiled again, and I found myself thinking about how right Zee had been. There was something oddly endearing about Lucy's earnest sweetness—and about the fact that she'd designed faux iPods that doubled as Tasers, "pointy things" and all.

"We'll take two cars," Chloe said. "Park them at least four blocks away from Peyton, preferably in separate directions. We'll rendezvous back here once the mission is over. Lucy, would I be correct in assuming that the Tasers have built-in communication devices?"

Lucy nodded. "In the headphones," she said. "That's why I picked the little iPod design—that and the fact that they come in colors."

"Are they pink?" I couldn't stop myself from asking the question.

"Nope." Lucy punctuated her answer with a shake of her head. "They're purple."

"I'm driving," Chloe said, not giving me the chance to mentally lament the color of my Taser. "Who else wants to drive?"

Before I could speak up, Lucy offered to drive, and Tara volunteered to ride with Chloe, shooting me a look that spoke volumes about the fact that I owed her one.

Five minutes later, I was in Lucy's car, listening to her music and wondering if I'd have been better off taking my chances with Chloe's manic driving.

"You don't like Kelly Clarkson?" Lucy asked, wide eyed.

I didn't answer.

"What about something old school?" she asked, eager to please.

"Old school? Like Cat Stevens? The Clash?"

"Weeelllllll . . ." Lucy dragged out the word and I read between the lines.

"You're not talking about 'old school' as in *NSYNC, are you?" I asked suspiciously.

"Spice Girls?" Lucy suggested hopefully. "Or maybe Ashlee Simpson's first album?"

"She has more than one album?" The thought was depressing.

"Or we could listen to the radio," Lucy said. "Or we don't have to listen to music at all. We could just talk."

"Let's talk." Those were definitely words I never thought I'd say, especially to a fellow cheerleader, but I was getting used to the fact that all of my preconceptions about my life, my future, and my teammates were turning out to be wrong.

"What do you want to talk about?" Lucy asked, and then she let out a preemptive giggle. "Noah?"

"Not funny, Lucy," I said.

Lucy just grinned. "He's just so . . ."

"Annoying? Deluded? Insane?"

". . . happy," Lucy finished. "He just seems really happy, you know?"

"You're one to talk," I said. "You're Miss Happy."

Lucy shifted lanes. "But it's like he doesn't even have to try. I mean, he almost got thumped at lunch, and he was grinning like crazy."

"Key word: crazy."

Lucy grinned wistfully. "Yeah," she sighed. "Crazy."

First the twins and now Lucy? The truly disturbing thing was that I couldn't decide whether she was teasing me or she was serious. At least with Brittany and Tiffany, I was relatively sure that they didn't actually find Noah studlike in the least.

"So," I said, more than ready to change the subject. "How about those Spice Girls?"

CHAPTER 27
Code Word: Ta-tas

In general, I think it's safe to say that people vastly under-estimate the amount of time the average spy spends standing around doing nothing. We arrived in the general vicinity of Peyton, Kaufman, and Gray approximately a half hour before the transaction was supposedly going down, and Heath Shannon didn't actually show up until a full hour after that.

Lucy and I spent most of this time hanging out in the ice cream shop next door to the tanning salon—Lucy's idea, not mine. But since I have never in my life objected to a banana split, it wasn't a horrible way to pass the time—especially considering that on the other side of the tanning salon, there was a lingerie store that made Victoria's Secret look like Baby Gap. Sparkly underwear was bad enough; I wasn't about to brave teeny-tiny nighties that looked vaguely like they belonged in a Madonna video—or worse.

Lucy stirred her ice cream absentmindedly. She was on her third cup of rainbow sherbet, topped with marshmallow fluff and rainbow sprinkles. I would have been impressed with her metabolism were it not for the facts that (a) I had a pretty great one myself, and (b) she actually only ate about a third of each cup, because by the time she got done stirring it up and twirling her spoon absentmindedly in the resulting goop, most of the ice cream had melted.

"We have visual contact."

It took me a second to realize that the voice in my ears was Chloe's. I'd been so distracted by Lucy's ice cream shenanigans and the enthusiasm with which she had been explaining the CW's fall lineup to me that I'd forgotten that I was wearing headphones.

"You ready?" Lucy asked, taking one last bite of her sherbet.

I nodded, and the two of us went to throw away our trash.

"I'm going in." This time, it was Tara's voice in my ear.

Lucy pulled me out of the ice cream shop, and—much to my dismay—down the street and into the lingerie store.

"We'll have a better view in here," she explained, gesturing out a side window. Sure enough, I could just barely make out the outline of Tara down the block. She was walking briskly, her arms full of shopping bags (no idea where she'd gotten them), and as we watched, she ran smack into a man-shaped object that I deeply suspected was Heath Shannon, even though it was kind of hard to tell from this distance.

"Here," Lucy said, digging into her purse and handing me a pair of white sunglasses with rainbow rhinestones embedded in the sides. "Try these on."

I did as instructed, and immediately noticed the change. I might as well have been standing a foot away from Tara. Whatever these lenses were made of, they were damn powerful binoculars. They also compromised my peripheral vision enough that I didn't have to worry about the large selection of holiday-themed bras to my left.

As Tara collided with Heath Shannon, he temporarily lost his balance, and she dropped her packages. He regained his footing, and as he helped her pick up her bags, I watched the way she used every excuse she could to touch his body, to move hers subtly against his. Had I been the average observer, I would have marked her for a high school Lolita, but with the glasses and my insider information, I concluded that she was stealthily slipping her hands in and out of his pockets with every soft touch.

The two of them finished gathering the packages and talked for several seconds before they continued on their respective ways: Heath toward us, and Tara in the opposite direction.

"I've got his wallet," Tara said a few seconds later, her British accent crisp in my headphones. "But no portable hard drive. No disk. If the Big Guys are right and this transfer was physical, he's still got the data."

"In that case," Chloe said, "he's all mine. Lucy, you guys should get into position, just in case. If I succeed on the Flick, fall back and use the tracker in my phone to follow us in case I need backup."

Unlike Tara, Chloe didn't bother turning the microphone in her iPod off when she engaged the mark, and I was treated to every second of the flirt half of her Flirt and Flick.

"Is there any way to turn the volume down on this thing?" I asked Lucy. I fiddled with the controls, and two sharp metal electrodes popped out of the end.

Ooops.

On the other end of our line, Chloe was doing a pretty good imitation of one of the twins. Personally, I thought she was pouring it on a little too thick, and she must have gotten that vibe as well, because she changed methods right around the first time Heath Shannon tried to excuse himself from her presence.

I won't go into detail about what her next method was, but let's just say it bore a suspicious resemblance to my FT and leave it at that. For the record, though, Chloe didn't do sullen and violently intriguing nearly as well as I did.

"Yikes," Lucy said, glancing down at her watch and sending me the signal that we were on. "It's getting late. We should probably go. Unless you want one of those Mrs. Claus bras?"

She didn't have to say anything else. Chloe had somehow managed to get Heath Shannon's number, but after that, he'd given her the brush-off.

It was now officially time for Plan C.

I headed for the store's exit, determined to put as much space between me and the Mrs. Claus bras as possible, but Lucy held me back, allowing a very large woman holding a very large package (which I could only assume was filled with very large, disturbingly risqué underwear) to exit in front of us. As we followed the woman out, I realized what Lucy had done.

Underwear Woman was blocking us from the view of any security cameras that may or may not have been surveying the area. We walked for a few more seconds and then slipped out from behind the woman to stand in front of a tanning salon with a smiling sun drawn on the glass windows.

Lucy nodded, first toward a billboard, then toward a post office mailbox, and then toward a Now Opening sign to our right. Based on the calculations we had for Peyton's surveillance equipment, this was the dead spot, the one place on this two-block stretch of Bayport that the Evil Law Firm of Doom couldn't monitor.

In other words, this little slice of upscale strip mall was our last shot at completing our mission without risking our covers. If Heath got past us, we'd have to fall back and intercept his car somewhere down the line and hope that he wasn't going to immediately transfer the files to his black market contacts.

Using the zoom-in sunglasses, I concentrated on appraising Heath Shannon—getting a feel for the length of his stride and trying to gauge what his strengths as a fighter might be. He was easily twice my size, and I had deep and abiding suspicions that he was carrying weapons more deadly than an iPod Taser.

Piece of cake.

I slipped the sunglasses off and handed them to Lucy. She tucked them into her purse, and then hooked one of her arms briefly through mine.

"This," she said seriously, "is going to be so much fun."

I counted backward in my head, my brain automatically calculating how much time I had left until the mark was within Tasering range. In any other circumstances, I would have loved nothing more than to bring my roundhouse out to play, but somehow, I didn't think that was quite subtle enough to fly in public. We didn't just need to take him out. We needed to take him out quietly.

Have I ever mentioned that *quiet* is not my strong suit?

Five. Four. Three. As he drew closer and closer, I sank back slightly on my heels, holding the Taser loosely in my hands.

Two, I thought, and then, a second before he was within my range, Lucy let out a high-decibel shriek.

"OMG!" She said. "You're, like, that guy! Who dated that girl!"

This so wasn't in the plan. And yet . . . Heath Shannon slowed his pace and smiled at Lucy. Apparently, in addition to dabbling in evil, he was also a whore for being fawned over by people who considered him a celebrity. I watched, absolutely bewildered, as our mark reached into his pocket to pull out a pen so that he could supply Lucy with the autograph she so clearly (and audibly) desired.

I'd been prepared to take him out. I'd timed it in my head, gotten it down to a precise movement. This, however, was unexpected. He was just standing there, completely distracted, chatting happily away with Lucy, as if he didn't have a care in the world. Tara hadn't managed to pick his pockets, and Chloe had only halfway seduced him, but Lucy's open adoration and obvious cheerfulness weren't running up against any barriers at all.

In a way, it made sense. Tara was sophisticated; Chloe was terrifying. Lucy was Lucy, and I had to admit that were I an international playboy, I never would have considered, even for a second, that she could have been anything else.

Realizing that standing there dumbly staring at the two of them wasn't the way to go about this, I repositioned my body so that I was standing directly behind the mark. He

220

sensed my movement, but as he glanced over his shoulder to assess the potential threat, I moved closer to his body and in one smooth move, dragged my thumb around the scrolling pad of my iPod, jammed the prongs into his back, and pressed the central button.

The Taser flared purple. I glanced around to see if anyone had seen, but everyone was too busy staring at Lucy, who was very conspicuously trying to rearrange her shirt in a manner that would make it possible to allow Heath Shannon to sign her left boob. I pocketed my Taser, and Heath Shannon went down.

I expected a riot then and wished that Lucy hadn't drawn so much attention to us, until I realized that that was exactly what she'd meant to do. People rushed toward us from all over. If the baddies at Peyton went back through their tapes and tried to determine who or what had intercepted their operative, they were going to have a great deal of difficulty. A crowd had formed when Lucy had begun shrieking, and when Heath went down, it just got bigger.

It was chaos. Someone from the tanning salon rushed out and asked if they could help, and Lucy nodded.

"Can you take him inside?" she asked. "I think he has low blood sugar."

That had to be the single lamest excuse I'd ever heard, but the tanning salon employees—some of whom may or may not have been affiliated with our bosses—were ecstatic at the idea of having a hypoglycemic almost-celebrity in their midst, and they carried him inside, at which point in time Lucy somehow convinced them that she was the president of the Heath Shannon Fan Club and that she knew for a fact that he'd been planning to go tanning that day, because he always went tanning on Thursdays, and would it be okay if he used one of their booths?

The guy in charge must have been on the Big Guys' payroll, because he didn't offer a single objection to Lucy's desire to drag an unconscious Heath Shannon into one of the tanning rooms. Once we got him alone, Lucy made quick work of checking his pockets, but came up with nothing.

She sighed. "I guess we'll have to strip him."

"What?" I seriously hoped she was joking.

She answered me by pulling off one of his shoes, and within ten minutes, she'd gotten down to his tighty whities, and we still hadn't found a disk of any kind.

"Ummmm . . . Toby?" Lucy's voice was small.

"Yes?" I was careful not to look at our unconscious mark. He might have been an international heartthrob, but there was such a thing as oversharing, and this definitely qualified, even if he was unconscious.

"Could you maybe check the underwear?" Lucy said. "I'm kind of . . . wellll . . ." She searched for the right word. "Shy."

"Shy?" I repeated. This, coming from the girl who'd practically begged him to sign her boob. Lucy "Never-Met-a-Stranger" Wheeler.

"About things like this," Lucy hedged. "Guys in underwear. It makes me . . . shy."

I opened my mouth, but when she offered me an apologetic smile, I couldn't refuse. Forty seconds later, we had the disk. I'd elaborate on how exactly we got the disk, but that information is classified. For the record, however, Lucy *really* owed me one.

Proving herself to be surprisingly scrappy and strong for her size, Lucy managed to hoist Heath Shannon's body into a tanning bed. She closed the lid, and together, the two of us used some ultrathin steel cables (which Lucy just *happened* to be wearing in her hair) to bind the bed shut, locking our mark inside.

When the Big Guys showed up (and I had a feeling it wouldn't take them long), they'd find Heath Shannon incapacitated and—more likely than not—just a little bit tanner.

"High five!" Lucy said. Glad that she hadn't demanded we herkie to celebrate, I obliged. By the time I'd settled into the passenger seat of Lucy's car, I was starting to feel like I'd been cheated out of the adventure of a lifetime. In my mind, I'd imagined that taking down Heath Shannon would involve a lot fewer theatrics and a lot more of me kicking ass. It was bad enough that I hadn't actually gotten to fight the guy, but the fact that the success of our operation was due in large part to Lucy's ability to convince celebrities to sign her boobs? Talk about disillusionment.

"What happened back there?" I asked. "Why didn't you tell me you were going to draw a crowd?"

Lucy glanced at me as she started the car, truly bewildered. "I thought you knew. It's standard procedure—if it's public enough that people are going to notice the mark going down, you draw enough of a crowd to mask the fact that you're the ones behind it. Peyton will probably run checks on everybody who entered the area, but since you Tasered him in the blind spot, they won't be able to connect it back to us, so they'll have a long list of suspects, and once they figure out we go to school with Jack and have for years, we'll be in the clear.

"Besides," she said, "what cheerleader wouldn't ask a guy like Heath Shannon to sign her breast?"

223

"My kind?" I suggested.

Lucy's face broke into a broad grin. "Did you just admit that you're a cheerleader?"

"Absolutely not."

"Don't worry. I won't tell anyone. After the thing with the underwear, I owe you one."

CHAPTER 28
Code Word: Smile

By the time Lucy parked her car in front of the school, I'd managed to come to terms with Operation Playboy. So maybe I hadn't gotten to go all Kung Fu Toby on an enemy operative, and maybe our success on the mission had had more to do with Lucy's breasts than with either of our abilities as secret agents, but no good could come from dwelling on the details. We'd incapacitated our mark and left him for the Big Guys to pick up. We'd confiscated a tiny disk that we'd already verified (via Lucy's CD player, which had more uses than playing horrible nineties girl band CDs) had information on it regarding operatives scattered throughout Asia, Africa, and South America.

We'd saved the day, and quite possibly dozens of lives. That—and the fact that Lucy had sworn never to mention the actual disk-getting methodology—was just going to have to be enough for me. For now.

When we got back to the gym, I reluctantly handed the disk over to Chloe. I was deluded enough to expect her to say something along the lines of "thank you" or "good job," but the words out of her mouth didn't even remotely resemble a compliment.

"Get dressed. Practice in ten."

I severely hoped she was talking about ten hours, because I'd just finished my second classified operation of the day, and I couldn't forget about the fact that I still had one left to go. I needed some downtime. I needed to change out of this outfit into something that didn't have the word CHEER embossed across it. I needed to take a shower and burn the memory of Heath Shannon's tighty whities from my mind. I did not need to deal with herkies and toe touches and hurdlers and handsprings and . . .

Even thinking the words had my still-dislocated crotch protesting in vain.

And yet, I somehow sucked it up enough to trudge into the locker room, where I found another pair of teeny-tiny pants (this pair opted for LIONS! over CHEER in the butt-message department) waiting in my locker. Beside me, Tara changed into her own shorts (no writing—lucky her) silently.

"Mission went well," I said. "Find anything interesting in his wallet?"

"Not really," Tara said. "Find anything interesting in his underwear?"

Her voice was so deadpan casual that it took me a minute to register her meaning.

"Lucy!" I yelled.

Tara grinned. "Your communicator was on," she said. "You were pretty verbal about your objections."

"What objections?" Bubbles asked. I swear, she came out of nowhere.

"Nothing," I said, shooting Tara a warning look.

"Nothing," Tara agreed.

"How were things here?" I asked, changing the subject before Bubbles could ask any more questions.

Bubbles didn't answer. I elaborated. "Party planning? Banner painting? Whatnot?"

Bubbles bit her bottom lip.

"Bubbles?" Tara prodded. "What's going on?"

"We were working on some stuff for the party," Bubbles said, "and our line of communication with Brooke and Zee went dead."

Tara took off then, running toward the Quad.

I turned my attention back to Bubbles, to grill her for more specifics, but she was gone. That girl was stealth incarnate.

When Tara came back five minutes later, I was more than ready for some answers. Whether or not I wanted to be, I was part of this now. This was my squad, my team. Something was going on, and someone was going to tell me what it was, or things were going to get ugly.

"Tara?" I didn't say anything more than her name.

"The line of communication with Brooke and Zee went dead shortly after they arrived in Al Jawf," Tara said. "Approximately half an hour ago."

"And that's bad?" I guessed.

Tara sat down to put on her athletic shoes. "It wouldn't be horrible," she said, her voice eerily devoid of emotion. "Sometimes the satellite signal fails; sometimes if you end up underground, the signal doesn't reach."

"Okay," I said. Tara stared down at her shoes, her face perfectly calm. It was that look that made me ask more. I was noticing more and more that when Tara was perfectly anything, it was a surefire sign that she was hiding something. Perfection was tricky that way.

"It wouldn't be horrible," I said, repeating her words. "But?"

"It wouldn't be horrible, but right before we lost the signal, April and Bubbles heard gunfire."

"Gunfire?"

"Shots were exchanged." Tara finished lacing up her shoes. "You'd better put yours on," she said, handing me an identical pair.

"Shots were exchanged?" I asked. "SHOTS were EXCHANGED?"

Tara moved quickly, and before I could prepare myself, she had me pressed up against the locker banks, her face close to mine. "Keep your voice down," she said.

I hadn't realized that my posh partner could sound quite like that. I could have fought her, and I almost did, but after the past forty-eight hours, I couldn't bring myself to do it. Yet.

"Shots were exchanged?" I whispered.

She nodded, eased the pressure off my body, and gestured with her head to the shoes. "You'd better put your shoes on," she said for a second time.

I looked down at the shoes, but didn't move to put them on. "Brooke and Zee were shot at, and we haven't heard from them since?"

Tara nodded.

"And you want me to put on my shoes so that we can go practice our halftime routine?"

Tara nodded again.

Around me, all of the others were suiting up, preparing themselves to Go, Fight, Win!

"We're not going to send in backup?" I asked, keeping my voice low.

Tara shook her head. "Our original orders were really specific. This is a two-person mission. No backup under any circumstances."

"And if the Guys Upstairs said it, it must be done," I said, rolling my eyes. "Forget the fact that they might not actually know everything. Forget the fact that Brooke and Zee might be in danger." I gave Tara a look that should have pinned her to the wall the way her arms had pinned me. "You can't just leave them there. We're supposed to be a team."

Tara didn't respond, but I wouldn't let it go.

"We can't just do nothing. What if they're injured? What if the operative they went to rescue is injured?"

"I alerted Central when I called in about the disk." Chloe spoke softly, appearing next to me. "They haven't heard from Brooke either, but they've got tracers on their agent, and he's on the move. Their statisticians think that, based on movement patterns, it's likely that Brooke and Zee are with him."

"And 'likely' is good enough for you?"

Personally, I was ready to take a little visit to Libya myself. It was totally and completely bizarre, but the feeling bubbling up inside of me was eerily similar to the one that made me bail Noah out of trouble again and again. Ginormous football players, international terrorists . . . what was the difference? Somebody was messing with something that was mine. That "loyalty" thing Zee had made such a big deal of was forcing me into action. Zee and Brooke were on *my* Squad. They were *my* . . . okay, maybe we weren't exactly friends, but maybe we could have been. Or maybe we would be, but right now, that didn't matter. I was ready to kick some butt.

"If Central hasn't heard from them by tonight, they'll send in some agents from the surrounding areas."

I opened my mouth to argue, but Tara lifted a hand to touch my arm.

"They'd be able to reach them before we could," she said. "And if something happened to Brooke and Zee, our cover's pretty much blown there. If they've captured two teenage operatives, none of us are going to be any less suspicious than Average Joe Spy."

"So we just stay here and do nothing?" I asked. I hated doing nothing.

"No," Tara said. "We cheer."

Whether or not cheering was preferable to doing nothing was a matter of some debate. On the one hand, practice would distract me from my insane urge to hijack a helicopter and fly it to Libya. On the other, I hated our halftime routine with the passion of a thousand fiery burning suns. It was a toss-up, really.

"B to the A to the Y to the Port, Bayport Lions take the court! L to the I to the O-N-S; when we leave you'll be a mess!"

My voice was loud and clear—and distinctly pissed off, but at least this time, I was getting the words right.

"Bay-port Li-ons." I clapped my hands five times like a good little cheerleading newbie. "Bay-port Li-ons." Clap, clap, clap-clap-clap.

By the time we got to the end of the routine the first time, my hands had gone numb from all the clapping, and they were turning a nice shade of borderline purple.

"It's called cheerleading," Chloe told me, rolling her eyes. "Not 'angry punks with self-mutilating tendencies.'"

"Don't clap so hard," Lucy translated. "Cup your hands like this." Clap, clap, clap-clap-clap. She demonstrated. "See?"

"And smile," Bubbles said. "Then you won't sound so angry."

"But I *am* angry."

"Doesn't matter," April said. She might have been as new to the secret agent game as I was, but she was a veteran cheerleader. "It doesn't matter if you just broke up with your boyfriend or if you're fighting with someone else on your squad or if you're cheering on a sprained ankle. When you perform, you smile. You're loud, you're proud, you're in charge, and you're on top of the world. Your team is the best. You're the best, and while you're cheering, that's all that matters."

Apparently, cheerleaders were supposed to be able to turn on the happy at the sound of a single "Ready? Okay!" Before I'd become one, it had never actually occurred to me that their smiles might be fake. They were on the top of the social chain. They were pretty and popular, and they had nothing to worry about except what color bloomers to wear under their cheer-skirts, and so they smiled. For the first time, I understood what Lucy had meant when she'd told me that cheerleaders were predisposed to being good spies. I could even understand why the Squad program might have been initiated in the first place. If you were the government, and you were looking for a group of athletic, beautiful teenage girls who were generally thought to be morons, but who were actually masters at manipulating their own emotions and showing the world (or the crowd, as the case may be) what they wanted it to see, there was a certain kind of person who fit the bill.

The kind who cheered.

"Let's try it again," Chloe said. "Without the anger management issues." She paused and then said the words that, as captain, Brooke would normally have yelled to start us off. "Ready? Okay!"

I forced myself to think of this as practicing in a different way. I wasn't practicing a halftime routine. I was practicing the innocent, ditzy look I'd give to an enemy operative before I clocked him with a seventy-mile-an-hour roundhouse. I was practicing keeping my emotions off my face and out of my voice. I was perfecting my cover, so that someday, I could be the one rescuing Brooke and Zee. Or Lucy. Or Tara, or any of the others.

"B to the A to the Y to the Port . . ."

Scarily enough, when I thought about things that way, I was good. My smile was broad, my eyes were bright, and my voice was nothing short of peppy.

Wherever Brooke and Zee were, I was just going to have to trust that they were okay. After all, when it came to the art of deception, I only had to look at the beaming faces around the room to come to the conclusion that I was completely surrounded by masters.

CHAPTER 29
Code Word: Sexy

After practice, I miraculously convinced the twins that I could handle my own hair and makeup for the party. They made me swear to exfoliate, and I had to sit through a tutorial on foundation, but it was a small price to pay for a little space and some time with my own laptop. After booting it up, I updated a few of my programs with bits and pieces that I'd picked up from the sparkly Squad laptop. Then I thumbed through my decrypting programs and wondered if there was anything potentially useful that the Big Guys, whoever they were, might not have access to.

And then I went to CNN's website and searched for any articles about shots exchanged in Al Jawf, Libya, earlier that day.

Nothing.

I was in the process of using the mother of all search engines to do the same thing when I sensed a presence in my room. I turned, half expecting it to be Bubbles with some kind of cream for my hair or gel for my eyes, but instead, it was Noah. He was wearing a collared shirt. The collar was popped.

"Are you wearing cologne?" I sniffed the air suspiciously and minimized the search window on my computer. "Scratch that. Are you wearing an absurd amount of cologne?"

"Why? You like?" Noah leaned against my bedroom wall.

"No. I don't like." I paused. "Do I even want to know why you're wearing cologne?"

Noah smiled then, and I knew I was in trouble. It was one of his crazy, charming, happy-puppy grins.

"Noah . . ."

Grin still in place, he inclined his head slightly toward me. "Shouldn't you be getting ready right about now?"

The word that ran through my head at that moment was a combination of about five words that I probably shouldn't repeat, but believe me, it involved an impressive number of interjections.

"Who told you about the party?" I asked Noah humorlessly.

"Toby, Toby, Toby . . ." Noah placed a hand on my shoulder. "Who *didn't* tell me about the party?"

I rolled my eyes. "Who invited you to the party?"

This time, the smile was less crazy, more hopeful. "You did."

I narrowed my eyes at him.

"Come on, Tobe. I'll be good. I promise. You won't have to save me even once. There'll be so many girls there that at least one of them will be dying for a piece of The Noah. I won't have to resort to working my magic on the so-called unavailable ones."

"The Noah?" He had to be kidding me. Between the title and the popped collar, I was starting to think I'd spent too much time growing up defending Noah, and not nearly enough beating sense into him.

"Just let me come with you. Please? Pretty please?"

I should have said no. I was going to the party for one reason and one reason alone, and that was the fact that if Brooke and Zee could put themselves in the line of fire for this mission, I could show up at a party and flirt with Bayport's Most Eligible Bachelor. I could convince him to take me to his dad's office. I could plant a new listening device (which Chloe had given me), and while I was at it, I could download information from at least one of the computers. I hadn't exactly been authorized to do the latter, but meh. Authorization, shmauthorization.

"Toby?"

"Fine."

Noah beamed at me.

"But let's get two things straight. One—I'm not bailing you out of anything. If you come home with a black eye or somehow dismembered, don't come crying to me."

"Deal."

Noah was eager to accept my terms, but he hadn't heard them all yet. "Two—you say nothing about whatever I end up doing tonight. You don't mention it to Mom and Dad. You don't tell your friends—who, by the way, aren't coming—and you don't even mention it to me. Capisce?"

"Your wish is my command."

I wished that I'd told him no, but of all the girls on the planet, I was the only one who was a sucker for Noah's hopeful face.

"Get lost," I told him. "If we're going to this thing, I need to get dressed."

I was less than surprised a few minutes later when I abandoned my laptop and opened my closet door to find that at some point during the day, my outfit had been selected for me. Sometimes it seemed like there were four of the twins instead of two. Except for the time I'd spent in class and working on Operation Playboy, I'd been with them for most of the day, and yet somehow at least one of them had made it back here at some point to play personal stylist.

For the first time since I'd joined the Squad, the selected outfit wasn't a skirt and a glitzy top—it was a pair of white jeans that looked dangerously low cut and uncomfortably tight. And a glitzy top. There was a note on the jeans ("wear thick blue belt with rhinestone buckle"), a note on the top ("wear with gel bra"), and a pair of high-heeled blue designer cowboy boots, with (shocker of shockers) a note attached. I read the last note and crumpled it. Apparently, the twins had decided that boots were my "trademark item" and they'd put out a fashion APB on new boot styles. They were expecting deliveries more or less daily.

Though I shuddered at a future filled with fashion boots, I couldn't help but think that it could be worse. I mean, they could have decided that a Chihuahua was my trademark item, and then I'd be stuck carrying a rat-dog around all the time.

Pushing the thought out of my mind, I carried my clothes into the bathroom and stripped. I showered quickly, dried my hair with a supersonic blow dryer that had magically appeared in my bathroom, and tried to apply my foundation. After the tutorial I had been given, I couldn't help but feel that one wrong move with one of these face sponge thingies, and I was going to somehow destroy the free world.

I skipped the mascara and eye gunk, but applied a small amount of lip gloss to minimize the chances of a drive-by glossing. Eyeing the white pants distrustfully, I began to put on the outfit: the glitzy turquoise thong I'd bought at

Victoria's Secret, the bewildering gel bra, the glitzy blue top, and finally, the white pants. They were made of a really thick denim that must have had at least some spandex in it, based on the way they stretched to grip my butt like a glove.

I checked my back half out in the mirror, just to make sure that the underwear wasn't showing through, and not at all because I was interested in what my butt would look like in the aforementioned stretchy pants.

Moving made me realize that something was off, and when I wedged my hand into the right front pocket of the pants, I pulled out a small piece of paper and a white choker with a blue gem on the end. The piece of paper was completely blank, but when I dampened it with the edge of my towel, bubble letters appeared on the page.

Choker = video/audio feed.

Whichever twin had written that message had signed it simply with a heart. My eyes scanned to the bottom of the page, and I saw the postscript.

PS: Don't worry—your underwear won't show through. Special-issue fabric.

And below that:

PPS: Wear the sparkly thong anyway. We'll know if you don't.

And that was that. The paper dried, the words disappeared, and I tore it into pieces before tossing it into the trash.

I put the choker around my neck, parted my hair down the center, and forced my feet into the boots du jour.

When I stepped out of the bathroom, Noah was waiting for me. His collar had, without a doubt, been repopped within the last five minutes.

"You ready?" he asked, playing it cool.

I weighed the situation. I hadn't managed to find out any information on Brooke and Zee, and I hadn't heard a word from the rest of the Squad. I mentally prepared myself to push those thoughts down and concentrate on the task at hand. To that end, I glanced down at my body. A full two inches of my stomach was showing, my newly gel-enhanced boobs were actually noticeable, and the sparkle from the belt was so intense that I thought it was going to give me an aneurysm.

I turned back to Noah. "Ready."

"You driving?" Noah asked.

At that exact moment, the doorbell rang, and I realized that when I'd made Noah the happiest goofy little freshman in the whole wide world, I'd forgotten one key detail about tonight's party.

I wasn't driving. Jack Peyton was.

CHAPTER 30
Code Word: Attraction

"You normally bring your little brother on dates with you?"

"Bite me. And watch the road."

From the backseat, Noah watched the interplay between Jack and me, fascinated. How could I have forgotten that I'd sort of agreed to let John Peyton IV pick me up at seven? What kind of idiot was I?

"Whatever you say, Ev," Jack said.

There it was again: the nickname, accompanied, as always, by the smirk.

"FYI, Smirk Boy, this isn't a date," I informed him tersely. "You're giving me a ride to the party. Once we're there, if you're lucky, you'll be one of the less nauseating people to interact with, and maybe I'll give you the time of day."

"Oh, Ev, stop. You're making me blush."

I know, I know. I was supposed to be flirting with him. I wasn't supposed to be trying to wipe the cocky smile off his face, but hey, it was my FT, and I'd do what I wanted to. Besides, he was just so . . . so . . .

"Great outfit, by the way. What? You didn't have time to

deface the belt buckle?" Jack took his eyes off the road just long enough to meet mine with a grin.

I could only hope that the sparkly buckle in question would give him the aneurysm and not me.

"It was a gift," I said dryly.

"From the twins?" Jack asked.

I was a teensy bit surprised that he was observant enough to have figured out who won the Most Likely to Give Toby Hideously Girly Accessories competition.

Jack laughed at the look on my face. "Please," he said. "This happens whenever anyone makes the Varsity Spirit Squad. The twins glitterfy them."

The way he spoke about the squad and the way it worked was somewhat unsettling. It wasn't that I expected the fact that I'd been majorly made over to go straight over everyone's head; I just didn't think that anyone would pinpoint the twins as the reason why, and I didn't think anyone would remember enough about makeovers past to know that this was a pattern with them.

"They call it the God Squad for a reason," Jack said. He shrugged and then glanced at me out of the side of his eyes. "You enjoying your high school divinity?"

"I call it the Bod Squad," Noah said, eager to join in the conversation from the backseat.

"Understandable," Jack replied, his tone gratingly solemn.

"The next one of you to call it anything," I said, "is going to end up with a sparkly belt buckle jammed so far up your butt that you'll be sneezing glitter for two weeks."

As a threat, it wasn't my best, but considering the fact that I was in a car with my oversexed younger brother, a guy who took a great deal of sadistic pleasure in rubbing me the wrong way, and a really obnoxiously sparkly belt, it wasn't half bad.

"Glitter?" Jack stared at me for a moment, his facial expression changing in a way that I couldn't quite read. Even if I hadn't been looking back at him, I would have felt his gaze. It was that tangible.

Then Jack treated me to another shrug. As he turned onto April's street, he shot Noah a conspiratorial look. "Is it me," he said, "or is she somewhat obsessed with my butt?"

I turned around to face Noah, and for once, he wisely remained silent.

As Jack pulled through the giant, open wrought-iron gate and onto April's absurdly long private drive, I took in both the incredible size of Château April and the way that Jack's eyes followed my every move.

Even from inside the car, I could hear the music blaring from April's house.

The private drive was lined with cars, and A-list teenagers spilled out, moving en masse toward the house. When Bayport High's Varsity Spirit Squad partied, it turned into a who's who of the high school world. The three of us got out and I wasn't actually that surprised when I saw a handful of football players at the door, sorting out the riffraff. The guys didn't so much as blink when they saw me, former Queen of Riffraff, climb up the front steps. Instead, they eyed my white pants appreciatively and greeted me with whistles.

"Toby," Chip said. "Good to see you."

I noticed that he didn't make a physical move on me. Wise decision, Chip. I wondered how his shin was doing, but didn't waste much time thinking about it. As Jack and I moved past the doorway, one of the football players leaned forward to stop Noah.

"Nice try, kid," he said.

Before one of the others could recognize Noah as the guy who was forever chatting up their girlfriends, I stuck my hand back and grabbed him by the popped collar. "He's with me," I said.

Noah grinned wildly. "I'm with her," he said, and when the football players grudgingly allowed him to pass, Noah couldn't resist. "Keep up the good work," he told them, reaching out and patting their lapels.

Jack choked back laughter, but I saw it in his eyes.

The smirk I could deal with.

Arrogance I could deal with.

Mr. Gorgeous finding my adorkable younger brother amusing? That one was a little bit harder.

Noah took off then, no doubt in a state of absolute ecstasy, and I was left alone with Jack.

"He seems like a good kid," Jack said.

"He's an idiot," I replied. "If it wasn't for me, he'd be dead by now."

Jack leaned back against a wall. "Do I sense a sweet side, Ev?"

It was too much. I was there, and he was there, and he wasn't being completely horrible, and I didn't know how to flirt. So I did the next logical thing. I ran. Well, I didn't actually run, seeing as how the fashion boots made that a physical impossibility, but I did leave Jack to follow Noah with a great deal of speed and very little explanation.

"I'll be back in a second," I called over my shoulder.

Jack crossed one foot over the other and continued leaning on the wall, his eyes still on me.

As I did my best to follow Noah through the crowd, the

song changed, and I grimaced. Either the DJ had a personal vendetta against everyone there, or everyone at the party other than me had completely horrible taste in music. This shouldn't have surprised me, granted, but honestly, is a little bit of the Pixies too much to ask for? Mayhaps some Sonic Youth? Anything that's not sung by an actress/singer or a rapper/pimp? When it comes to music, slashes are never a good thing.

I caught up with Noah, and proving once more that it is completely impossible that we could possibly share any DNA whatsoever, he grinned broadly. "I love this song." A group of girls strutted by, moving their hips to the music as they walked, and Noah raised his eyes heavenward. "I *really* love this song."

As much as I hated to interrupt his prayer of thanksgiving, I felt compelled to reissue my warning. "If you get into a fight, you're on your own."

My words had less than no impact on his cathartic experience.

"Toby!!"

I only knew one person who spoke with two exclamation marks in her voice.

"Hi, Lucy."

"Isn't April's house amazing? Doesn't it look . . ."

Like something out of *Laguna Beach*? Or possibly what it would look like if Lindsay Lohan and Usher made a music video together?

". . . like totally amazing?"

"Amazing," Noah repeated.

Lucy smiled at him. "Hi!" She punctuated her greeting with a wave.

Feeling strangely compelled to protect both Noah and Lucy from inevitable disaster, I tried to warn Lucy that waving at my brother while wearing a tube top could have major consequences, but a hand on my shoulder stopped the words in my mouth.

"Your outfit is so cute," Brittany said, her eyes sparkling.

"You have such incredible taste," Tiffany chimed in.

I rolled my eyes, but with Noah standing there, I couldn't stop their self-congratulations.

"Your necklace is off center, though," Britt said. "Here, let me." She reached up and fiddled with the charm around my neck, turning it ninety degrees to the right. "There," she said, and the real meaning behind her words (and the fiddling) didn't escape me. She'd turned on the video and audio feed in the necklace. I was officially good to go.

If only I knew how to go about seducing someone.

No sooner had thoughts of seduction crossed my mind than I caught Jack's eye. He was still standing where I'd left him, but had since been surrounded by a mass of girls, all vying for his attention. The smirky smile was back on his face.

"Go talk to him." Tara's voice was soft—her words were encouragement, not an order.

"I should probably stick with Noah for a while," I said. "You know, just until I'm sure that—"

"We'll take care of your brother." Tara nudged Brittany, who nudged Tiffany.

"Hey, Noah," the twins called in unison, and moments later, an arm around each twin, Noah left me behind in the dust.

I buried my head in my hands. "He'll be impossible to live with now."

Tara smiled, and not so subtly, she nodded her head in Jack's general direction.

"You know," Lucy said thoughtfully. "Your brother's kind of cute."

Not again.

"No matter what you do," I said, "do not let him hear you say that."

Lucy giggled and shrugged.

I turned back to Tara. "The twins won't . . . they won't do anything to him, will they?"

Tara shook her head, her eyes filled with mirth, and then she nodded toward Jack once more. "I'll keep an eye on them," she promised. "I'll even drive Noah home. You—"

This time, I nodded toward Jack before she could. "Yeah, I know. I know."

"Think of it as going into battle," Tara said.

"Yeah," I muttered, thinking of the way Jack had been with Noah. "Just look how well that turned out for Brooke and Zee."

I didn't mean it to come off sounding flippant, but it did. Lucy didn't seem to notice, and Tara took no offense.

"Brooke and Zee are on their way back from the spa," Lucy said brightly.

"The spa," I repeated, remembering the cover story. "And the . . . uhh . . ." I knew nothing about spas and was having a great deal of difficulty coming up with a code word for gunfire.

"The mud bath?" Tara suggested. "It turned out just fine." She lowered her voice. "Brooke was wearing one of Lucy's special bras, so there was no mud-related damage."

I remembered the bulletproof push-up bras Lucy had gushed about my first day in the Quad and then turned back to the weapons designer in question, who was singing along with Hilary Duff, my brother and his supposed cuteness completely forgotten—out of sight, out of mind. She was smiling and bouncing and moving around like someone with more energy than she knew what to do with.

And she'd saved Brooke's life.

"Now go." This time, Tara actually gave me a little shove on the shoulder. "Do your thing."

At that moment, Jack saw me looking at him, and for my benefit, he put his arm around another girl.

I snorted, ripped my belt off and dropped it on the floor, and marched over to do my thing and wipe the smirk right off his face.

CHAPTER 31
Code Word: Want

"Why, Ev, what a pleasant surprise."

If this was his way of getting back at me for chickening out on our date, he was more delusional than I could possibly say. He was my mission, not my boyfriend, and I was not jealous.

"Guys," Jack said, smiling at his legion of loyal fans, "this is Everybody-Knows-Toby." He paused. "Although," he said, looking thoughtful, "I suppose you all already knew that."

Oh yeah. He thought he was really cute.

The girls clustered around Jack obviously thought so, too, but I remembered what Zee had said. These girls weren't his type—Jack had Conditioned Cheerleader Aversion, and most, if not all, of the girls were either JV cheerleaders or varsity wannabes. As such, they were completely torn about what to do once I showed up. On the one hand, they would have liked to devour me whole for taking even a microscopic bit of Jack's attention away from them. On the other hand, I was varsity, and that meant that their futures were in my hands.

"Of course," one of the girls said, offering me a plastic smile. "Everybody knows Toby."

Another girl tilted her head to the side. "Are you the one who's related to Calvin Klein?"

"Those are great boots."

"Did you really date Prince William?"

They were on a roll now.

"Actually," I said, lowering my voice, "I didn't date Prince William, but . . ."

Jack watched, bemused, as all of the girls leaned toward me, eyes wide.

" . . . but I heard that Jack did."

Two of the girls frowned at me. One cast a suspicious look at Jack. The fourth was a little behind on processing and just stood there, smiling and nodding.

Jack grabbed me by the elbow. "Excuse us, ladies," he said. "Toby"—he emphasized his use of my actual name—"and I were going to go grab some punch."

With a great deal of expertise, he steered me away from the girls before I could suggest that he'd dated any more of the world's most eligible bachelors. Smart boy.

I didn't know where he was taking me until we ended up outside on a veranda. Alone.

Uh-oh. Not good, I thought. We were supposed to end up alone, but not here. Somehow, I had to get him to take me to his dad's office. I was also unsure as to his state of mind. Some guys—okay, most guys—would probably greatly resent the insinuation that they'd dated the heir to the throne of England.

I tensed my body slightly. If Jack was feeling like lashing out at me, I wanted to be ready to lash back. Actually, I wanted my foot to be ready to lash back. The rest of me would just go along for the ride.

Jack opened his mouth, and I waited for him to yell. "Did you see their faces?" he asked quietly. "I can't believe you . . . and they . . ."

I shrugged. He didn't sound particularly murderous.

"Ev, you told them that Prince William and I were an item."

I scuffed my foot into the ground. "Better you than me."

"Better me than you," he repeated, and then he laughed, loud and long. "You're . . ."

"Clever?" I suggested.

"You're something," he finished. "When I figure out what it is, I'll tell you."

I had to remind myself that this was Brooke's ex. Chloe's ex. He had a substance abuse problem, and the substance was cheerleaders. He hadn't even known who I was pre-Squad. He was my mission, and I was not the girl who fell for a guy just because he had a really contagious laugh.

"So what are we going to do out here?" I asked. I meant to sound somewhat seductive, but it came out sounding confused. What was I doing? More to the point, who was watching me make a fool of myself through the handy-dandy necklace camera?

"What do you want to do out here?" Jack didn't move toward me at all with the words. I appreciated the respect for my personal space.

"Why don't we race?" It was a stab in the dark, but I never claimed to be good at this.

"Race to where?" Jack asked. It was a pretty small veranda.

"To the car," I said. "Winner decides where we go from there."

Given the fact that I was almost positive that I could beat him in a fair race, it was a stroke of genius.

"Race to the car," Jack tried the idea out by saying it out loud.

I nodded.

"This thing really isn't your deal, is it?" he asked.

"What thing? The party?" I asked, planning to press the whole "race to the car" thing.

"The party," Jack confirmed. "The squad, the whole popularity thing." He paused. "You'd rather those girls think that I dated Prince William than that you did."

"Your point?"

"Why are you a cheerleader?"

He sounded suspicious. Darned Cheerleader Aversion.

"If I tell you, can we race?"

He nodded. "Why the hell not."

I mulled the question over, trying to come up with an answer that was at least partially true. "I like to do things that people tell me I can't," I said finally. "And nobody ever thought I'd make the Squad."

Least of all me.

"Huh," Jack said. And then, without another word, he bolted off the veranda and back into the party. It took me a couple of seconds to figure out that he was headed to the car.

"Cheater!" I yelled after him. I quickly scanned the surrounding area. He had enough of a head start that there was no way I could beat him taking the same route. Luckily, there was one other route available. Casting a single dubious look at my boots, I climbed on top of the railing, jumped off the veranda, and landed on the ground outside, a full story below. Not knowing how much time I'd bought myself, I ran full blast for the car.

By the time Jack got there, I'd taken off my boots and was pretending to buff my nails.

He looked from me back up to the veranda. "You jumped."

I nodded.

"Cheater."

I could feel the smile spread across my face. Ah, the sweet taste of victory.

Gallantly, he walked around to my side of the car and opened the door for me. I snorted. He ignored me.

After he'd settled himself in the driver's seat, he turned to me. "So," he said. "Where are we going?"

It was on the tip of my tongue to say his dad's office, but something stopped me. I wasn't the first one to use Jack to get to Peyton. If I asked to go there directly, who knew what kind of memories I was going to stir up? The last thing I wanted was for him to compare me to Chloe or Brooke.

"I don't know where we're going," I said slowly, "but I know what we're doing."

Jack waited.

"Actually," I said, divinely inspired, "I know what you're doing."

"What I'm doing?"

"It involves a Xerox machine and your butt," I said. He blanched, and I continued. "Such is the price of defeat."

"You want me to xerox my butt?"

I shrugged. "It beats this place. Where's the nearest copy shop?"

Jack, still unsure whether I was mentally unstable or just

highly unpredictable, turned the car on and put it in drive. "I've got someplace else in mind," he said.

"Does it have a copy machine?" I asked. Translation: is it your dad's office?

Jack didn't answer. Instead, he smirked and pulled onto the road. "You know, Ev," he said, "this obsession with my butt is getting old."

CHAPTER 32
Code Word: Pressure

"Where are we?" I had a feeling we were in the underground parking complex attached to the law firm, but I asked the question anyway. "That's like the fifth gate we've gone through."

Jack shrugged. "Security."

"This must be the most secured butt-copying facility of all time."

Jack whipped his car into a parking space. "It's my dad's office," he said. "They're kind of anal about security." He smiled. "Pun intended."

We got out of the car, and Jack punched a code into a panel on the wall, and the glass doors slid open for us.

"Evening, Jack."

"Evening, Mike." Jack preempted my question. "He's one of the night watch. We have full-time security."

"What are you guys securing here? Nuclear weapons?" I could practically feel Chloe (or whoever was on the listening end of my feed) groaning at that question, but it's what I would have asked if I hadn't known anything about Peyton at all.

Jack shook his head. "It's a law firm. We have some high-profile clients." He whipped out a key, and once we were in the elevator, he used it to access the top floor of the building.

"If it's so secure," I said, "why do you have a key?"

Jack stared straight ahead as he answered. "It's a family thing. My dad gave me one the day I turned sixteen."

"Does he expect you to join the biz?" I asked.

Jack's face hardened. "Something like that."

Zee could have read more into his expression than I could (and, I thought, she probably would if my necklace was catching all of this on tape), but I got the feeling that Jack wasn't exactly anxious to take over the evil empire. Maybe that was why he used his access to bring girls to Peyton to do inappropriate things with copy machines.

The elevator doors opened, and I was shocked that everything looked so normal. There was a large (and incredibly posh) reception desk in front of a glass wall that had the firm's name embossed on it in scripty letters. The ceilings were high; the floors were wood. Jack immediately took a left, and I followed. I'd memorized the layout, so I knew that we were moving conveniently toward both the copy room and his father's office.

As we entered the copy room, Jack narrowed his eyes at me. "If you tell anyone about this," he said, "I will kill you."

He sounded mockingly matter-of-fact, but given our surroundings, I couldn't help but take his words a wee bit seriously.

Jack bowed then, and without further ado he approached the copier, turned around, and went to work.

My hand went automatically to my neck, covering the necklace. No one on the Squad needed to see this.

As it turned out, though, Jack copied his butt like a professional. He hopped up on the machine, and with a little maneuvering, slid his pants down in the back.

I averted my eyes, even though I couldn't see anything.

The next thing I heard was the sound of the copier. Moments later, Jack was back by my side. "The price of defeat," he said, handing me the Xerox.

I couldn't help it. I burst out laughing. "You take defeat so well," I said, looking at him out of the corners of my eyes. "You must be used to it."

"Now, Ev," Jack said. "That was almost a compliment."

I shrugged, letting my hand fall away from the necklace. "Almost is about as much as you're going to get, Butt Boy."

"You know," he said. "You're really not very likeable."

"Color me heartbroken."

It took about two seconds for the smirk to take hold of his face, and I knew what he was going to say before he said it. "Your turn." He looked toward the copier.

"I won," I said. "Winner doesn't pay the cost of defeat."

I was feeling pretty cocky, but then he said the three words that put the nails in the coffin of my dignity.

"I dare you."

I have this thing about dares. It is physically impossible for me to turn one down. My cheek twitched, and I glared at him.

"I double-dog dare you."

"Fine," I grumbled, overcome with the urge to punch him in the stomach. "But that means you still have to pay the cost of defeat."

"And what might that be?"

Something that would get me inside his dad's office. What would get me inside his dad's office?

"I'll let you know."

For the sake of my own dignity, I will not go into any of the details of what came to pass in the next few minutes. Along with taking things in and out of my bra, photocopying my butt in a stealthy manner was not a skill I possessed in any abundance. It figured—tonight was the one time I wasn't wearing a skirt.

Eventually, however, I managed it. Jack, being the gentleman that he was, turned around completely.

As I walked over to hand him the finished product, all I could think was The things I do for my country.

"So what's the price of defeat?" Jack asked, the corners of his lips twitching madly.

My mind whirled. I needed to think of something that would (a) get me into his dad's office, and (b) make him pay for my loss of dignity.

The answer came to me then, and my own mouth pulled up in a smile that was nothing short of evil. "You got a scanner?"

Five minutes later, we were in his dad's office, and Jack was composing an email.

"Who am I sending this to again?" he asked.

"You know who," I said. "And you know what to say."

"Claiming this is a picture of Prince William's butt has *got* to be illegal." Jack stalled for time.

"Yeah. Butt forgery. I'm sure it's a felony." I was implacable, and Jack groaned as he typed in the names of his admirers from earlier that night.

"Do I have to sign it?" he asked.

I took pity on him. After all, I was inside his father's office. I could afford to have some mercy. "No," I said. "It'll be coming from your email account. I think that will suffice."

He attached the scanned copy of his butt and hit send.

"Remind me never to lose to you again," he said.

"My heart bleeds for you," I said. "Really."

While he'd been typing, I'd been messing with my gel bra. I now had the bug in my hand. It was small, nearly invisible, and equipped to cling to any surface. All I had to do was find one. As this thought raced through my head, the phone in the office began to ring, and I visibly jumped.

"Do I make you nervous?" Jack asked.

"No," I said, torn between being scornful and coming up with an excuse for my jumpiness, lest I tip him off to the fact that I had ulterior motives for what had, in all truth, been one of the best nights I'd had since my family had moved to Bayport. "I have phone fear."

"Phone fear." Jack repeated my words, no tone whatsoever in his voice, but his lips curled up. Reflexively, my lips mimicked the motion, and even though he didn't move, it suddenly felt like the two of us were standing really close together.

The phone rang again and again, and with each ring, Jack's eyes bored deeper and deeper into mine. I silently begged the phone to stop ringing. If it didn't, something might happen here. Something big.

Something unexpected.

Something new.

Heeding my wishes, the phone stopped ringing. For a split second, there was silence, and then the answering machine picked up. "John. It's Alan. I need to talk to you. It's about Jack."

At first, I was disturbed by the fact that someone was calling the evil law firm to talk about Jack. The two of us were standing mere feet apart, my entire body felt flushed, and Jack had never averted his gaze.

"Who was that?" I asked, my throat constricting with something I couldn't quite describe.

"My uncle. He and my father don't get along." Jack didn't offer any more explanation, and in the back of my head, somewhere behind my mind's acknowledgement of the way my skin was humming and the rising ball of lovely dread in my stomach, I realized that Jack's uncle sounded very familiar.

"So," Jack said.

"So," I repeated.

He inched toward me, and the look in his eyes made my heart jump.

All thoughts of voices gone, I stepped backward. Slowly, he advanced on me, and I backed up until my shoulders were pressed against the paneled wall. Trying to concentrate on something other than Jack's lips, which were moving closer to mine by the second, I pressed my hand firmly against the wall, finally slipping the bug I'd been sent here to plant into place.

Mission complete.

"Care to share your thoughts with the class, Ev?" Jack asked. His face was so close to mine that I could feel his breath on my cheeks.

My thoughts were as follows.

He was going to kiss me.

I wanted him to kiss me.

I hated that I wanted him to kiss me. How *one of those girls* could I get?

Kissing him would be wrong. He was my mark. I was using him.

The entire Squad would probably watch this footage on repeat as soon as April's party was over.

In that moment, I made three impulsive decisions.

I grabbed the charm around my neck and twisted it, turning the camera off completely.

I leaned forward and beat him to the punch, planting the world's biggest, longest, hottest kiss on his mouth.

And then I punched him in the stomach, turned, and ran. It wasn't until I got far enough out of the office and away from Jack that my mind started working again and I realized why the voice on the answering machine had sounded so familiar. I'd heard it before. It was a voice that had told us to infiltrate and bug the building I was standing in now.

Jack's uncle was our Charlie.

CHAPTER 33
Code Word: Fire

Despite my postrealization, postkiss stupor, I made it out the big glass doors and into the elevator before Jack realized what (or rather, who) had hit him. Thanks to my nimble fingers pressing the "close" button with great fervor, the elevator doors closed just as Jack started to come after me, and I made it out of the building and into the parking garage before I realized that I was completely and utterly screwed.

I hadn't driven here. Jack had. Jack, whose father was the head of the evil law firm. Jack, whose uncle was apparently the voice behind our orders. I shook my head to clear it. What was with me and forgetting about Jack driving? And I called myself a secret agent. I ran out of the garage, knowing that Jack wouldn't be more than a couple of minutes behind me.

Jack, who was quite possibly the best kisser known to womankind.

"Need a ride?"

If you'd told me that I would ever, ever, under any circumstances be glad to see Chloe Larson's little red car, complete with an eye-rolling Chloe in the driver's seat, I would have suggested you get your head checked. But there she was, and I wasn't about to look a gift cheerleader in the mouth. I ran to the car like a madwoman, flung open the door, and jumped in.

"Go," I said. "Go, go, go!"

Thrill Driver that she was, Chloe needed no more encouragement, and seconds later, we were flying down the street. Fearing for my life, I grabbed for the seat belt.

"How'd you know?" I asked. Forget what I said about the whole looking the gift cheerleader in the mouth thing. My mind was doing some quick mental additions, and the fact that Chloe was Cheerleader Ex Number Two on the Jack front had me more than a little suspicious. Had she been planning on crashing our nondate? Or had she heard what I'd heard on the answering machine and thought to get me out of there fast? "And what were you doing so close to Peyton?"

Chloe was silent for a moment, and then she fessed up. "When your video feed went dead, I got a little worried."

Back up there, Cheer-Girl, I thought. Chloe? Worried about *me*? Was this supposed to be one of those "what's wrong with this picture?" quizzes I used to do in the waiting room at the dentist's office? What had happened to Chloe Your-Mere-Presence-Offends-Me Larson? What had happened to all of her issues?

"And besides," Chloe continued. "You alone at Peyton with Jack?" She rolled her eyes. "You couldn't even handle standing next to him at the party. In case you haven't noticed, you're kind of new to the whole boy thing, and I thought someone needed to be here to do damage control when you had the big meltdown."

I read between the lines: ninety percent of Chloe had

been here for the Toby-Makes-a-Fool-Out-of-Herself show (and possibly to pick up the Jack pieces after it all went down), and ten percent of her had been vaguely concerned that I might be dead or something because I'd turned off my necklace cam.

At this point, a ninety-ten split with Chloe was about as much as I could possibly ask for.

"I did not have a meltdown," I grumbled.

Chloe didn't say anything.

"I didn't!" I insisted. Sharing an incredibly impassioned kiss with someone and then belting them in the stomach and pulling a runaway bride (minus the bride part) was not a meltdown.

"Did he kiss you?" Chloe's voice was matter-of-fact, but her eyes were just a little bit lethal.

"Ummm . . . no." Technically, I had kissed him.

Chloe let out a breath. "Maybe the twins are slipping," she said. "They were positive that he was going in for the kiss before the feed died."

I stuck as close to the truth as possible. "I sort of . . . errr . . ." I took a deep breath of my own. "I punched him in the stomach."

"Are you demented?"

I took stock of the situation. I'd just kissed my mark, who happened to be the most eligible bachelor at my high school, the son of an evil lawyer whose name was constantly on the top of CIA watch lists, the nephew of the voice behind our operation, and the ex-boyfriend of not one, but two blood-thirsty varsity cheerleaders. And then I'd punched him in the stomach and run.

I had to face the facts. For once, Chloe's insult was right on target: I was obviously completely demented.

To distract her from that oh-so-apparent fact, I turned to the portion of this twisted equation that didn't have me still going disgustedly weak at the knees.

"Jack's uncle." That was all I got out, all I was able to say.

"What about him?"

If Chloe knew something, she wasn't telling, but that didn't enlighten me at all as to whether or not she knew, because even if she did, Chloe would make me dig for it.

"His voice." Why was it I could only manage two-word sentences? Was this some kind of postkiss affliction?

"What about it?" Chloe wasn't giving an inch.

This time, I tried for three words. "I recognized it."

I half expected her to say "what about it?" but she didn't. Instead, without even looking at me, she said, "No, you didn't."

The way she said it made me even more convinced that I had.

"Yes, I did."

"No." Chloe's voice was sharper this time. "You didn't."

Sure, I thought. I didn't recognize the voice, just like I didn't kiss Jack. A lie for a lie. When Chloe turned off the highway a second later, I realized that we weren't headed back to the party, or toward my house. I couldn't quite imagine her being all gung ho on girl bonding time given the mounting tension in the car, so I was pretty sure we weren't going back to her house for a sleepover. That didn't leave too many options.

"Where are we going?"

Chloe didn't answer. Now that I'd told her that Jack hadn't kissed me, and she'd refused to offer me any real answers to the questions I wanted to ask about Jack's uncle, I had ceased to matter and was more or less invisible.

"Chloe!"

"Where do you think we're going?" Chloe asked. "While you were flirting—badly, I might add—with Jack Peyton, I was at the party, monitoring your mission and tying up ends on the Infotech case."

Ends? What ends? If things had gone according to plan, I'd more or less trashed their system. I'd also downloaded all of their encrypted files, so really . . .

"The files." My mouth thought faster than my brain did. "Did you decode them?" If she was looking for a way to distract me from the voice I had most definitely recognized, she'd found it. I wasn't sure which answer I was hoping for, but it mattered to me. A yes meant that we'd be able to know for sure if any other aliases had been compromised. It would also give me the chance to poke around in whatever program they'd been using to hack the CIA, and the thought had me practically salivating. On the other hand, a yes might also mean that Chloe had somehow decoded them, and despite the fact that she'd rescued me (however inadvertently) from impending postkiss doom, the thought of Chloe decoding *my* files made me want to punch something. If, on the other hand, the answer to my question was a no, I might actually get the chance to decode the files myself.

"The Guys Upstairs took care of the decode," Chloe said.

The Big Guys. Aka Jack's freaking uncle. I had to wonder—what did that say about the Big Guys? The law firm was a family business, so much so that Jack had his own key. If one of our superiors was part of that family, why did he need me to go in and plant the bug?

I didn't mull over the questions; they were so enormous in my mind that they pretty much mulled over me. Chloe whipped her car into a parking space, and we made our way into the school, to which Chloe had her own set of keys.

"The perks of working for the government," I said, my heart only half in it, as the rest of it was still being mulled.

Chloe smirked. "Our faculty sponsor is Mr. J," she said. "I told him we needed keys, and he gave them to me and told me not to tell anyone. I swear, that's one vice-principal who *worships* cheerleaders."

That was so totally wrong. There had to be something highly illegal (or at least against school board mandates) about giving keys to the school to teenage cheerleaders.

Then again, this was Bayport, the land of evil law firms and CIA agents with questionable connections and boys I'd kissed who I shouldn't have. In the scheme of things, everything was relative.

Chloe and I went to the Quad through the locker room, and five minutes later, we were in the main room, and summaries from the decoded files were on the larger-than-life flat-screen. We sat in silence for a full five minutes, taking in the reports and working them over in our tech-savvy minds. This was probably the closest Chloe and I would ever come to bonding.

"Huh," I said finally. "So that's how they did it."

"They had an inside tech source with low-security clearance who opened a back door for them, and since they designed the beta version of the security program, they were able to belly up to the rest of the system." Chloe blew a strand of highlighted hair out of her face. "That's totally cheating."

I had to agree—with a freebie entry into part of the system and knowledge of the way the whole thing was set up, breaking the newer codes wasn't that impressive. Hacking is like finding your way through a labyrinth, and those Info-tech weasels had a tour guide and a map.

I found myself looking at Chloe out of the corners of my eyes. First the bonding, and now complete Toby-Chloe agreement. What was the world coming to?

"So what now?" I asked.

Chloe shrugged. "Now we let the big guys do what they do."

"And that would be . . . ?"

That was the exact moment when the techie bonding ended. "What do you think?" she said. "They'll make some arrests, reconfigure the security system, and try to figure out a way to implicate Peyton as the conduit between Heath Shannon and Infotech."

From the way Chloe said the word *try*, I got the feeling that pinning anything on the law firm might prove difficult. It more or less figured. I mean, every group of cheerleading superspies has to have their archenemy, right?

If only I hadn't kissed the archenemy's heir apparent. Or punched him in the stomach. Or led Chloe to believe that my lips had never touched his. Or found out that our arch-enemy and our big boss might be one and the same.

If only, I thought, I hadn't enjoyed doing almost all of the above.

"Are we done here?" I asked. Our case was over—the op-eratives were safe, Heath Shannon was in custody, and Info-tech had been shut down indefinitely. Add to that the fact that I'd just bugged Peyton and ignore what I'd discovered about the Voice, and I was going to go out on a limb and call this operation a success. That said, I, for one, had no burn-ing desire to spend any more time than necessary inside Bayport High. For most of my high school existence, I'd made it my mission in life to spend as little time inside these hallowed halls as possible. Go Bayport.

"Got someplace better to be?" Chloe asked.

"It's been a long night," I said, unimpressed by her scoffing. "Need I remind you that I xeroxed my butt to plant the bug at Peyton?" I gave Chloe a look of my own. "Or that for some godforsaken reason, I'm wearing a thong?"

Oh, the indignity of it all.

"Trust me," I said. "You do not want to mess with me right now."

Chloe, showing a remarkable amount of restraint, turned off the television, locked down the Quad, and drove me home. In a move worthy of an evil genius, she exacted her revenge for my "don't mess with me" spiel by playing bubblegum pop music full blast the entire way.

Point, Chloe.

As she pulled up to my house, she smiled sweetly. "Don't forget," she said. "Tomorrow's a game day. You should probably listen to the playlist tonight. You don't want to look like a complete spaz on the field."

I translated her tone to mean that looking like a partial spaz was the most I could hope for. Anxious to get away from both Chloe and the "music" in the car, I reached for the door, but Chloe spoke again.

"Oh, and by the way," she said. "Your little brother said to tell you that you greatly underestimate his incredible appeal to the fairer sex. I think the twins were putting ideas in his head."

I was going to kill Noah. And the twins. And possibly Chloe. It would be therapeutic, really.

I opened the car door.

"Sweet dreams," Chloe said.

I came this close to telling her I'd made out with Jack, but I didn't. I was almost positive I could take her in the cat-fight that would ensue, but then we'd be one short for our halftime performance, and my head was going to explode if I had to memorize a new formation.

I walked up to my front door, and when I reached for the doorknob, the door flew inward. Noah stood there, smiling at me.

"Ask me how my night was," he said.

I looked over my shoulder. Chloe was gone, but wherever she was, I was positive she was smirking in victory.

"Toby, just ask me," Noah ordered. "Or better yet, touch me."

"Noah, I'm not going to—"

"Just touch me."

I reached my hand out to thwap some sense into him, but he jumped back. "Careful," he said. "Don't burn yourself, 'cause I'm on fiiiiiiiiiire!"

And then he broke into a victory dance, moonwalk and all.

When I got my hands on them, Brittany and Tiffany were dead girls.

CHAPTER 34
Code Word: Halftime

"Hello, girls."

This time, I had my "good morning, Charlie" impulses well under control, but really, my response had nothing to do with control and indeed nothing even to do with the fact that the cheerleading uniform I was wearing was highly uncomfortable. It had everything to do with the fact that hearing the Voice again sent me flashing back to that night, to the kiss, to everything.

John. It's Alan. I need to talk to you. It's about Jack.

"I know you girls have a big game today, so I won't keep you, but we wanted to express our sincere appreciation for your work on this case. Heath Shannon is currently in custody and has agreed to provide us with information on his terrorist contacts in exchange for a light sentencing."

I noticed that there was no mention of Heath Shannon similarly betraying Peyton, Kaufman, and Gray, which I took as signifying that somehow, Mr. Playboy found the law firm more intimidating and potentially lethal than his terrorist contacts. Try that for mind-boggling.

John. It's Alan. I need to talk to you. It's about Jack.

"Infotech has been effectively shut down. Coincidentally enough, they've also had a major turnover in management. Apparently, several of their lead executives have fled the country."

Given Heath's decision, I wondered what the executives were more afraid of: the government or Peyton's undoubtedly unpleasant methods for tying up loose ends.

"Toby."

The Voice spoke my name, and I bit back the urge to speak back, to yell out that I knew who he was and to demand to know why he wanted to talk about Jack.

"The bug you planted at Peyton has been up and operational for the past two days. Though we don't expect it to last indefinitely, it will be invaluable until we can find an alternative means of collecting intel inside the firm."

An alternative means like, perhaps, being related to the guys who own it?

Tara gave me a look that told me I should reply, and though I managed to refrain from voicing my silent question, I couldn't stop a smart-mouthed one from leaving my lips instead. "Does that mean I get a gold star?"

The Voice didn't show a single sign of chuckling. "It means," he said, "that we'll keep you."

I hadn't known that not keeping me was even an option. It was a testament to how far I'd come in the past couple of days that I somehow found the idea of not being on the Squad anymore incredibly aversive.

"We've analyzed the information that you confiscated from Heath Shannon," the Voice continued, and I tried not to think of what exactly that "confiscation" had entailed. "And we've reassigned our operatives accordingly. Any information Peyton got from these hacks is now obsolete."

270

We'd stopped the metaphorical sickness from spreading. We'd assessed the damage, and we'd treated the symptoms. To put it in cheerleading terms, we'd gone, we'd fought, and we'd won. And because I'd had the words to our cheers and chants burned into my cranial region by that blasted iPod, I knew for a fact that after the Bayport Lions made big with the go-fight-win, the first thing we did was do it again.

And now for the words I never thought I'd say: Go Bayport.

"As always, girls, we'll be in touch." The Voice paused slightly, and I waited for another cryptic announcement. "Good luck with your game."

And then, there was silence.

So that's it. My first mission. I broke a code that sent Brooke and Zee into the line of fire (literally) in Libya. I hacked Infotech's secured system, acquired their files, destroyed their system, and helped the guys upstairs safeguard their system against future attacks. With Lucy's help, I took down a freelance heartthrob/operative and retrieved the stolen data. I seduced the school's most eligible bachelor, infiltrated an evil law firm, and bugged it like a pro. I found out that one of our superiors was more than he appeared, and I wore hideously uncomfortable boots and indecently short skirts. I got Stage Sixed, became one of *those girls*, photocopied my butt, and partook in what, in all honesty, was my very first kiss. And then I punched the guy and ran.

All in all, it wasn't a bad showing, except, perhaps, for the last part.

As the ten of us left the Quad and filed out onto the football field, I found myself at the center of conversation. The twins combined their dating expertise to conclude (in the absence of any knowledge about the kiss) that I was sending Jack mixed signals. Thank you, Captain Obvious. Zee, after dissecting Jack's psyche a bit more, told me that, if anything, I'd increase my chances with him by playing the intrigue card.

I tried to tell them that I wanted nothing to do with him, but for some strange reason, nobody believed me. I also couldn't convince them to change the topic of conversation, even as we took our positions on the sidelines. We'd safeguarded national security and captured a playboy who'd ratted out terrorists, our Squad captain now owed her life to a bulletproof push-up bra, and the first football game of the year was officially starting, but somehow, my alleged love life was *still* the topic of conversation.

That's pretty much how my first mission concluded. I still didn't know anything about Jack's uncle, or about why the CIA needed cheerleaders to infiltrate Peyton, Kaufman, and Gray when Peyton blood ran in one of their own. I didn't know what "Uncle Alan" wanted with Jack. I didn't even know what *I* wanted with Jack.

That's *almost* how my first mission ended, anyway. There was one other tiny thing.

"You ready for this, Toby?" Brooke asked me an hour later, in a tone that suggested I probably wasn't.

I'd just spent a record amount of time on the sidelines, cheering and chanting with a huge, fake smile on my face, and she was still doubting me.

"Brooke, it's a halftime routine. It's not rocket science." I rolled my eyes. "I'll be fine."

"And now, for your pleasure, the nationally recognized heart of Bayport—the Bayport High Varsity Spirit Squad!"

The announcer's voice rumbled out of the loudspeakers,

and the crowd burst into applause, hoots, and hollers (in that order).

We took our positions on the field. I ignored the way my cheerleading skirt rubbed uncomfortably against my legs. I thought about my last mission and my next one and the importance of never letting anyone see more than you wanted them to see.

I smiled.

"Ready? Okay!"

"B to the A to the Y to the Port . . ."

It was official: there was no turning back.

If you'd told me at the beginning of my sophomore year that I was going to become a government operative, I would have thought you were crazy, but if you'd told me I was destined to become a cheerleader, I would have had you committed, no questions asked. Then again, if you'd told me right after our halftime performance that our second mission would be more lethal, more scandalous, and more filled with kisses than the first, I wouldn't have believed you.

It just goes to show how wrong I can be, because as I cheered, my smile forcing the world to view me as nothing more than a girl in a skirt, the beginnings of my second mission, more dangerous than I could have imagined, were already headed my way.

"Go, fight, win! We'll beat you again. BAYPORT!"

ACKNOWLEDGMENTS

More than anything else I've written, this book was a work of revision, so I owe a great deal of *The Squad* to my wonderful editor, Krista Marino. Thank you for the suggestions, the questions, and making me work hard, book after book. Thanks also to my agent, Elizabeth Harding, for believing in this series as a series; to my mother, Marsha Barnes, for reading multiple drafts, laughing so hard she cried, and being on hand for late-night phone calls of the midrevision freak-out variety; and to Neha Mahajan, for comments, support, and loving Jack. You guys are the best.

I'd also like to thank my family, who are without question my biggest fans; my readers, whose emails, reviews, and comments never fail to brighten my day; my friends at both Yale and Cambridge (especially Mike Lombardo), who let me babble on about cheerleading secret agents without ever giving me so much as a single weird look; and Chelsea Render, who knows how to bring out my inner spy.

Finally, I'd like to give a nod to anyone who's ever been underestimated, whether or not you were wearing a cheerleading skirt at the time. This book is for you.

Jennifer Lynn Barnes earned a bachelor's degree from Yale University and a master's from Cambridge University. A former competitive cheerleader, she was named an All-American Cheerleader by the National Cheerleading Association in 1997. She can neither confirm nor deny any experience she may or may not have had as a secret agent, but she can tell you that she's the author of three other teen novels: *Golden, Tattoo,* and *Platinum*, as well as *The Squad: Perfect Cover*'s sequel, *The Squad: Killer Spirit*. Jennifer wrote her first book when she was still a teenager, and she is currently hard at work on her next. Visit her online at www.jenniferlynnbarnes.com.

*Toby Klein is ready
to bring it.*